Remembrance
OF
Blue Roses

YORKER KEITH

1

I have heard a wise man say that love is a form of friend-ship, and friendship a form of love; the line between the two is misty. I happen to know that this holds true because I have roamed that misty line. Time has passed since then, but I cher-ish the memory of the blue roses in grace and perpetuity — our blue roses. It all began with a fortuitous encounter.

* * *

On a fine day in early April 1999, I was sketching in the sculpture court at the Metropolitan Museum of Art. I felt hes-itant working in such a public space, but this was a homework assignment for the art class I was taking. The object of my sketch was a sculpture of an adorable young woman, a nude, reclining on a moss-covered rock surrounded by an abundance of flowers. The smooth texture of the white marble sensually expressed her lively body, which shone with bright sunlight beneath the glass ceiling of the court.

My drawing materials were simple, just a number 2 pencil, an eraser, and a sheet of heavy white drawing paper. The assignment was to capture the skin of a figure in as much detail as possible. I had almost completed sketching the woman's body and was working on the rock and flowers. I was not doing badly, I thought, for a small crowd of museum visitors had gathered around me, showing approving faces and nods.

"Ah, this is excellent!" one man exclaimed.

I recognized the voice and turned to see Hans Schmidt, standing amid the crowd wearing a big grin.

"What a surprise!" he continued. "I didn't know you had such an artistic talent, Mark. How are you?" He came forward and firmly shook my hand.

I greeted him, then pointed to my drawing. "I've been working on this for a while. I wasn't sure how it would come out. But it's coming along all right, I guess."

"I don't know much about drawing, but this looks great." He gestured enthusiastically to a young woman next to him. "What do you think?"

"It's pretty." Her voice sounded like a bell.

"This is Yukari, my wife." He guided her toward me, his hand lingering at the small of her back.

I swallowed. I knew Hans was married, but this was my first time to meet his wife. *Hans's wife is Japanese? How lovely she is. Hans, you devil, you're a lucky man!*

"Pleased to meet you." I gently shook her small refined hand. "I'm Mark Sanders. Hans and I are good friends."

Hans's wife appeared to be in her late thirties, or late twenties? I could hardly tell, because Japanese women often looked much younger than their age. She was willowy, of medium height, with a fine complexion, dark eyes, straight nose, and shiny dark brown hair that hung to her shoulders. For a Japanese woman, she had a touch of a Western woman's body, the round breasts and a curvy waist. Despite her conservative dress, she reminded me of the nude I was sketching — though I quickly banished the thought.

She gazed directly into my eyes with keen curiosity. "Do you come here often to sketch? It's really nice."

"Well, yes," I answered, "I visit this museum often. But to sketch? No, this is the first time. You know what? It's so embarrassing."

I dabbed some sweat from my forehead. We three burst out laughing.

"Hans, I'm almost done. Can you come back in ten minutes or so?" I said. "Then we could go to the terrace for a cup of coffee."

"Sounds terrific," said Hans. "We'll be walking around the sculpture court. When you're done, just join us."

Hans took Yukari's arm and started moving leisurely toward other sculptures. She smiled at me and went along with him. Hans tried to hold her closely at her waist, but she discretely slipped away. I didn't understand what it meant. I presumed that as a Japanese woman she was timid to show open affection.

I hastily added finishing touches to the figure, rock, and flowers. Since the figure had been almost completed, the rest went quickly and easily — or so I felt after having seen Hans and Yukari.

*   *   *

I had known Hans for some time because both he and I worked at the United Nations New York Headquarters as international civil servants. He was German, aged forty-two, tall and slim, with blond hair, high forehead, and grey eyes. He had a Ph.D. in economics from the University of California at Berkeley, and worked as an Economic Affairs Officer in the Department of Economic and Social Affairs of the Secretariat, which was the administrative body of the UN. His job there was to maintain and operate a global econometric modeling system, called EGlobe.

We had originally met in a French language class. Being at the UN, we were required to be proficient in at least two of its six official languages: Arabic, Chinese, English, French, Russian, and Spanish. In my case, I added French to my native English. My French was hardly adequate, though, so I was working my way through the seven-level French program.

In level six I met Hans, who had just started the program from that level. We ate lunch often together in the cafeteria and practiced our French. His grasp of the language was much better than mine. Also, since he used computers heavily for his work, and since I had a good friend, Shem Tov Lancry, an Israeli, in the Information Technology Services Division of the Department of Management, I introduced them, so Hans was able to receive technical advice from Shem Tov.

I packed up my drawing materials, and we three went to the balcony above the Great Hall of the museum, where drinks and desserts were served while musicians played chamber music. We each ordered a glass of red wine.

Yukari Asaka, I learned, was a professional violinist, a member of the Parnassus Symphony Orchestra, which was regarded as the best orchestra after the first-tier orchestras in New York, such as the New York Philharmonic, the Brooklyn Philharmonic, and the Metropolitan Opera Orchestra.

"How did you meet?" I asked them.

"One evening," Hans began, "I went to a concert by the Parnassus at Carnegie Hall. After the concert I visited a back-stage room to meet the soloist who had played a piano concerto with the orchestra. On my way out I found a small velvet bag on the stairs between the backstage rooms and the main stage. Inside I found a woman's cosmetic kit and a wallet. I was reluctant to give it to a stagehand, so I brought it home, called the telephone number in the wallet, and left a message that I had the velvet bag. Almost at midnight a woman called me. It was Yukari." Hans caressed her shoulder.

"I was so depressed that night," Yukari said. "When I was leaving Carnegie Hall after the performance, I realized my bag was gone. I had known that even backstage rooms for orchestra members were not safe, but this kind of thing had never happened to me before. I searched everywhere with no luck. My friend brought me home by taxi. Lost money was one thing, but I was exhausted just thinking about reporting the lost bank cards, credit cards, driver's license, union card, and so on. At my apartment I saw my answering machine blinking. The message sounded like a voice from heaven."

Her English was good, though she spoke with a Japanese accent, which sounded exotic to my ears. Was I fascinated by her way of speaking, or by herself? I didn't know — maybe both.

"Next day," Hans took over, "we met, and I returned her bag." He raised his glass to Yukari and took a sip.

"I think I dropped it while I was returning from the ladies' room to the dressing room. But thanks again, Hans." She too raised her glass and took a sip.

Hans beamed. "After that we kept seeing each other, and one year later we got married. That was a little over two years ago. Since then I've been a happy man."

"Do you have children?" I asked.

Hans laughed. "Not yet, but we are working on it."

Hans's tone sounded honest, and he seemed truly happy. Yukari looked down and kept quiet, but she did not appear negative, so I assumed that she was just shy about the topic of child-making.

When we found that they lived on the upper east side of Manhattan, not far from my apartment, Yukari raised her face. "Soon I'll invite you for dinner," she said. "I'm a good cook. Do you like sushi?"

"I love it!" I said with great enthusiasm.

Yukari smiled at me. Hans caught it. He seemed to be delighted with her. I assumed that he was pleased with his wife for her willingness to entertain his close friend.

"Do you play any instruments?" Yukari asked me.

"I used to play the piano when I was a kid," I replied. "But I have to be careful in New York, where so many people are talented. I'll tell you my fiasco." I paused and sipped my wine. "This was only a few years ago. A friend invited me to a dinner party at his apartment. His wife was taking piano lessons. After the dinner, as the entertainment, his wife played the piano, some Beethoven sonata. She was a good pianist for a student. Then her teacher played. Since she was a professional, she played a Chopin polonaise excellently. Then my friend insisted that I play, for he had known that I used to play the piano. As a guest I felt obliged, though I was terribly reluctant, because I had not played for years." I took another sip, flushing at the memory. "One piece in my limited repertoire was Mozart's *Sonata 16*, which consists of many variations of the theme. The last variation is that famous Turkish march." Here I tururu'ed my tongue, mimicking the melody of the march. "I thought I could manage the theme. You know that, right?" Again I imitated the familiar melody. "It's short, anyway. So I went to the piano and bowed to the audience of about ten people. Then I started playing. They provided me the music, but since I had not practiced for years, naturally I made a lot of mistakes. My cheeks burned, and sweat poured down my face, blurring my eyes so I couldn't even read the music."

I exaggerated wiping the sweat from my face in despair. We laughed. I was happy to see Yukari laughing heartily.

"That's funny," she said. "I don't meant to put you down, Mark. But I do understand how you felt, because even I sometimes go through that kind of humiliating experience."

"Thank you for defending me," I said. "It was the most embarrassing moment in my life. Since then, I've stopped saying I used to play the piano. Today is an exception, because you're a musician."

Yukari nodded repeatedly, supposedly, I guessed, appreciating my recognition of her as a professional violinist, or giving me moral support. I felt good.

"Mark, I need to tell you this," Hans said. "I have a passion for opera, so I'm taking voice lessons and an opera workshop at the Evening Division of the Juilliard School. I want to be called a semi-professional opera singer." He proudly swelled his chest. "Meet a great tenor."

Hans was full of surprises, I thought. I threw him a big thumbs-up. Yukari waved her hand in half-approval and half-dismissal.

"If Yukari had been a pianist," Hans insisted, "I would be a much better tenor by now, since she would help my voice practice."

Yukari laughed off his comment.

Hans gazed at his wife with admiration. "I have no complaints as to her being a violinist," he said, "because I've always wanted to marry a woman who is more than just a classical music lover."

He kissed her cheek. Yukari smiled. How adorable that smile was.

*   *   *

At age forty-five, I was a Human Resources Officer in the Administrative Support Division of the Department of Peacekeeping Operations. After graduating from George Washington University with a BA in psychology, I worked for several years in the federal government, then went to the Marshall School of Business at the University of Southern

California. With a newly obtained MBA, I came to New York to work for the UN, where I have been for over ten years.

Our division had been headed by a British director, a competent, well-respected administrator and a real gentleman, who handled complex administrative support tasks for the peacekeeping operations with fine diplomatic skills. I had worked closely with him on interesting projects and had been promoted rapidly twice.

Then the director retired. He was replaced by an American woman with considerable political power but lacking any professional competence in administrative support for peacekeeping operations. She reorganized the division, sidelining several staff members who had been close to the former director, including me, and bringing in many of her friends. She promoted four of her friends to senior officers' posts, at least one of which had been meant for me. I was given trivial assignments.

Partly because of the aggravation at the office, my marriage also crumbled. I had been married for four years to a beautiful Swiss woman, Francine Le Bret, whom I had met at the UN. She was a warm person with a kind heart, who genuinely loved me. Our married life had been peaceful. As my idea of marriage included raising a family, I had wanted children. Unfortunately we could not conceive, and after four years of disappointment, I lost interest in our marriage and divorced her. Not conceiving a child could not be a reason for divorce in New York State. But I forced my lawyer to creatively fudge legally acceptable reasons for divorce. In this respect my lawyer did a good job. Francine wanted to stay together, but my determination for the breakup was so strong that she could not resist. Four years ago we were finally divorced. I knew it was unfair and unjust to her. But I couldn't help it.

Surely I was punished for my despicable act. After our divorce, one of my close friends, Shem Tov, took pity on Francine, and he consoled her. That grew into love, and they got married. Then, making the matter worse, or better, I don't know which, she became pregnant and bore a beautiful baby boy, whom they named Jacques. God damn me! I had divorced her for nothing. If we had stayed together, the children would have come.

My life, both public and private, being so disarrayed, I felt bitter. I shut myself off from any social activities. In the office I did what I was asked to do like a machine without soul, tasks that were of no importance anyway. After work I went straight home and watched TV or read books. Nothing seemed particularly interesting or exciting.

There was one exception. A few times a week, after work, I went to the Art Students League on West 57th Street, where usually I took one drawing class and one painting class per semester. I sometimes went to the life sketch class, too, where a nude model was provided without an instructor for quick sketching for those students who wanted to improve their drafting skills. Sometimes, at the end of a semester, the instructor would organize a class show in a gallery of the League to exhibit the best works of the students. My works appeared occasionally. It gave me a little enjoyment, my only indulgence.

Such was the state of my life when I met Hans and Yukari at the museum. Embarrassed, I couldn't tell them the details of my office life or my private life. I mentioned only that I still worked in the human resources area, and I was divorced. They seemed to accept this as evidence of my private nature and did not press too much.

However, both Hans and Yukari appeared unreservedly open to me, and in my heart, I welcomed the opportunity to befriend them.

2

In New York, April was a busy month for cultural events, as the 1998-1999 season was coming to an end. Since Hans was an opera singer (semi-professional, as he called himself) and Yukari was a professional violinist, I wanted to invite them to a concert. Fortunately I found a good one on a Friday evening at Carnegie Hall. The Chicago Symphony Orchestra would perform Brahms's *Serenade No.1* and *Violin Concerto*, featuring a guest conductor and a well-known violinist, Inge Wunderlich.

On the evening of the concert, I guided my guests up to the Second Tier, which provided the most satisfactory acoustics in my opinion. We sat in one of the boxes with Yukari in the center, Hans to the right, and me on the left.

This was the first time I had seen Yukari and Hans on a formal occasion. She wore a long black silk skirt and a long-sleeved white blouse. Her pale, graceful face was radiant with anticipation. A string of small pearls shone at her slender neck.

I felt her appearance reflected a modest mixture of elegance, strength, and fragility.

In contrast, Hans wore a dark business suit, perfectly tailored to flatter his tall frame and European posture. His high forehead and well-groomed short blond hair suggested his intelligence, with a discrete touch of cultivated passion and creativity.

Yukari looked completely at home, since she had performed at Carnegie Hall many times. "Thank you again, Mark," she said. "This is quite a treat. I'm really looking forward to hearing Brahms's violin concerto, because it's in my repertoire, and I love Inge Wunderlich."

"Yes," Hans added, "the program is excellent, because being German, Brahms is my favorite composer."

I beamed, pleased by their delight.

The concert opened with *Serenade No. 1*, consisting of six movements. The piece created a cheerful and bright, yet tender and sweet atmosphere in the hall, like a wedding party. I felt light-hearted, and I sensed Hans and Yukari feeling so as well.

The *Violin Concerto* followed after a short intermission. The orchestra and the soloist played the dazzling first movement. Then came the famous Adagio. The winds and strings gently accompanied in *pianissimo* the rhapsodic main theme of the violin solo, entirely sustained with profound intimacy and longing. The melody seemed to purify the heart of everyone in the hall, where absolute silence was kept.

As I listened attentively to the violin solo, I heard the almost inaudible sound of a sob from my right, and I glanced toward Yukari. I had the impression that she was oblivious to the stream of tears on her face, so absorbed was she in the music.

The third movement, the finale, started with an intoxicating rondo theme, in which the pure tone of the orchestra and rich, serene violin solo were united in glorious harmony. The climax occurred as the violin descended and the orchestra concluded the last chords. The audience responded with loud applause and a standing ovation. Hans, Yukari, and I stood and shouted "Bravo," applauding until our hands grew numb.

After the concert we took a nightcap at a nearby restaurant. I felt very content and close to Hans and Yukari, and I judged they felt the same way.

"Yukari," I ventured, "may I ask a question? You don't have to answer if you don't want." Without waiting for her to reply, I came directly to the point. "If I'm not mistaken, you were crying during the second movement of the violin concerto. Why?"

"I was," answered Yukari, not sadly but with a tone of acceptance. "I don't mind telling you. That movement and Inge Wunderlich's inspiring performance made me remember the sunniest days of my life."

I raised my eyebrows, inviting her to continue.

"I went to the Curtis Institute of Music in Philadelphia," she said. "This was a big thing for an eighteen-year-old Japanese girl — coming alone to the United States from Tokyo to study music. My parents financially supported me on the condition that after the graduation, I would go back to Japan." She paused, seemingly nostalgic for her younger years.

"You were a brave girl then." I couldn't help saying this.

She nodded with a smile. "An insatiable desire to go abroad runs in my family. So even at age eighteen, I feared nothing. In the school, I studied with Madame Jeanne Bouvier, a famous violin educator at the time. I received a Bachelor of Music degree and subsequently a Masters in violin performance. Then I had a clash with my parents, because they insisted I return to Japan, reciting the condition we had agreed upon when I left home. But I refused to go back." She sighed. "You have to know that a traditional Japanese family would never allow their daughter to live alone in a foreign country. So I understood my parents' wish, which was reasonable. But I adamantly refused. Finally they yielded. They allowed me to stay in the US for a few years to see whether or not I could make a living by my violin. If thing did not go well, I was to go back to Japan. To this I agreed, because I didn't want to be unreasonable to my parents, and I knew that I would face a daunting challenge. There was a good chance I might fail. But I wanted to try."

"Amazing," I said. "You have a strong will, and your parents are very understanding."

"Yes," Yukari said, "but I was a rebellious daughter." She paused for a moment, swirling her tea. "My father asked his friend at the Japanese embassy in Washington DC to help me obtain an O-1B visa, a so-called artist visa. Also he managed to get a recommendation for me from the deputy minister of foreign affairs, who was our distant relative. Since I was one of top students at the Curtis, the school also wrote a recommendation for me. I got the visa, which would have been impossible without those referrals."

"So a young Japanese female violinist debuted in the US … impressive," I murmured.

Yukari giggled a little. "Not with a fanfare. But I spent two years in Philadelphia as a freelance violinist, performing here and there as a member of full orchestras, chamber orchestras, or even as a soloist sometimes. My future seemed promising."

Hans had been listening quietly until then, but here he joined in the conversation. "You never told me those details of your early career," he said to Yukari. "Now I begin to understand your strained relationship with your parents."

I kept quiet, but thought, *Really? Why hasn't she told him? Why is she telling now? What's going on?*

"Yes, it's complicated," Yukari told Hans. "But let me continue." She sipped her tea and resumed. "Then an opportunity arrived, and I auditioned for a position in the Los Angeles Philharmonic. To my delight, I was accepted. I moved to Los Angeles in August of that year and started performing with the LA Phil. I was only twenty-six."

Hans and I clapped our hands and shouted, "Bravo!"

Yukari blushed. "I was proud of my achievement," she admitted. "I felt I could conquer the world, so I worked hard. I still occasionally went back to Madame Bouvier in Philadelphia to check how I was doing. I performed in the LA Phil with many famous conductors and soloists for four years, determined to rise to solo violinist someday. This was the best period of my life." Her face shone.

"So you took a huge chance, and you succeeded," I said. "You deserve to feel proud of yourself."

"Yes, this is great," Hans said. "What happened next?"

Dark clouds appeared on Yukari's face, and her eyes welled up. "Then I was diagnosed with leukemia."

"Oh, no!" said I and Hans together.

I stared at Hans. How could he not know this?

"I was admitted to a hospital in LA for chemotherapy," Yukari went on. "I lost my hair, my beautiful dark brown hair, completely. I lost my physical strength too. Playing the violin professionally was out of question, as my mere survival was at stake." Her face grew pale, and her voice started trembling. "I was depressed, of course. I even contemplated suicide or hoped to die of leukemia rather than become too weak to play the violin for the rest of my life."

I sighed. Hans did the same.

"Fortunately, after a series of tests and medications, the doctors finally seemed to find the right medication for me. The disease went into remission." Yukari's face recovered a little light.

"Thank God," I uttered. "Your parents must have felt relieved."

"I didn't tell them about my illness."

"What?" I raised my voice. "Why? You needed them."

"No, if I had told them, I knew they would force me to go back to Japan. My life as a violinist is here. I didn't want to go back."

"Maybe, but ..." I found no word to go on.

"I stayed in the hospital for a while," Yukari said. "I was on a medical leave, so the LA Phil still paid my salary. My health insurance covered medical bills. My friends visited the hospital often, which gave me moral support. I was fortunate under the circumstances, particularly since I didn't have any family here to look after me."

"I'm glad," I said in relief.

"The problem was my parents," Yukari said in a tone of demur. "They used to call me at my apartment in LA from time

to time. I guess they did so during my hospital stay. Since I
didn't answer — as I was lying in a hospital bed — they called
the administrative office of the LA Phil, and the staff told them
of my illness."

"Uh oh. Did your parents call you at the hospital?"
I asked.

"Yes, immediately," Yukari answered. "They created a big
scene, particularly my mother. She cried and cried."

"Of course ..." I said.

"Luckily, by then the leukemia had gone to remission.
But right away both my father and mother came to LA from
Tokyo. I asked the hospital staff not to allow them to come
to my room, but they didn't listen because the visitors were
my parents. So my father and mother came into my room. As
expected, my father insisted that I return to Tokyo. I refused.
My father grew adamant this time, but then I threatened to kill
myself if they brought me to Tokyo by force."

"No!" I said. "Your parents were right. They were only
concerned for your well-being."

"I know, but I stubbornly refused to be taken back."
Yukari glowered, her lips tight. "My father, usually a gentle person, lost his temper and exploded. Most likely everyone on the
same floor must have heard him shouting. I didn't care. I didn't
want to go back. Period. There was absolutely no space in me
to compromise. But my father didn't give up either. Finally my
mother broke down and implored my father to back off. They
arranged for a part-time caretaker to look after me once I was
released from the hospital. Then they went back to Tokyo. My
father was still furious, but I remember my mother's sad face.
Sorry, Mom, I was a bad girl." She wiped tears from her cheek.

"Now I understand why you rejected the idea of going to Tokyo for our honeymoon when I proposed," Hans said.

How sweet Hans was to propose that, I thought. *But he didn't know until now that she had a problem with her parents? Why?*

"Yes," Yukari replied to Hans. "How can I face them? You see, I'm a black sheep as far as they are concerned."

"How did you manage after that?" I asked.

"After two months or so, finally the hospital released me," Yukari resumed. "Then I stayed in my apartment for about three months. I was weak. The caretaker visited me every day for a few hours and took care of my daily needs, like medication, cooking, cleaning, and laundry. I felt grateful to my parents for their thoughtful arrangement, as they paid the bill for the caretaker. Gradually I regained my strength. Finally, to my great relief, I recovered fully, and most wonderful of all, I was able to play the violin professionally again."

"You survived the ordeal," I said. "You are a courageous person. I admire you."

"You could have told me this before," said Hans, sounding hurt. "But thanks for telling us tonight. Now I understand you much better."

Here too I wondered as before, *Why has she been withholding something so important about her life from Hans?*

"Eventually I went back to the LA Phil and started playing again with them," Yukari said. "Coincidentally, during this period they changed the music director. The new conductor was a gifted man, but I didn't like his personality, because I felt he was using us orchestra members to fulfill his ambition. So in less than one year I quit the LA Phil and came to New York.

After spending a few years as a freelance violinist, I managed to get hired by the Parnassus Symphony Orchestra."

"So it was a long journey for you," I said. "But you're quite an adventurer."

Yukari gave a little shrug. "I'm grateful that I was able to settle professionally in New York," she said. "But I still don't have the full physical strength required of a solo performer. In the Parnassus, I play second violin. I just don't have enough energy for a concert master or principal player."

"But at least you are pursuing your career in New York," I said, "a cultural center of the world, overcoming the past hardship. I think that's a great achievement."

My compliment did not cheer her up. She gazed at her hands, exhaling weakly.

"Sometimes I envy soloists," she went on, as if this were what she had wanted to say all along. "This evening, when I was listening to Inge Wunderlich, I couldn't help thinking that that violinist could have been me if it weren't for the leukemia." She frowned at the injustice. "Inge Wunderlich was a child prodigy whom Herbert von Karajan adored. She was spoiled, always behaving seductively and provocatively. But she was gorgeous, and after all she was Karajan's protégé, so she became very famous. Then a few years ago, she lost her husband in a car accident. Now she is a single mother, supporting her two daughters. I think the experience matured her. She is now much more composed and low-key, and her music has much more depth. This is why I was so moved by her performance this evening."

I wanted to say something to Yukari to show that I understood her feeling. But I held my tongue, as she seemed about to reveal something very personal.

"Still, I kept saying in my mind," she whispered, her lips trembling, "that that soloist could have been me — even though I now know my limitations. I cannot be that, I know.... It's sad. Particularly if I look back to the time I was performing in the Los Angeles Philharmonic." Her eyes flashed with determination. "So I mustn't look back. At least I survived the leukemia. This is me. Imperfect, but I have to accept it — and then move forward. Shouldn't I?"

Yukari lowered her head and quietly sobbed. Hans tenderly caressed her shoulder without a word.

3

For a few days after the concert, I felt guilty for bringing Yukari to such an emotional state. I wanted to cheer her up. My painting class was holding an exhibition at the Art Students League, so I invited Hans and Yukari, promising myself to engage in no more sad talk.

As a rule, class shows were held only for one evening per class. Our show happened to be on a Friday. I had brought the best painting I had completed during the semester. It portrayed a young woman, sunbathing in the nude on a summer garden chair.

When Hans and Yukari arrived, the gallery was already crowded with guests, students, and faculty members. I greeted them, and with glass of wine in our hands, I showed them the works of my classmates, moving toward my work.

"This is my painting," I said, throwing my hand toward it in exaggeration. "What do you think?"

As I stood quietly, my friends studied the painting. The young woman was sitting on a white wicker chair in a garden. She had short brunette hair with a white rosebud at her right ear. The sun shone abundantly on her flesh, which I'd rendered in a bright orange color with a hint of pink. Beside the chair stood a basket full of flowers. The background, an array of greens, suggested grasses and trees.

I explained that a classroom in art school was usually bare and unattractive, and the model sat on a regular chair — most of the time paint-stained. That was not really picturesque. Therefore, the white chair, the white rosebud at her ear, the flower basket, and the greenery in my painting were from my imagination, based on some scenes from fashion magazines.

"Does the nude bother you?" I asked Yukari, since I didn't want to do anything to upset her this evening.

"Oh, no," she replied matter-of-factly. "I'm a musician. I do appreciate anything beautiful. But why do painters paint nude figures so often?"

"First of all," I eagerly answered so she would understand the real reasons, "a nude figure is aesthetically pleasing. A female nude, a male nude, children without clothes, they are all beautiful." She inclined her head, encouraging me to go on. "Also, the body is something we are most familiar with. If we make a mistake — for example, drawing one hand longer than the other — we can immediately recognize the error. So a nude figure is considered a good subject for beginners who need to develop their artistic skills. Actually a clothed figure is more difficult to paint or draw than a nude because the clothes distort the shape of the body."

"I see," Yukari said agreeably. "Do you consider yourself a beginner?"

"No," I said with a little pride. "I'm already an intermediate student. But I enjoy painting both nude and clothed figures."

"Hmm," said Hans, grinning. "Of course you enjoy a nude, particularly a female nude, right?"

"Oh, no," I protested. "It's not as you might think. Painting a nude is a very serious business. You have to concentrate. The figure becomes simply an *object d'art*. You cannot have any distracting thoughts. By now, to me, a nude figure is nothing but a beautiful object."

"Yes, I understand what you mean," Yukari said, rescuing me. "Even though your painting is a nude, I rather feel a healthy and pleasant female body sunbathing. I even feel I wouldn't mind sunbathing like that."

Oh, yes, I said in my mind, *I like this. A Japanese girl can say that? Great! I want to paint her in the nude if she agrees. But would Hans go for it? Forget it.* I cooked up the poker face of a serious artist.

Hans had been looking around at one painting after another, apparently concentrating on the nudes. I observed that he was enjoying these figures with a suggestive grin. He drew close to Yukari and me, and whispered, "Wow! All these naked women! I can't help it. I'm aroused." He stuck his forefinger straight up.

He and I roared. People in the gallery stared us with smiles, probably guessing what we were talking about.

"It's not funny!" Yukari spat, shaking her head. "Hans, you must pay more respect to art, because I see only beautiful art objects. Students must have spent a lot of time and effort to come up with these works."

"Sorry," Hans immediately said. "I didn't mean to make fun of it."

"Yes, you did," she replied, pursing her lips.

I was surprised by her strong reaction to Hans, though I appreciated what she said. She moved away from him, pretending to examine other paintings. I hastily followed her to alleviate the awkward air. As we were looking at still-life paintings, Hans came shyly to us. We strolled for a while in silence.

"But seriously, Mark," Hans said finally in an apologetic tone, "your work stands out from other paintings. You have a gift."

Yukari nodded in a gesture of reconciliation. Probably she didn't want to spoil the evening. I saw clearly Hans appearing relieved.

"Someday you must paint all of us together — clothed, of course," he said.

"That's a great idea," Yukari told me, ignoring Hans. "Please do. I can't wait."

*　*　*

The following Monday, Hans called me in my office and thanked me for the past Friday evening. He conceded that he would be more careful about commenting on artworks before Yukari. He then said that on Saturday, his opera workshop class at Juilliard would hold an informal concert, marking the end of the spring semester. He asked me to come with Yukari.

That Saturday evening Yukari and I met at Juilliard and went into an auditorium called the Theater, a small, cozy recital hall for the students. This being Juilliard, however, it was well-built with excellent acoustics. As we entered, the friends and family members of the students steadily filled the theater. We sat in the middle, and soon Hans came to greet us.

"Good to see you," he said, beaming with excitement. "This evening you'll hear a great German tenor — that would be me — singing great Italian arias."

At this I laughed, but Yukari showed an indifferent face, as if she didn't hear him.

"Why don't you sing German lieders or arias from German operas?" I asked him, just to make small talk, so as to avoid another awkward situation.

"I like German lieder," Hans replied immediately, as if he had already prepared for this question, "those of Schubert, Brahms, Schumann, and even Beethoven. They are exquisite. But essentially they are art songs for baritones. I'm a tenor. I want to show off my tenor voice. I like German opera too, particularly Wagner's. They are musically and theatrically spectacular. But there's not much acting involved. Most of the arias and ensembles are sung just standing, whereas Italian operas have plenty of action in addition to their musical and emotional appeal. I'm trying to specialize in Bel Canto opera, represented by Rossini, Donizetti, and Bellini." Here he pointed out the programs Yukari and I were holding. "This evening I'm going to sing a trio from *Il Barbiere di Siviglia* and another trio from *Armida*, both of which Rossini composed. The former is sung by a soprano, a tenor, and a baritone, while the latter is sung by three tenors."

The ceiling lights flickered, indicating the call of singers to the backstage.

"I have to go. Wish me luck." Hans kissed Yukari's cheek, chuckled at me, then ran off to the backstage.

Soon after, the concert began. Some students sang solo arias, and others sang duets, trios, or quartets in varying combinations of voices. There was no orchestra; the instructor played the piano. Students acted the scene on the stage while singing, but they wore their regular clothing — suits or dresses. According to Yukari, being Juilliard, even though the workshop was an evening class, the quality of students was very high.

While listening, I had the impression that Yukari had moved slightly closer to me in her seat. As the program proceeded, she tenderly held my hand, which caught me off guard, like a thunderbolt striking me. I didn't understand what it meant. I turned to her. She smiled. I thought she was just trying to be friendly. This was unusual even for an American woman, so it was beyond my imagination that this would come from a Japanese woman, especially one I had met only recently, and most of all, who was the wife of my close friend. But I just let it go because we were amongst other audience.

Hans's turn came for a trio from Act 3 of *Barbiere*, the storm scene. Yukari withdrew her hand from me. Hans as Count Almaviva and a baritone as Figaro entered the stage, sneaking into Dr. Bartolo's house to take Rosina, his ward, and to run off. The recitative started. They met with Rosina, a soprano. As it turned out, Hans had a beautiful lyric tenor voice. The Count confessed that he had disguised himself as a poor student whom she loved, but actually he was Count Almaviva, and he declared his deep love to her. Astonished but

happy, Rosina sang the soprano theme of joy. The Count followed the same theme. Figaro unsuccessfully urged them to
hurry to escape from the house. As the music approached the
climax, Rosina, the Count, and Figaro sang together, scurrying
joyfully toward the windows. Just before they reached the lad-
der at the window, the scene abruptly ended.

The audience warmly applauded. However, to my surprise, Yukari yawned, not openly, but discretely, though I didn't
miss it. I clapped my hands in approval of Hans's performance.
But her applause appeared just polite and obligatory.

An intermission followed. Yukari held my arm and led
me to the entrance foyer, leaning her head on my shoulder.

"Mark, I like you," she said timidly, but clearly. "I wish I
had met you before Hans."

"What are you talking about?" I said, making an effort to
suppress the tone of rebuke. "Hans is my close friend, and you
don't know me well enough."

"Since we met at the museum, Hans has told me all about
you," Yukari said, clinging to my arm as if it were a piece of wood
amid thrashing river water. "By now I know you well enough."

We came to a corner of the foyer, where we could maintain some privacy.

"I'm thinking of divorce; please help me," Yukari said in
one breath.

I thought I had heard her wrong. I blinked my eyes, feeling totally puzzled.

"I'm serious," she said. "I'm not crazy."

"No," I said, firmly, but I hoped without sounding cold. "I
didn't hear this, all right? Hans is a good man, and I wouldn't
betray him."

"But he slept with another woman after our marriage." Her voice cracked.

"I don't believe you," I shot back. "Don't play with me."

"It's true," she said, her eyes imploring me to believe her. "We hired a housekeeper, a young Filipino woman, whom Hans found through his Filipino colleague at the UN. I understand there are many Filipinos working at the UN. This woman was a younger sister of the wife of one of them. She came once every two weeks, usually on Thursday afternoon. She was in her late twenties and very pretty. She took care of all our housekeeping needs. After a few months we trusted her and let her come even while we were not at home. One Thursday I had an afternoon rehearsal, but it ended much earlier than scheduled, so I went home early. Then I found Hans with this woman in our bed."

I gasped. *Is this possible? Hans? That cool academician, devoted international civil servant, and sweet husband I know?* "I still can't believe you," I said plainly, "because it's completely out of character for him."

"I did love him when I married," she said. "Do you think I would want a divorce unless something happened between us? Do you think I would fabricate such a disgusting story?"

I was stuck. I couldn't simply dismiss her claim, but I needed more information to make a judgment one way or the other.

Hans arrived with a bottle of water in his hand. "Ah, here you are," he said, grinning broadly. "How was I?"

Hans seemed too preoccupied with his singing to notice the awkwardness between Yukari and me. Yukari composed a polite face.

"Congratulations," I told him right away, feeling relieved by his appearance. "You were wonderful. You can reach those high notes comfortably, and your singing perfectly expressed the happiness of a young lover."

He shone, clearly very pleased. But he whispered that he had to save his voice for the next piece, and sipping water, he returned to the backstage.

Yukari resumed. "Hans has begged me for forgiveness. He admitted that it was his mistake, and he swore that he would never do it again. He asked me to give him another chance. So I thought I would let it pass. But now I regret it, because I think he is still seeing that Filipina occasionally." She sounded earnest.

I shook my head. "Really? I just can't believe it."

The intermission ended. Yukari and I went back to our seats.

In the second half of the concert, the arias and ensembles were more complex, aggressive, and risky. Indeed, some students could not reach high notes at the climax, and some made mistakes on the rhythms or entry cues, though all were generously forgiven by the audience.

Hans's turn came again, this time in a trio from Act 3 of *Armida*. The stage was dark. Suddenly the lights came up, and three tenors stood in the middle of the stage, spotlit. They bowed to the audience. Then all of them at the same time ceremoniously pulled an enormous white handkerchief from their jacket pocket, shook it with a huge exaggerated gesture, and held it in their left hand with a showy pose, audaciously suggesting that they were equal to the famous Three Tenors:

Carreras, Domingo, and Pavarotti. Roaring laughter came from the audience —including me. Yukari remained unmoved.

The theater grew quiet, and the trio started with recitative, then each of three tenors came into singing. The tenor who sang Rinaldo must have been an advanced student. He performed excellently in the demanding part. Hans sang the somewhat-less-demanding role of Carlo. The other tenor sang steadily in the role of Ubaldo. The waves of three tenor voices haunted the theater.

I was too disturbed by Yukari's exposé to enjoy the trio ensemble. I mechanically faced the stage, but in my mind I was trying to understand what she had said in the foyer. Yukari, too, appeared too upset to listen to the trio. Again she yawned a few times.

As the trio ended, the audience clapped furiously with laughter, praise, and approval. They shouted "Bravo" many times. The three tenors bowed a few times and acknowledged the audience together by raising both hands in a V shape and waving their signature handkerchiefs. The audience cheered and clapped endlessly — except Yukari and me.

After the concert, as usual, we stopped at a nearby restaurant for a nightcap. For a while we talked about the singing of the students at the theater. Yukari remained polite but did not participate in the conversation. As I felt her tension, I wanted to find some neutral subject.

"Opera arias and ensembles are good," I said. "But Hans, how about choral music? What's your favorite chorus piece?"

"Oh, that's easy to answer," Hans replied immediately. "I love Brahms's *German Requiem* best. Do you know it?"

"I'm not too familiar with it," I said in honesty. "Why is it so special to you?"

"You must hear it. Someday I'll invite you, if I find a good concert for it," Hans said thoughtfully. "The music is so exquisite, peaceful, and spiritual that we feel as if the music is refreshing our courage to live our life and keep going. Whenever I hear it, I feel inspired, and the courage grows in my heart."

Yukari raised her face and quietly gazed Hans. I thought this was a good sign. She seemed to recognize a warm, humane side of him.

"When I die," Hans said out of blue, "I would like the *German Requiem* to be played at my funeral. I would be very happy."

This was a sad remark, I thought, but it came so naturally from him that I simply accepted it without protest.

Yukari slowly opened her mouth, the first time since we came to the restaurant. "Hans, please don't worry, I'll take care of it." She spoke with compassion. "But I would much prefer not to see you dead."

Again I sensed we were headed in a dangerous direction.

"Okay, so much for that," I said. "Let's talk about something else."

"Then I'd like to ask a question, Mark," Yukari said, "if you don't mind."

"No problem," I answered. "Shoot."

"You said the other day you're divorced. What happened?"

This was a personal question I would never discuss with casual friends. But I felt Hans and Yukari were close enough to tell about it. Besides, this was a much better topic than the potentially explosive subject of the delicate relationship between Hans and Yukari.

So I told them about my marriage with Francine, my disappointment, divorce, the subsequent marriage of Francine and Shem Tov, and their baby boy, Jacques. I tried to be as objective as possible. In conclusion, I confessed honestly my stupidity.

Yukari listened intently, then asked, her eyes wide open, "Are you saying that you divorced your wife just because you didn't conceive a child?"

I shrugged. "That's the primary reason. There were other minor issues, but those, I must say, we could have worked out."

"But by New York State law, you can't divorce your wife for that reason," she said in a reproachful tone.

It appeared that she had done some research on divorce. I felt that what she had been telling me about Hans might be true.

"I know," I said. "My lawyer did a good job."

"I can't believe it." She raised her voice. "You may not realize it, but you did the worst thing a man can do to a woman. Women do not tell this to men, but when a woman becomes mentally ready for marriage, and when she meets a man, the first thing she thinks of is what kind of child she would have with him, taking into account his intelligence, personality, appearance, and family background, some of which she may not know yet. But only if the imaginary child is acceptable to her will she start dating the man. I may be exaggerating a little, but this is how women think."

She paused for a breath. I saw that she was trying not to hurt me. I thought that all she was saying was reasonable and I should have known, though it was too late now.

Searching for words carefully, Yukari resumed. "What I mean is that the desire to have a child with a man she loves is an instinct to every normal woman. So it's terribly shameful to a woman to be told that she can't have a baby — or even worse, that she is worthless if she can't. Besides, how did you know it was your wife who couldn't produce? It may have been you." She broke off, appearing to realize she was going too far. "Sorry, I didn't mean to put you down. But my point is that you can't divorce your wife simply because you didn't conceive a child in four years. No, it's wrong, Mark." She shook her head disapprovingly.

Yukari's words struck deep inside me. "Yes, I was wrong," I told her. "I've already admitted this. I learned it the hard way, and I deserve the punishment I received. Now Francine and Shem Tov are happy with their adorable Jacques."

Hans spoke gently, seemingly trying to soften the situation. "I think a child is a gift from the eternal. It may take time. Yukari and I have been married two years, and we don't have a child yet, though we hope it'll come soon."

I thought how sweet Hans was for saying that. But Yukari looked down at her hands as if she wanted to move away from the subject.

Then she met my eyes and asked point-blank, "Do you meet your ex-wife even now?"

"Yes," I answered. "Since Francine works at the UN as a Conference Officer, we often run into each other, and we talk. She still loves me, she says, even after my unforgivable act. Besides, because Shem Tov is a good friend of mine, we often socialize, and many times she comes with him. I even see Jacques occasionally. I like the boy." I sighed. "That child would have been mine if I had not divorced Francine. I realize how foolish I was."

"I didn't know Shem Tov's wife is your ex-wife," Hans said. "I have to be careful when I meet them next time, so I don't embarrass you or Francine."

"Mark, I was going to suggest that you reconcile with your ex-wife," Yukari said. "But that option seems out now."

Was it my imagination that Yukari looked happy?

*   *   *

On Monday, Hans and I met at the cafeteria, supposedly to practice our French, as the spring session was nearing an end and we would have to take a final exam. But I spoke English, complimenting him on his "semi-professional" singing. He was pleased. We talked about how funny it was when the three tenors waved their white handkerchiefs.

To my relief, Hans didn't seem to know of Yukari's disclosure to me about his unfaithfulness and her contemplation of divorce. I was still in a state of disbelief. I hoped that somehow this was a misunderstanding between Yukari and Hans, and they would resolve it soon. I had no wish to bring this matter to Hans. I pretended that I knew nothing about it.

"By the way," said Hans, "Yukari's spirits have lifted, and she is cheerful now. You have a magic power over her. I guess she likes you very much."

"Well, that's too bad," I shot back immediately. "She is married to you."

We had a noisy belly laugh for several seconds. Deep down, however, the situation between the three of us tormented me.

4

One Saturday evening Hans and Yukari invited me for dinner. They lived in a highrise on a tree-lined block of East 89th Street just off Park Avenue at the edge of Carnegie Hill, one of the most prestigious locations in Manhattan. The apartment was a clean one-bedroom with a view of Park Avenue. The sunny living room held a basic set of furniture, a few bookcases lined with economics and music history titles, a desk equipped with a PC, an upright piano, stacks of music scores, a metronome, and a music stand. A dining table and four chairs stood in one corner.

Next to the piano, a bookcase stored three violins. According to Yukari, the first was made by a classic Italian master, the second by a modern American craftsman, and the third by a contemporary Japanese violin maker. She used the first two for performances and the third for practice. She opened the three cases for me, assisted by Hans. The instruments all looked magnificent. She chose the Italian violin and tuned the strings with the bow.

"I'm going to play the second movement of Brahms's *Violin Sonata No. 2*," she said, "known as the *Thuner Sonata*. He composed this during his summer retreat at Thun in Switzerland. It's considered one of his best works."

She played the entire movement with professional concentration. The music sounded like a light-hearted spirit enjoying the fresh warm air in a sunny field, singing a flower song. Was it because of the violin, the music itself, or her skill? Hard to tell. Probably all three together. I enjoyed listening to her performance right before me, because I sensed the tone was more personal than in a public concert. Hans appeared proud of her. When she completed the movement, he and I applauded warmly and yelled "Bravo!" She acknowledged us by curtsying.

"This violin is about two hundred years old," Yukari said. "But as time passes, it produces the sound better and better. It's amazing."

A timer alarm sounded from the kitchen. She gently replaced the instrument into the case as if handling her own baby. Then she went into the kitchen to attend to her cooking.

"Speaking of the sound," Hans said, "except for Yukari's violins, our apartment is nothing fancy. But one good feature is the thick walls between the apartments. Even when I sing in a loud full voice, the neighbors don't complain."

"I practice the violin every day for a long time," Yukari called from the kitchen, "sometimes even with my colleagues. No problem to the neighbors. It's hard to find this kind of apartment in Manhattan."

"Another good thing is the closeness to my church," Hans continued. "I don't go to church every Sunday, but I try to go at least once a month, in addition to special occasions, like Easter and Christmas. I'm a Lutheran, and there is a Lutheran church at the corner of 88th Street and Lexington Avenue, only two blocks from here."

I called to Yukari in the kitchen. "Are you a Christian?"

"Yes, I'm a Methodist," she answered. "When I was going through the ordeal of leukemia, one of my friends in the LA Phil, who happened to be a Methodist, gave me a copy of the Bible. It comforted me. So after my discharge from the hospital, I attended a Methodist church near my apartment and eventually got baptized. Here I go to Hans's church with him, even though it's a different denomination. I like the service, because I find it soul-refreshing, and they provide excellent music."

"That's nice," I said. "I'm an Episcopalian, and I occasionally go to the Heavenly Rest at Fifth Avenue and 90th Street. The Methodists branched out from the Anglican Church, to which the Episcopal Church is affiliated. So Methodists and Episcopalians are brothers and sisters."

"I didn't know that," Hans said. "But the Episcopal Church and the Lutheran Church work together. We can even exchange priests if needs arise. So we three are close in faith. You must come to my church someday."

"That's a good idea," said Yukari, emerging from the kitchen. "Well, Mark, dinner is almost ready." She smiled at me as the hostess of the evening. "I'm a good cook, but you'll have to excuse my limited repertoire. I never had time to go to a cooking school, which I would like to do some day. Since this is our first time to invite you, I'm preparing sushi as the main course with salad and Japanese custard soup called *chawan-mushi.* I hope you'll like it."

I had brought two bottles of red wine. Hans and I helped her set the table. I felt happy because I didn't observe any tension between Hans and Yukari. I thought that at the worst, she was trying to be a good hostess for me so as not to embarrass Hans. Preferably I hoped that she might be reconsidering her thought of divorce. Whichever the case might be, I welcomed the congenial air between the two.

When we all sat at the dining table, Yukari said, "There is one good custom in Japan, which Westerners don't have. Before we eat we always say *Itadakimas,* which can be literally translated as 'I take the meal,' but it actually serves as an informal grace, or Western equivalent of *bon appétit.* So let's say together, Itadakimas."

We did. And without a further ceremony, we began eating. For the salad and soup, we used Western utensils. The Japanese salad dressing, Yukari's own recipe, tasted like a mixture of Italian dressing, mustard, and soy sauce, which was quite new to me, and it stimulated my appetite.

According to Yukari, the custard soup, chawanmushi, was made of shiitake mushrooms, ginkgo nuts, fish cake, fish meat, soft vegetables, and other ingredients I had never heard of, mixed with egg white in medium cups, and steamed.

"This is great!" I said. "I've never had anything like this before. It all melts in my mouth and tastes delicious."

"Thank you," Yukari said, seemingly pleased. "My mother makes excellent chawanmushi, and I have loved it since I was a little girl — though it's difficult to make. I'm glad today it came out all right."

"I like this too. I wish you made it more often," Hans said to Yukari. "But I understand that it takes a lot of work. So I have to be content with getting this on special occasions."

Then came the main course. Each of us had one large plate, on which Yukari had arranged sushi colorfully and beautifully, including tuna, yellowtail, salmon, red snapper, shrimp, eel, sea urchin, and others. She showed me a traditional way of using chopsticks and eating sushi. We ate with enthusiasm. The crispy wine made the sushi lively and kicking, which made us drink the wine more, which made us eat more sushi.

"Sushi looks simple to make," Yukari said. "But actually it's hard to make good sushi." She pointed to her plate. "First of all, the cooked rice is important. I use Japanese sushi rice, not American rice, which is not really for sushi. And I use a Japanese rice cooker, which cooks rice perfectly." She plucked a grain of rice from her sushi. "Not only that, we have to tender the cooked rice for sushi. We use white rice vinegar, sugar, salt, and some secret ingredients that each Japanese family carries. This is a challenge because the liquid must not have any color so the rice remains white. We mix this liquid with the cooked rice and stir the rice gently. Then the rice grows sticky, yet its text becomes firm, so the rice and fish stay together when we attach the fish filling to the rice ball." She demonstrated so we could see that the rice was indeed glued together, yet each grain had its firmness. "The last thing we need is fresh fish. In Japan, a sushi chef personally goes to the fish market every day very early in the morning, like four o'clock, and buys the freshest fish for sushi. Here in Manhattan, I go to a Japanese grocery store, where they sell sushi-grade fish."

Indeed, the fish fillings on top of the rice balls looked very fresh and piquant. I couldn't resist taking another piece — red snapper, my favorite — into my mouth.

"Only Japanese can make good sushi like this, if I may say," Yukari concluded. "Don't go to so-called Asian sushi bars or restaurants, which are owned by Korean, Chinese, Thai, or Vietnamese. I have nothing against them, but they really don't know how to make sushi."

"Well, I've learned something," I said. "Sushi looks like a piece of raw fish on top of a rice ball. But actually a lot of work is involved — it's an art. I'm glad tonight I'm eating the real thing, prepared by a Japanese."

"Me too," Hans said. "Now I can appreciate it more when you make sushi, Yukari."

Hans and I raised our glasses to Yukari, then as she did the same, we sipped more wine. I had never eaten so much sushi. My stomach felt quite full. Hans, too, appeared happy with the dinner, and, I guessed, with Yukari.

Over dessert and tea, our conversation turned to our family. Hans suggested Yukari go first to explain her family background.

"I was born to a traditional Japanese family," she began. "I have to give you a little history lecture so you will understand better. Bear with me, all right?"

I was very much intrigued, so I eagerly gestured for Yukari to go on. Hans, too, nodded and relaxed to listen to her lecture.

"During the Tokugawa Shogunate period," Yukari resumed, "my family, the Asaka, was a wealthy clan, hereditarily serving as treasurer to a *daimyo*, a warlord, in the Harima region. In the middle of the nineteenth century, the Shogunate government decided to send the first Japanese ambassadors to the United States. My great-grandfather served as a low-ranking treasury officer in the embassy."

"My goodness!" I exclaimed. "This is a real history lesson. You see, America is a relatively new nation, so I'm interested in this kind of history, particularly if your family is involved, Yukari."

"You've never told me this before," Hans said. "Please go on."

"President Buchanan and his government welcomed the envoys in Washington DC with great fanfare," Yukari continued. "They formally exchanged the Commerce Treaty ratifications, which was the main purpose of the embassy. The envoys attended a presidential banquet and other state functions, such as visiting factories, shipyards, and hospitals. They traveled to Baltimore and New York, and were also enthusiastically welcomed. Then they went back to Japan. My great-grandfather enjoyed this mission, observing all this with his own eyes."

"So your great-grandfather was one of the first Japanese diplomats to the US," I said. "I'm dumbfounded and impressed."

"Hear, hear," Hans said. "Go on."

Yukari smiled modestly. "By the time the embassy returned to Japan," she continued, "the political tide in Japan had completely changed. Now the Royalist movement had the power over the Shogunate government. Eventually the Shogunate government collapsed, and in 1867 all power was restored to the emperor. This was called the Meiji Restoration."

"What happened to your great-grandfather?" I asked.

"I'm coming to that," Yukari said. "The daimyo my great-grandfather served was a close ally of the Shogunate. After the Restoration, therefore, the emperor's new government destroyed the daimyo's castle and completely stripped his power and authority, which affected all those who served him. In addition, the Restoration was an extraordinary transition from an old feudal social system to a modern industrialized democratic society. The old establishment mostly withered. My great-grandfather, too, could not adapt well to the new society. He suffered bankruptcy and lost all his estate, which had been immense. He died in financial disgrace."

"I'm so sorry," I uttered, sighing.

"Yes, that's too bad," Hans seconded.

"Well, so much for the history lesson," Yukari said. "Actually my family story starts from here. But without mentioning my great-grandfather's disgrace, you wouldn't fully understand it."

"I have to hear the rest," I said. "Please go on."

"Yes, do continue." Hans leaned forward, clearly as eager as I to hear more.

"Okay, next comes my family legend about my grandfather, which I heard from my father repeatedly," Yukari amiably responded. "When my grandfather came to the age for higher education, our family had absolutely no money for it. One day he slit his little finger. Using the blood from the finger as ink, he wrote a petition to the governor of the new prefecture, which included the Harima region, asking for a scholarship for a university education. The 'blood letter' was considered a sacred pledge and commitment. The governor recognized my grandfather's name, as our family had been prominent in the region.

Finding that our family had lost its estates, the governor sympathized with my grandfather and granted the scholarship."

"I'm glad," I said. "How courageous he was!"

"Absolutely," Hans echoed.

"My grandfather went to China and studied Chinese
government administration, which was considered one of the
most sophisticated civil service administrations in the world
at the time, because China had to govern its vast geographical territory and its huge population, a mix of different races,
languages, religions, and cultures. During the Sino-Japanese
war, from 1894 to 1895, he provided outstanding intelligence
and strategy development services to the Japanese military
establishment in China. After the Japanese victory over China,
which stunned the world, he was lavishly rewarded."

"So your grandfather reestablished your family grace,
didn't he?" I said, feeling genuine joy and respect for her grandfather. "He was a real adventurer, like in a novel."

"Your great-grandfather would have felt proud of his son,
if he had lived to see that day." Hans added.

"I agree," I said.

"You can understand why this is our family legend,"
Yukari said, beaming with pride. "Now my father's story." She
composed herself and resumed. "My father went to the School
of Law at Kyoto University, formally called Kyoto Imperial
University at the time, to prepare for his career in the government. After receiving a Bachelor of Law degree, which was
equivalent to a Masters degree in the US, he managed to get
a scholarship to go to Berlin University in Germany. He studied law, political science, economics, and history there. Then
World War II broke out, and he returned to Japan."

"Wait a sec," Hans interrupted. "My grandfather taught architecture at Berlin University until Berlin was divided between East and West after the war. But his field of study seems different from that of your father."

"That's an interesting coincidence," Yukari replied. "Anyway, let me continue. My father worked for the Ministry of Foreign Affairs in Tokyo. Since he spoke German, and since Germany was a Japanese ally, he had a high-profile job in the ministry. But when Japan lost the war, MacArthur's occupation force came and started hunting for war criminals. My father left the ministry quietly, simply to avoid prosecution. He went into the private sector and worked for a big construction company as Executive Vice President until his retirement."

"This is the father who came to Los Angeles when you stayed in the hospital for leukemia?" I asked.

"Yes," Yukari answered. "He is over eighty now. Since he married late, my mother is still in her sixties. But fortunately they are both still living."

I remembered something. "You said the other day, 'An insatiable desire to go abroad runs in my family.' Now I understand what it means. You are an adventurer, like your great-grandfather, grandfather, and father."

"Yes, that's it," Yukari said. "When I refused to go back to Japan during my illness in LA, as I told you before, my father was furious. But over time he accepted me, as I proved that I am one of the Asakas. My mother told me later that my father now feels proud of me."

"This is one of the greatest family stories I've ever heard," I said, gazing at Yukari in admiration. "You are part of that great story."

"I'm proud of you, Yukari," Hans said happily.

"So this is my story," Yukari concluded. "Now, Mark, why don't you tell us your family background?"

"Yes, Mark, you go next," said Hans.

I sipped tea, contemplating whether or not I should tell my family background from the root. It didn't take long to come to the conclusion that, since Yukari had told her family story in detail, including her great-grandfather's disgrace, I should do the same, though from a different perspective.

"Okay, then I have to start from a slightly shameful origin," I began. "My family is related to the current Sir John Carl Graham, the eighteenth baronet in England, who is listed in *Debrett's Peerage & Baronettage*." Here I paused. "Do you know *Debrett's*? It's a book that lists all the titled families in Great Britain. It's a must-have book for the social-status-conscious people in Britain, which means practically everyone."

"Wow!" Hans exclaimed. "So your family is listed in that book? Impressive!"

Yukari jumped in. "Japan abolished the title system after World War II, so we don't have that kind of issue any more. But people still seek a traditional family status in secret."

"I live in a republic, the United States of America," I hastily added. "So I don't believe in those titles. But hear me out, since it is part of my family heritage." I sipped my tea again, then resumed. "My family story goes like this. The tenth baronet, Sir Thomas Graham, was a very handsome and easygoing gentleman with the reputation of a lady's man. He had a beautiful, intelligent wife who oversaw the day-to-day management of his estate in Kent. Unfortunately, at age thirty, which was very old for a woman at the time, she still had not produced a child."

"Oh, no," Yukari cried. "Don't tell me he did what you did to Francine."

Hans laughed, but immediately said, "Sorry."

I grinned. "Worse than that. Sir Thomas flirted around carefree with ladies in London society. While he and his wife discussed divorce often, her desperate prayer was answered, and she finally conceived a child. However, it was too late. He had found an attractive lady of seventeen and secretly made her pregnant. The prospect of a pleasurable life with the young lady was so irresistible that he forcefully divorced his wife of eleven years and remarried the younger woman."

"My goodness," Yukari said, "a bad tradition runs in your family."

We all laughed, though my laughter was mixed with chagrin.

"Now my family story really begins," I continued. "Sir Thomas's ex-wife was then discretely sent off to Washington DC with generous financial provision. There she gave birth to a baby girl. The child grew up to become a beautiful lady in Washington society at the time of President James Buchanan. This is my great-great-grandmother, Anne Graham Sanders."

"So your family, too, is an old one," Yukari said.

"Yes, for an American family," I answered, "because here we really don't have many old families. I don't know whether this was the proud origin of my family or the disgraceful origin."

"Wait a minute," Yukari interrupted. "When my great-grandfather visited Washington DC, Buchanan was the president. What a coincidence."

"Yes," I said, intrigued by Yukari's comments. "Anne Graham married a government official named Sanders and started two family traditions. First, she kept 'Graham' as her middle name and instructed her children to do the same. Second, she made a replica of the Graham coat of arms as our family regalia, which has been passed down through generations to the present day. Since her mother had been formally divorced, and since only men can carry the coat of arms of their family, strictly speaking, Anne Graham Sanders was not eligible to carry that coat of arms. So the traditions she started seem to me a sort of protest against the unfair divorce of her mother by Sir Thomas." I paused a little to gather my thoughts. "We still have the replica of the coat of arms at my parents' house in Washington DC. I like it: a dove with an olive branch in her beak, a symbol of peace, flying forever forward above the globe. The motto, '*Promovere*,' is my motto too. Move forward … it suits me."

"I like that," Yukari said decidedly. "It's my motto too: move forward."

"So here I am, four generations after Anne Graham Sanders," I said, wrapping up. "My formal name is, therefore, Mark Graham Sanders. Sometimes I go by Mark G. Sanders, but most of the time simply Mark Sanders. As I said before, I live in a republic, so I'm a believer in equal opportunity, and I don't believe in birthright. So my family heritage doesn't play much of a role in my life."

As I concluded, I had an impression that Yukari's face shone in tenderness toward me. Yes, we shared a similar old family background, though in different countries. But what did it mean to us? Anyway, she was married to Hans.

"Now, Hans, it's your turn," I said.

Yukari kept quiet.

Hans polished off his tea. "Okay," he said. "My family background is not as colorful as yours, Yukari and Mark. But it goes something like this." He took a deep breath. "My grandfather was a professor of architecture at Berlin University, which was founded in the early nineteenth century and became the center for German intellectuals, taught by Humboldt, Hegel, Fichte, and many other renowned professors."

"Good old days in Germany, eh?" I said.

"That's right," Hans replied with pride. "My grandfather had a glorious academic life, as all professors in Germany enjoyed their privileges at the time. But the Nazis came to power and intimidated the university faculty. They burned books and expelled professors and students, and even murdered some of them. Fortunately they dealt leniently with the Department of Architecture, due to its close ties with Albert Speer, who was Hitler's personal architect and the Minister of Armaments and Munitions."

I hoped Hans wasn't going to get into the war, since the topic was unpleasant and Germany — and Japan, too — had been enemies of the US and its allies.

"My grandfather was a typical academician," Hans continued, "who loved research and had absolutely no interest in politics or even in world affairs. The war did not change anything for him. He went to the university every day for work as if no bombs had been falling on Berlin. Then Germany lost the war, and the country was divided. Berlin was in the middle of East Germany, but it was further divided into four blocks, administered by the U.S., U.K., France, and the Soviets. The

Soviet soldiers occupied the east side of Berlin, where the university happened to be located."

"Then what happened to your grandfather?" I asked, relieved he had skipped much discussion of World War II.

"I'm coming to that," Hans said. "In Germany at the time, professors were part of the upper-class establishment. My grandfather could not stand the East German authority that now controlled the university. So he moved to the west side of Berlin with his family. This broke his spirts, since he had lived very close to the university for his entire life until then." He paused. "You should know that the Berlin Wall was created only in the early 1960s, so until then people on the east side were able to move freely to the west side. This is what my grandfather did."

"I see," I said. "I didn't know they could move freely within Berlin."

"The worst was yet to come," Hans said. "In West Berlin, a group of students brought books, while tutors started teaching in a villa provided by the US authority. This was the beginning of the Free University of Berlin. My grandfather actively involved himself in establishing the Free University. My father grew up under the protection of my grandfather and eventually became a young faculty member of the Free University."

"So your family is an academic family," I said.

"Yes," Hans replied. "And I experienced a historic moment of tragedy in Berlin. In August 1961, the Soviet authority began building the concrete wall, reinforced by landmines, virtually imprisoning West Berliners in the midst of East Germany. This completely broke my grandfather. His only comfort was that he had brought his family to West Berlin before the wall was built, which had been a right decision, no matter how painful it was. Soon after, he died of a broken heart."

"Your grandfather was a good man," I said. "I sympathize with him."

All this time, I noticed that Yukari had been keeping quiet. I thought it was a dangerous sign. But there was little I could do.

"I feel sorry for him too," Hans said. "I was born in the late 1950s and was only four when the Berlin Wall rose. Even at that age, I still vividly remember my grandfather putting me on his shoulders and desperately trying to show me the university from the west side of the wall, standing on tiptoes on a bench, saying, 'Hans, remember. That's Berlin University, the pride of Germany, my university.'" Hans sighed. "Now that the Berlin Wall is torn down and Germany is united, if my career at the UN does not work out for me, I might go back to Berlin and teach economics and econometrics at Berlin University, my grandfather's university. I have a Ph.D. from Berkeley. I could do that."

"I hope that won't happen," Yukari said abruptly, speaking for the first time since Hans started telling his story.

"Sorry, I didn't mean to scare you," Hans said apologetically. "I was just thinking of it as a contingency plan. Me too, I hope that won't happen. I believe in the UN, so New York is my place to live and work."

"I'm glad," Yukari said.

"By the way," Hans said, "Mark, you mentioned your family coat of arms. I have something of that sort. I didn't pay much attention to it until now. It bothers me. Let me bring it."

Hans went to the bedroom and quickly returned with a small black box.

"I found this when I was cleaning my grandfather's room," he said. "I thought it was just a stationary box without any specific value, so I've been using it to store small things. But look at the top."

He showed us the box. On the top, indeed, was a small crest painted in gold.

Suddenly Yukari shouted, "How did you get this?"

Hans seemed completely astounded by her reaction. "As I said, I found it in my grandfather's room. Is this something special to you?"

"This is a Japanese lacquer box," said Yukari, gazing at the box with her eyes almost popping out, "commonly used to keep documents like letters in the old days in Japan. What surprises me is that this crest is my family crest."

"Really?" I and Hans uttered at the same time.

"See here," she continued, pointing at the crest. "This four-cut lozenge is called *takedabishi*, and it is enclosed inside a ring. I can't believe it. But indeed, this is my family crest. … Excuse me for a minute."

She ran to one of closets. Using a stepstool, she brought down a cardboard box, from which she withdrew a collapsed fan. She came back and showed it to Hans and me.

"This is nothing fancy, but just a Japanese fan." She opened it, displaying a beautiful flower pattern inside. "When I left Tokyo for the US, my parents gave me this so I would remember my family heritage. Look here at the top of the fan. This is my family crest."

I studied it. Sure enough, it bore the same design, though slightly smaller. I cried, "My goodness, it's the same!"

"It's the same!" Hans repeated like a parrot.

"Then the question is: how did your grandfather get it?" said Yukari.

"Your father must have met my grandfather in Berlin," Hans said, "and given him this box, probably as a token of friendship. Is it possible?"

Yukari sank in a deep thought, then said, "To think of it, although my father never studied architecture, he was very interested in it, and he often visited Japanese castles to enjoy the structure and beauty. So it's possible that he went to see your grandfather for discussions on architecture, something like a comparative study of European castles with Japanese castles. It would be quite plausible, indeed."

An idea flashed in my head. "You said just several minutes ago that your father worked for a big construction company after leaving the foreign ministry. It makes sense, because he was interested in architecture."

"I've never thought that way," Yukari said. "But I must say it makes a lot of sense."

"I'm convinced, Yukari," I said, "that your father met Hans's grandfather and gave the box to him."

"Unbelievable," Hans said. "But me too, I feel sure that's what happened."

"W-w-wait a minute," I said, stammering. "In my parents' house in Washington DC, we have a pretty Japanese doll. It's very old, but well kept in a glass box. Although the glass box is modern and American-made, the doll is genuine Japanese-made. My mother told me that it is one of our family treasures, passed down from generation to generation. The base of the doll is a black lacquer panel. If I'm not mistaken, at the corner of the base this same crest is painted in gold. Is it possible?"

"Fantastic!" Yukari exclaimed. "Let's suppose it is my family crest. Then my great-grandfather must have given it to your great-great-grandmother, Anne Graham Sanders. This is possible, because the officials of the Japanese embassy were introduced to the society ladies at social occasions."

"Hmm ... this is getting really far beyond my imagination," I said. "Did you say your great-grandfather was a treasury officer in the embassy, Yukari? ... Aha! Anne Graham Sanders was married to Nathaniel Sanders, my great-great-grandfather, the Deputy Secretary of the Treasury Department at the time. As I recall, Anne was a close friend of Harriet Lane, the niece of President James Buchanan. Since Buchanan was a bachelor, the vivacious Harriet served as the de-facto mistress of the White House, welcoming and entertaining the guests with charm and grace. So it's very possible that Anne and Nathaniel were with Harriet when she was entertaining the Japanese embassy at a ball or other occasion. The Japanese treasury officer, your great-grandfather, must have presented the doll to Anne, the wife of the Deputy Treasurer, as a memento for friendship. ... That's it, I'm sure. Faaantastic!" I couldn't resist clapping my hands.

"Yaaay!" Yukari, too, cried in joy, applauding wildly.

"Incredible!" Hans said, leaping to his feet.

"This is more than just a coincidence," I said, shaking my head at the marvel. "We were destined to meet."

I warmly clasped Hans's hand, then hugged Yukari, my first hug to her. Both Hans and Yukari responded affectionately

with smiles and nods, even a kiss from Yukari, her first kiss
to me.

"Mark," Yukari said, her face radiant, "we are all practically related."

5

At the United Nations, June was dubbed "j-UN-e," a month of hospitality events organized by the UN, the Member States, and the local communities, as the General Assembly session was now in recess until it reconvened in September. One of the traditional events was an evening concert at the General Assembly Hall, sponsored by one of the Member States, to which the UN staff members and diplomats of the Member States were invited for free. This year the German government had brought the Gewandhous Orchestra from Leipzig. The program consisted of Beethoven's *Egmont Overture* and Brahms's *Symphony No. 1*. Hans secured two tickets for Yukari and himself, while I managed to get a ticket as well.

Since the orchestra was one of the best in the world, the huge chamber was crowded with UN staff, diplomats, and their guests. We heard many different languages being spoken. Hans greeted several of his colleagues and introduced Yukari to them. He also saluted several diplomats who represented their countries to the Second Committee, which discussed economic and financial issues. Hans knew them because he regularly attended the committee with his director whenever they discussed EGlobe, in which Hans played a major role.

"*Bonsoir,* Mark!"

I heard a sweet voice and turned away from Hans and Yukari to see Francine with Shem Tov.

"*Ah, Francine!* Ça va?" I said, practicing my French.

"*Ça va trés bien, merci,*" Francine said in her elegant French, and hugged me. "*Et toi?*"

In her late thirties, my ex-wife was graceful, slender, of medium height, with brunette hair and hazel eyes. She still used "*tu*" for me, the more intimate form of address in French.

"*Trés bien, moi aussi, merci,*" I answered, and switched to English before I embarrassed myself. "How is little Jacques?"

"He is just fine," she said, beaming. She still spoke with a melodic French accent, though she had been in the US for a long time. "He started babbling something. I think he is forming some primitive words."

"That's nice," I said, again thinking that this boy could have been mine. My heart ached, but I felt grateful to Francine for treating me as an old friend in spite of my shameful behavior. How generous she was.

"This evening a babysitter is looking after him. So this is our night out," she said, breaking into a broad smile.

"You'll be surprised how fast the baby grows," Shem Tov joined in.

He was about forty, a little taller than Francine, with a muscular frame since he had completed his mandatory military duty. He was handsome, with dark hair and dark eyes. His cheeks and chin were clean shaven, but looked almost blue.

"Good to see you, Shem Tov." I shook his hand warmly.

Hans greeted Shem Tov and Francine, then introduced Yukari.

Francine hugged Yukari. "Ah, you are Japanese, yes?" she said. "I once tried to learn Japanese. It was hard. Maybe you can help me?"

"My pleasure," Yukari answered, smiling.

"I lived in Japan for five years when I was a boy," Shem Tov told Yukari, "because my father served as the Israeli ambassador to Japan. I went to an American school in Tokyo and had my Bar Mitzvah in a Jewish community house there. I have a lot of good memories of those days. Someday I want to visit there again."

"Is your father still in Japan?" Yukari asked.

"No, he is already retired from the foreign service," Shem Tov answered. "But he is still quite active in Israel."

"I was going to perform in Tel Aviv once as a solo violinist," Yukari said nostalgically. "But that was cancelled because I became ill."

She had not mentioned this to me. I thought that this must have been one of many sad disappointments she'd had to face during her battle with leukemia. I could understand why she didn't want to tell me.

"She is a professional violinist, Shem Tov," I said with pride.

He widened his eyes. "Wow, I'm impressed."

"Shem Tov is a cultivated man, Yukari," I said. "He loves attending concerts."

"I want to hear you perform," Shem Tov said to Yukari. "Please let me know when you have your next concert. We'll come."

"Thank you, I'll do that," Yukari said, smiling. "But now I play in an orchestra."

"Wonderful!" Francine said. "Shem Tov and I are avid classical music lovers. I'll look forward to hearing you play."

Luckily we found five consecutive seats in the middle of the chamber and sat, in the order of Hans, Yukari, me, Francine, and Shem Tov.

Before the podium, where the Secretary-General, the president of the GA, and the vice-president sat during the sessions, the several rows of delegates' tables had been removed and a stage constructed, large enough to accommodate the orchestra members, their instruments, and the conductor. At the front wall of the chamber, behind the podium, large HD TV screens hung on either side of the huge UN emblem.

Shem Tov leaned across me toward Yukari and said, "See those big flat TV screens? The Japanese government donated them. I work in the IT division. My boss is Japanese. His group, called the Systems Management Section, manages the computer data center. Japan is the second largest contributing country to the UN budget after the US. So Japan has a lot of presence in the UN."

"That's nice to hear," Yukari answered, observing the TV screens and the surroundings. Since this was her first time in this chamber, she appeared fascinated.

"Another group of our IT division manages the conference technology support, including those TVs," Shem Tov added. "This evening they'll simulcast the performance on the

TV, and the host government, Germany, will pay the bills for operating the facility."

"I'm a Conference Officer," Francine said. "So I know it costs a lot of money to operate those conference facilities. Fortunately, IT simplifies our job to run conferences smoothly."

"What kind of work does the Conference Officer do?" Yukari asked.

"When the General Assembly session is on," Francine replied, "this chamber is like a madhouse. The order of the speakers must be carefully arranged, because the speakers are all dignitaries representing their countries, like presidents, prime ministers, foreign ministers, and even kings and queens. Interpreters have to be arranged in a timely manner. The verbatim must be recorded accurately and promptly, after which they must be translated into all six official languages, regardless of the original language of the speaker. Then they must be put into a computer system that stores all UN official documents, called the Official Document System, so the world public can read it within a day on the Internet. We Conference Officers coordinate all these activities. GA has many committees and commissions, and there are many other conferences by the Security Council, the Economic and Social Council, and non-governmental organizations. I'm in charge of the Fifth Committee under GA, which deals with budgetary and administrative issues."

"My goodness, it sounds like a complicated job," Yukari said in admiration.

Francine nodded, seemingly pleased. "Yes, it is."

I was glad that Shem Tov and Francine seem to like Yukari. But I noticed that somehow Hans appeared to be trying to hide himself from other people in the chamber. I wondered why.

"Ah, look," Francine cried, pointing to a dark handsome man two rows before us. "That's Justin Tugutu, a Tanzanian, who is in charge of ODS. He is a colleague of Shem Tov, and I also work closely with him for my job. Hi, Justin!" she called and waved.

The pleasant-faced man in his mid-thirties looked back, and on seeing Francine and Shem Tov, broke into a big grin. "Hello, Francine and Shem Tov. How are you? No need to feed documents into ODS this evening, eh?"

"Yes," Francine replied, "this evening is for enjoyment."

"Yeah, let's enjoy ourselves," Justin said.

The conductor came to the stage, and the audience warmly welcomed him. Without much ceremony, he began the *Egmont Overture*, a short piece, but it set a solemn mood. The TV screens showed the conductor and the orchestra members in action, in wideshots and zooms from several angles that helped the audience to better appreciate the performance.

Then the orchestra played Brahms's *Symphony No. 1*, which was renowned for its full energy and spirit. In the first movement, after a sublime introduction, the main allegro theme energetically sprang up, keeping its forward momentum, but lingering with some tenderness and climaxing in a serene coda distinguished by a solo violin. I saw Yukari's smile. I observed, too, Shem Tov and Francine watching Yukari's reaction. And was it my imagination, or was Francine studying me as well? The next two movements passed rather quickly, building the expectation for the fourth movement, the Finale. The orchestra performed the famous hunting horn theme exuberantly, leading into the solemn, grandly striding melody and culminating in the frantic ending.

The audience burst into applause, which the conductor and the members of the orchestra delightedly acknowledged. With a few encore pieces, the concert was over.

Since it was not late in the evening, we decided to go to the Delegates' Lounge and relax. On the way we stopped at the restrooms. The men came out first, and we waited for Yukari and Francine.

Two Asian women appeared, and one of them, pretty-looking, accosted Hans. "Hello, Hans, how are you?" she said, kissing him. "You haven't called me lately. Don't be so cold. Call me, okay, sweetie? I'll take care of anything you want." She winked.

Hans backed off, trying to hide himself without success, because he couldn't find anything to cover him. Reluctantly he faced the woman and said, "Ah, yes, I'll do that."

Then he completely ignored her, and said to me and Shem Tov, looking toward the ladies' room, "Women take a long time, eh?"

The two Asian women walked away.

"I wish those Filipinos would leave the UN," Hans said. "The work at the UN is a public service, so everyone who works here must have a spirit of public service. But those Filipinos come here just to make money so they can feed their family. Nothing wrong with that by itself, but they should be doing it outside the UN, not here." He stressed "not here" loudly.

"I agree," Shem Tov said. "When I started working for the UN, the first thing I noticed was the number of Filipinos working here. I said to myself, 'Why on earth so many Filipinos here?' They don't seem to have anything to do with the works of the UN. They are nothing but parasites. It's just not healthy for our organization."

It was essential that each UN staff member uphold a spirit of public service, as befit our role as international civil servants. At the UN promotion was subject to the limited post availability, and those who worked hard were not necessarily rewarded financially. Therefore, the spirit of public service, or the satisfaction of serving the people, provided the primary motivation to work hard for the UN. What Hans and Shem Tov had criticized was the lack of this spirit of public service in several ethnic groups of developing countries at the UN, the most notable one being Filipino.

The UN employees consisted of two categories: Professional and General Service. The Professional staff were recruited internationally and worked in their professional fields, such as political science, economics, sociology, law, accounting, information technology, personnel administration, and the like. The General Service staff were recruited locally and worked as clerks, secretaries, messengers, and manual workers. In this way the UN could maintain a global perspective in the professional fields, while contributing to the local economy of the host country, in our case the US, by hiring local residents, either US citizens or greencard holders, in the non-professional fields.

Filipinos came to the US on tourist visas and somehow got hired as the General Service staff, using their vast underground network at the UN, circumventing the policy of local recruitment. It was not an exaggeration that Filipinos dominated the population of the General Service staff. This was a fact everybody knew at the UN, but we couldn't discuss it openly in public, because we didn't want to be labeled racist, which was a taboo at the UN. So we talked of it only privately.

I suspected that the Asian woman who had kissed Hans was his former Filipino housekeeper, with whom he had had an affair, according to Yukari. She was not a UN staff member, so the woman next to her must have been the UN staffer who brought her to this evening's entertainment. Most likely Hans had suspected that his ex-housekeeper might appear this evening. He clearly didn't want to run into her, which was why he had been keeping a low profile during the concert. The exchange between them appeared to suggest that Hans had not seen her for a while. Did this mean that he had severed the illicit relationship with her? If so, this was a piece of good news. But he hadn't refused her invitation to call her. Did that mean he was still keeping up their relationship? Those vulnerable people with dubious visa status would do anything to secure their visa, including sex. I felt sorry for Yukari.

However, Hans' remarks about Filipinos in the UN seemed to reveal that he was resentful of the Filipino community, including his ex-housekeeper. Did this mean that Hans was trying to get rid of her? If this was the case, there was hope for his marriage. But I was not sure at all.

Francine rejoined us. "Sorry for keep you waiting,"

Shortly after, Yukari emerged. She appeared not to have seen the two Filipino women. I saw Hans taking a deep breath, probably feeling relieved, as he had barely escaped a catastrophe.

We moved on to the Delegates' Lounge. This was where behind-the-scenes negotiations and bargaining took place among diplomats over drinks, tea, or coffee. It was beautifully decorated with paintings, sculpture, and tapestries that had been donated by the Member States. The bar was closed already. We sat at a table.

Hans seemed to feel a need to clear from his mind the encounter with the Filipino woman. Composing himself, he said, "This concert has a symbolic meaning. Leipzig used to be in East Germany. The Gewandhaus Orchestra, one of the greatest cultural institutions in the world, had been administered poorly, like everything else in East Germany. Now that Germany is united, this orchestra has regained the excellence and glory of the pre-communist era. I think the German government wanted to show this to the UN and the world. That's why they brought the orchestra here and funded the simultaneous broadcasting."

"I'm sure it is so," Shem Tov said. Then he asked Yukari, "What did you think of the concert?"

"When I go to a concert," Yukari replied, "I just want to enjoy it. So I try to avoid being critical. I did enjoy this evening's concert, because true to its reputation, the Gewandhaus Orchestra performed excellently. But I couldn't help noticing that some of their instruments were shabbily maintained, not really in top shape. I felt sorry for them. They are still carrying the injuries of the past. I hope the situation will improve."

"That's true," Hans seconded. "I noticed it too. I hope the ghosts of the past will disappear soon."

This sounded to me like Hans was speaking of the Filipina. I was wrong. He was talking of World War II.

"By the way, Shem Tov," Hans said next out of blue, "I went to Israel when I was a doctoral student at Berkeley. My sole purpose was to visit the Holocaust Museum in Jerusalem in order to express my contrition for what my country did to your people during the war."

At the UN it was safer to avoid this kind of sensitive subject, particularly between a German and an Israeli. I was astonished, therefore, to hear Hans speak so openly. I was about to change the subject.

Determined to speak out, however, Hans continued, his voice trembling. "No words can express what I felt there. I was not born yet, but that does not absolve me from the responsibility for your people. Such horror must not happen again. In the museum, I pledged myself that I would work toward that goal. This is why I came to the UN. Will you forgive me?" He was almost crying.

An odd silence enveloped us for some time.

Shem Tov appeared profoundly affected. After a white, he cleared his throat and said, "I appreciate what you've said. You were not born at the time, so it's not your fault. But yes, let us try to prevent that kind of thing from happening again. Me too, this is the reason I came to the UN. You and I share the same goal."

"Then you'll forgive me?" Hans repeated.

"It's not a question of forgiveness," Shem Tov replied immediately. "We cannot erase the dark fact of the past. So our responsibility now is to work together for preventing it. Come, let's shake hands." He presented his hand.

Hans clasped it firmly. As if that were not enough, he embraced Shem Tov.

I saw Yukari and Francine dabbing their cheeks. I, too, was deeply moved.

"Well," Shem Tov said, "I'm very happy this evening, because I've come to know that Hans and I share the same fundamental goal for our life; I became acquainted with the lovely Yukari; and of course Mark is my close friend and Francine is my dear wife."

"Japan is a peace-loving country now," Yukari said. "I'm proud of being part of it."

"Yes, as a Swiss," Francine said, "I want to mediate peace among all people."

"Me too," I said. "I believe in the UN. This is why I'm here. But let's not ignore the reality that the UN is not functioning as well as it should, because it's infested with those parasites who leech the money from the organization for their personal purpose, neglecting our mission for the public service. So within that reality, let's do our best."

I saw Hans and Shem Tov enthusiastically making thumbs-up, while Francine and Yukari applauded.

"Let's pledge ourselves for peace," I proposed.

The five of us formed a circle, holding hands: Yukari, Hans, Shem Tov, Francine, and me. We kept a moment of silence for our pledge.

Then, with the squeeze of hands that travelled around the circle, Shem Tov solemnly pronounced, "I have a feeling that this is the beginning of our long-lasting friendship."

* * *

The next day I had late lunch at the cafeteria. I was walking toward the elevator bank to go back to my office, when
I ran into Francine. She was just coming back from the UN
Childcare Center, where she had given Jacques lunch and
played with him. Since this was a less-busy time for her job, she
proposed we take a walk together in the UN garden. I didn't
have any urgent work at my office, as usual, so I happily agreed.

The fresh green of the lawn and trees warmed our hearts
as we strolled the garden. After a while, we sat on a bench
under the cherry trees.

"Francine," I said, "Hans and I had been friends for some
time. But recently I met his wife Yukari, whom you met yesterday. Hans, Yukari, and I are now good friends. On one occasion, she told me that I had done to you was the worst thing
a man could do to a woman. Since then I've been thinking of
our relationship. I believe that Yukari is absolutely right. I have
done a terrible injustice to you. It's easy to say this. But I really
mean it. I hope you can forgive me."

"Mark," she replied, "I am a kind of person who cannot hate anybody. Hatred is just not my nature. When we got
divorced I was sad and depressed, but I didn't hate you. That
sadness gradually disappeared. Now I am happy with Shem
Tov and Jacques."

I sighed. "You are an angel. I now wonder how I could
have divorced such a sweet person who loved me so much. If
we had stayed together, as you wanted, we would have gotten
Jacques, and both of us would have been happy. I realize how
stupid I was."

She gently put her finger to my lips. "Don't say that. It's done, and it cannot be undone."

"I agree, but I want you to know how sorry I am."

"I'd like you to move on, Mark. Yesterday I saw an opportunity. From a woman's intuition, I know you love Yukari."

I felt a pang at my heart. "Excuse me?"

"Don't be embarrassed. Any woman would see it in you."

"Yukari is Hans's wife, so she and I are just good friends."

"That's what you think in your brain, but your heart feels otherwise."

I may have recognized a warm feeling toward Yukari, but I had been suppressing that feeling and forcing myself to believe that we were just good friends. Besides, Hans was my close friend. I had no desire to betray him.

I replied simply, "I've never thought that way."

"Be honest to your heart, Mark," Francine said. "Yes, it's true that she is married to Hans, your close friend, which creates a complication. I don't know how you should proceed in this situation, so I cannot give you any advice. But I want you to be happy with Yukari."

6

Late June, soon after the evening concert at the General Assembly Hall, Shem Tov, Francine, and their little Jacques left for their four-week summer vacation to stay in his parents' home in Israel. Shem Tov told me that he had some personal project to undertake there, which he promised to discuss with me on his return. But he didn't reveal what it was.

Hans and I decided to spend the Fourth of July together with Yukari. Since the day fell on a Sunday, we would not have to work the next day.

It was a sunny, hot summer day, but the air was dry and comfortable. We met at the Fulton Street subway station around three o'clock in the afternoon. We walked leisurely to South Street Seaport, then to Battery Park. Streets were closed for pedestrians. Many people were strolling among the street entertainers and street vendors.

Yukari walked between Hans and me. To my surprise, she held my hand at her right and his hand at her left. She appeared happy with that. I was more surprised that Hans seemed quite content with it, as if it were most natural. So while I felt pleased because Yukari was holding my hand, I also felt odd because Hans was next to her.

We stopped for lemonade, and rested here and there. In the park we listened to a jazz and pop concert, while overlooking the Statue of Liberty in the harbor under the golden sun.

Then we went to Little Italy for dinner. We chose a cozy restaurant, which was crowded with patrons. As we settled at a table, Yukari went to the ladies' room.

Sipping cold water, Hans said, "Since we had dinner in my apartment, my love life with Yukari has improved."

I thought he was joking. "What are you talking about?" I asked.

But Hans looked earnest. "Somehow your presence helps Yukari and me stay closer," he said. "I'm grateful to you. I need you."

I thought that this may have been the reason that Hans had not seen that Filipino woman lately. Yukari may have put her thought of divorce on hold. This was good for both him and Yukari. And this may have been the reason he had been content when Yukari held hands with both of us as we walked.

"I still don't know what you're talking about," I said in an intentionally light tone, pretending my ignorance of their marital strain. "But if you're enjoying your love life with Yukari, I'm happy for you."

Yukari came back.

For the appetizer, we ordered steamed calamari, smoked oysters, and Caesar salad to share at the center of our table. For the main course, Yukari had steamed red snapper; Hans, grilled lamb chop with sausage; and I, grilled swordfish. Plus a bottle of red wine.

As we ate and drank, I narrated a brief history of American independence, like the one we learned in the elementary school. Yukari and Hans knew most of it, but they listened to me with keen interest. It appeared to me that they wanted to hear a standard version of the American independence story from American.

When I finished my lecture, Yukari asked, "Why do you use fireworks on the evening of July Fourth?"

"Ah," I answered immediately, "to remind us that our independence was hard won after many battles and bombardments. The fireworks are a peaceful substitution for the gun battles and cannon bombardments. So we celebrate today with fireworks. The noisier, the better."

"I see," Yukari said. "That makes sense."

I added thoughtfully, "Sometimes I wonder how the mother of Anne Graham Sanders felt when she celebrated July Fourth for the first time in Washington DC. Probably she wanted to sever all ties with England and to start her new life in America. So the fireworks must have bolstered her courage to do so. Especially today, therefore, I feel my family heritage to the core as American."

Yukari raised her wine glass and cried, "Happy birthday, America!"

"Thank you," I said, raising my glass. "To America!"

"Hear, hear," Hans said, raising his glass. "To America!"

We gulped generous swigs of wine.

Then I said to Yukari, "To Japan!"

"*Arigato*," Yukari said. "To Japan!"

Hans yelled, "To Japan!"

Then I did the same to Hans. "To Germany!"

"*Danke*," Hans said. "To Germany!"

Yukari cried, "To Germany!"

Each time as we shouted, we raised our glasses and drank. We were drunk with the spirit of Independence Day and our patriotism. Other guests in the restaurant smiled at us.

A waiter nearby frowned and grumbled jokingly, "How about Italy? You're now in Italian territory, you know."

We yelled back immediately, "To Italy!"

Loud cheers, bravos, and laughter came from all waiters and waitresses. Then, as if it were a competition, a well-dressed gentleman at one of the tables stood and spoke solemnly in a strong foreign accent.

"*Excusez-moi*," he said. "Don't forget France. We gave America the Statue of Liberty."

We toasted high. "*Vive la France!*"

The French gentleman nodded repeatedly with deep satisfaction, because, I wishfully guessed, our French grammar was correct and our diction was excellent. The ladies at his table laughed happily.

The enthusiasm spread like contagion to every patron in the restaurant. They were mostly American. They roared back with full energy.

"Happy birthday, America!"

As the sun set we left Little Italy and went to the UN to watch the Fourth of July fireworks. At the gate Hans and

I showed our UN ground pass, as well as a special ticket for Yukari. We left US territory and entered the international territory of the UN compound.

It was already past nine o'clock. The UN was closed to the public, but the garden was crowded with staff members, diplomats, and their guests. Hans, Yukari, and I made our way through the crowd, stopping to greet colleagues. We managed to find space at the edge of the terrace overlooking the East River, Yukari standing between Hans and me.

The fireworks display began with sudden shower of fire, punctuated by a crackling explosion of new sparks. Lights followed fiery lights, round-shaped, broom-shaped, fountain-shaped, or in bullets of many colors, accompanied by loud sizzles and booms. Some disappeared instantly, while others fell slowly from the sky to the water. Bright, colorful, and noisy, on and on they went as if never-ending. The crowd oohed and clapped.

Again Yukari gently held both me and Hans with her hands to each side. The luminous flashes and exuberant explosions in the hot, dark summer night stimulated us with passion for life. They shone only briefly, but they did their best to make the dark sky beautiful. Without words, Hans, Yukari, and I communicated this to each other through our connected bodies, our faces alive with joy. I felt delirious.

In a dashing fury of flashes and bangs, the show came to the end.

We felt it was too early to go home. We needed to calm our excitement. For some time, therefore, we strolled around the garden. Summer roses bloomed in abundance in the flower beds. Under the moonlight their many colors appeared mysterious, and their sweet aroma wafted on a gentle breeze. Yukari stopped here and there to lean close to the petals and take a deep breath, fervent with the perfume. Lit by the moon, surrounded by the blue-tinged roses, Yukari in her willowy light-blue summer dress looked like a fairy.

Behind her the General Assembly Hall building and the Secretariat building, the symbol of the UN, stood majestically in the summer night. I saw in Hans his burning pride at working for the UN. It reminded me of my early years there.

Still we felt wide awake and stimulated, so I invited Hans and Yukari to my apartment on 78th Street. No sooner had I proposed it than they cheerfully agreed.

This was their first visit to my apartment, which was a standard one-bedroom, distinguished only by many paintings and drawings, all my own work, that hung on the walls. The sunbathing nude they had seen at the Art Students League had earned a prominent spot in the living room. They studied my works attentively and paid me compliments.

I had asked my parents to send me the Japanese doll, explaining the heritage of the three families. Pleased to hear the story, they had mailed it to me immediately. The doll in her glass box was standing on one of side tables, a young lady in a traditional Japanese kimono, dancing, holding a fan in each hand. It was a delightful scene. I showed it to them, and we confirmed the crest of the Asaka at the base. We embraced each other in joy.

The apartment was comfortably air-conditioned. I served a bottle of cool white wine, a soothing refreshment after so many hot hours outside.

It was past midnight. We were all pleasantly tired and wanted to sleep. I invited them to spend the night in my bedroom while I slept on the sofa in the living room. They readily accepted my offer.

What happened next — I don't know why it happened.

Yes, we'd had a little too much wine that day. From my point of view, however, a more accurate explanation would be that we were intoxicated with our closeness to each other. In the three months since our first encounter, how much we had discovered of each other … how intimately and historically related we had found ourselves … the many tastes and interests we shared. Despite our different nationalities, we'd come to feel we could trust each other with no reservation. We felt like family, or even more than that.

Yukari took a shower and came out, wrapped in a large white bath towel.

"Oh, that felt so refreshing," she said. "I even washed my hair. Mark, may I use your hair drier?"

She was holding my drier in one hand, clutching the towel with the other. Her skin was almost pink from the hot shower and probably the wine, too. With her wet dark brown hair straight to her shoulders, she looked as natural as a Japanese version of Aphrodite emerging from the sea.

"Ah, Yukari, you look very beautiful," Hans said. "Mark, would you draw her? I'd like to have your drawing of her. Yukari, please take off the towel." He spoke as matter-of-factly as if he had asked her to pass the butter.

"You can't be serious," I protested.

"On the contrary," he shot back, "I'm quite serious. There are many accomplished figure drawings and paintings in this room. I've always wanted a portrait like that of Yukari. You've said that to you a female nude is nothing but an *objet d'art*. And Yukari, you've said too that you wouldn't mind sunbathing in the nude. So please, both of you, do me this favor," he implored.

"I don't mind if Mark draws me like this." Yukari pointed to the white towel around her body.

She looked like an excellent model for a standing nude pose, half nude anyway. I couldn't refuse further. I took out a box of conte pastels, the best medium for quick figure drawing. I fastened a sheet of gray drawing paper on a drawing board, then chose conte bars in flesh, white, and brown colors. I was about ready.

"Oh, no. Yukari, you must take off the towel." Hans waved insistently. "Please respect the artist."

"Well, I wouldn't do it for anyone else. But Mark, I can trust," replied Yukari, still hesitating.

"Okay, do it, Yukari, do it," Hans encouraged her.

She was almost willing.

"Yukari, to the eyes of Mark, you're simply a beautiful object. Go ahead."

She was almost ready.

"Yukari, please," begged Hans.

"Well then ... tah taaaah!"

To my astonishment, Yukari dropped the towel, completely exposing her naked body. Her fine white skin glowed a rosy pink. I found her firm, jutting breasts indescribably pleasing. Her pretty nipples swelled to a deep red. Her legs were long and lean. Her waist tapered in smooth crescents. Her tight, round buttocks flipped up, inviting. Her small delta was covered with thin dark brown hair.

"Ole! Yukari, dance, dance!" Hans clapped excitedly.

Yukari started dancing, smiling, waving an imaginary rose in her right hand, and singing lightly a soprano phrase from *Carmen*.

"Ta, ta, la, la, la, ta, ta, ta, ta ..."

I quickly picked up a flesh-colored conte bar and started drawing. I had done several exercises in drawing a dancing model, so I wasn't afraid of a moving figure. I swiftly drew, catching her moves. The moment probably lasted only a few minutes. Then she rushed into the bedroom, still naked, but laughing.

Hans brought the towel and my drier to her in the bedroom; then he, too, took a shower. In the meantime I carefully added finishing touches to the figure, applying more flesh color for the body, brown conte for shades, and white for highlights, and smoothing the conte texture to express the fine skin and feminine shape. Against the gray background, the figure leaped out as if she had been dancing in the air. I felt confident that I had captured Yukari's lovely body in motion. By the time Hans came out of the bathroom, I had completed the drawing.

He approached, wrapping his waist with another white towel. "Oh, beautiful," he exclaimed. "Yukari is really dancing, isn't she? I love it. May I show it to her?"

He held the drawing paper by the edges and intently stared at the figure on the paper. I noticed something growing behind the towel at his front, raising the damp fabric like a tent. With that, he went to the bedroom.

The noise of the drier blowing abruptly stopped, and Yukari's voice murmured something in a high-pitched hoarse tone, followed by the sounds of bare skins touching passionately. I hurried into the bathroom. The hot shower felt wonderful, washing away all the sweat of the day. I came out of the bathroom wearing my bathrobe and tried to dry myself in the living room.

Soon I heard hot and steamy moans of pleasure coming from the bedroom. I realized that Hans had not completely closed the door and the light was still on, spilling into the hallway. I tapped the door lightly.

"Ahem, excuse me. Hans, you forgot to close the door completely. I'm glad you're enjoying yourselves, but please tone it down a little. My neighbors will wonder, because the walls of my apartment are not thick like yours."

"We're having a real good time," Hans shouted.

"Mark, you don't know what you're missing," Yukari tossed out.

"Oh yeah? I was once married, remember?" I threw back.

"Yes, yes, that's it. … Soooo … gooood. …there … Ohhhh … Ahhhh … Uhhhh …" Yukari sounded as if she were floating in heaven.

"I give up. Have fun. Good night." I closed the door.

"Thank you for the lovely drawing. I like it very much. Good night." It was she.

"Yes, thank you. Good night." It was he.

"You're welcome, Hans and Yukari."

Back in the living room I lay on the sofa, pulled a blanket to the top of my head, and fell into a deep sleep.

I didn't know how much time had elapsed. I felt someone was kissing my lips repeatedly, and I awoke. I saw Yukari leaning over me, still completely naked, in the twilight of the early morning. I thought I was dreaming. But she smiled at me.

"Mark, thank you again for the lovely drawing," she whispered. "I'm glad you saw my naked body, because I wanted to show you. So actually I was making love to you, in my mind. And I've never experienced such an intense orgasm before. It was all because of you. I'm so happy. ... I love you, Mark. ... Have a sweet dream ... my dearest."

She tenderly kissed me again, then returned to the bedroom.

Thinking this was surely a dream, I drowsed off.

7

What should I make of this? I wondered for a few days after our night together in my apartment. One part of me tried to convince myself that I'd been dreaming, which was very plausible because I had drunk much wine that day. Most likely it was my silly, absurd fantasy, even erotic, as I had somehow unconsciously desired Yukari. At the same time, however, the other part of me wishfully thought or hoped that it had really happened, that Yukari had come to me, said those words, and kissed me. If — though this was a big IF — that had been the case, what should I do? I couldn't find an answer, because I didn't want to betray either Hans or Yukari. I was trapped between my two dear friends. However, one thing of which I was absolutely certain was that it was not me who had slept with Yukari, but Hans, her husband. I found nothing improper there. I breathed a little easier and decided to let it run its course.

At the United Nations summer was usually a slow period, as there was no General Assembly session or major conferences. The staff members took a long vacation to enjoy the summer and recharge for the fall when the new GA session would begin. Hans had always taken off a few weeks in the summer. Usually he visited a resort area in the United States or Canada, or sometimes went to visit his parents in Berlin. This summer, however, it was different.

According to Hans, the previous December the GA had adopted a resolution in which the GA requested that the Secretary-General submit a report on economic development at the next GA session. Hans's director, Pierre Skoog, a world-renowned Swedish economist, was responsible for writing the report, and Hans was the primary economist to draft the report, as it would be based on the economic indicators compiled from the EGlobe system he was in charge of. The final draft would have to be completed by the end of August so there would be sufficient time for editing, translation, and printing of the final report to the GA. Hans had to stay in New York and work on the report.

This did not prevent him from enjoying after-work hours and weekends, however. One day Hans and I met in the cafeteria for lunch. With unusual excitement, he described a top-secret project on which he wanted me to be a partner. Since the evening of the Fourth of July, the image of Yukari in the light-blue dress among the roses in the UN garden had been haunting him so often that he had done careful research on the roses. He learned that roses of a blue color were extremely difficult to produce and that only a few strains of blue roses existed, most of which were patented. However, he finally found one in the color he was looking for. It was called "Blue Earth," a hybrid perpetual rose of almost white with a faint hue of blue. It bloomed twice a year, in the early summer and in the autumn. He wanted to plant the roses in the UN garden and to show the bloom to Yukari. He had already made a reservation to purchase a few trees of Blue Earth from a florist.

We looked at each other. We knew that it would be risky to undertake such a naughty project without being discovered by the security guards or the gardeners.

"That's why it's top secret," Hans whispered. "Let me explain my strategy. I've been thinking. It'll work."

He confided his plan, in which I would be an accomplice. Strictly speaking, it was not allowed. But I thought it was innocuous enough. In addition, I found the idea of surprising Yukari very tempting. I agreed to participate.

The following Saturday afternoon we met in the UN garden. I carried a medium-size pad of watercolor paper, a box of watercolor paints, and two glass jars, while Hans carried a big, empty canvas duffel bag and two plastic water containers full of water. Just as on the Fourth of July, there were many roses in full bloom in the flower beds. We chose a spot in the beds where the soil was bare. Hans had brought our roses to his office the previous day, having gotten cleared by the security guards at the UN entrance by explaining that these were plants to decorate his office.

Sitting on a nearby stone, I started painting with watercolors, mixing paints on a palette, dipping and washing sable brushes in the water jars. Hans sat beside me with the duffel bag on the ground, still flat and empty. He pointed out plants and commented on his preference for the location of our roses to be planted.

Sure enough, soon a security guard came by to inspect our activities. His face looked familiar, and he also recognized me. I said to him cheerfully that the roses were so pretty that I couldn't resist painting them. Hans seconded me with exaggeration. The security guard gazed around at the roses in the beds, my painting, painting tools, water jars, water containers, and the duffel bag. My watercolor of the roses in the garden was pretty good, I thought. Convinced that I was simply painting the roses, the guard soon left us.

As soon as the guard disappeared from sight, Hans went to his office to fetch our rare roses. Several minutes later he came back with the duffel, now conspicuously thick. He unzipped the bag and brought out a hand trowel and three rose trees. He quickly dug three deep holes in the soil of the bed we had chosen, set each rose-tree root bundle in its own hole, and covered the roots with the soil. He poured water on the spots abundantly from the water containers. The rose trees were already about four feet high with several buds that were about to open. They stood securely.

Once this was completed, according to our plan, the rest should be taken care of by the regular gardeners who maintained the flower beds and pruned the roses. They wouldn't be able to distinguish the roses we'd planted from the other roses in the beds. It would take only several days for our roses to bloom. Hans and I shook hands and grinned. Our conspiracy had been successfully accomplished.

The following Friday Hans brought Yukari to the UN garden after work. The place was still bright with sun. Our three rose trees were swaying gently in the breeze, proudly upright. Each had a few branches with several light blue buds now in full bloom. The texture of the petals was silky smooth. The blossoms were highly fragrant, and their exquisitely sweet aroma wafted in the humid late-afternoon air.

We stood before them. Hans opened his arms and introduced our blue roses to Yukari. He explained what we had done. Her eyes opened wide with delight.

"How wonderful!" she exclaimed.

Hans told her that blue was the color of the UN, and that it was therefore very proper to have roses of blue color in the UN garden. He also mentioned that Yukari's blue dress had inspired him to form this secret plan. While today she wore a simple white cotton summer dress, it matched nicely with our blue roses. I understood perfectly why Hans had wanted to do this. He seemed very proud of what we had accomplished. Of course, so was I.

Yukari held her hands against her heart. "Thank you for doing this for me," she said with reverence. "They are beautiful. Our blue roses. Our secret."

She embraced and kissed both Hans and me.

*　*　*

For musicians in the New York metropolitan area, summer was always a challenging period because of the season break. Many patrons went to their summer houses in the Hamptons or the Berkshires. Consequently, there were fewer musical activities in the city, and many musicians, too, went to resort areas to work at music festivals.

Since Hans had to stay in Manhattan to prepare for the SG's report to the GA, Yukari had no choice but to stay with him, so she worked odd jobs as a freelance violinist. This provided Hans and me with unusual opportunities to enjoy concerts in which Yukari participated. Many were held outdoors in an informal setting, like Central Park, Washington Square Park, and Bryant Park. We watched Yukari playing the violin more than we listened to the music. After the concert, we collected her and went home together.

Sometimes we stopped by the UN garden to admire our blue roses. Once, at Hans's request, I brought my watercolor painting kit and quickly painted Yukari next to our blue roses, as watercolor painting didn't take much time. How graceful she looked among our blue roses, and in my watercolor. As I presented the finished work to her, she smiled and gave me a kiss, Hans happily applauding.

One of the major summer music festivals in New York was held at Lincoln Center. Groups came from many parts of the world to perform classical music, jazz, dances, and musical dramas, outdoors and indoors. One evening Yukari played in one of these concerts at Avery Fisher Hall.

Hans and I sat on the right side of the second tier, close to the stage, so we could see Yukari better. The program was all baroque music. The first half was an excerpt from Handel's *Water Music*. There was no better music than this to please an audience on a summer evening, as it had been composed to entertain King George I during a water party he held on the Thames River. Brass instruments pumped continuously cheerful waves, and wind instruments blew joyful breezes, while string instruments simulated the merry-making.

The second part was performed by a small chamber orchestra, which made the concert very intimate. Short pieces by Bach and Vivaldi were followed by the last piece, Pachelbel's *Canon in D*.

This famous canon was played by the string section only, so there were probably fewer than twenty musicians on the stage. The audience fell into a profound silence as the opening theme presented a basic chord progression to be repeated throughout the entire work. Then the violin entered with an extremely simple melody, which was successively carried over by other strings. The theme was repeated in a harmonious combination of different strings at various pitches. I found the intimacy of the music entirely absorbing and meditative.

Yukari played gracefully with total concentration. Although there were other violins playing, I was certain that I distinctly heard the sound of her Italian violin. How serenely her violin sang. How touchingly she played. How confident she appeared. How beautiful she looked.

When it was over, Hans and I leaped to our feet and applauded enthusiastically. The audience followed with a standing ovation. Seeing us from the stage, Yukari gave us a big smile and we exchanged nods.

After the concert we met at the central plaza between Avery Fisher Hall, the Metropolitan Opera House, and the New York State Theater. Many people were enjoying the plaza. We sat close together, Yukari in the middle as usual, at the edge of the fountain. She clasped my waist and Hans's with her hands.

The stars were bright in the summer sky. The pearly moon looked almost blue, the blue of our roses in the UN garden.

Call it friendship, love, love-triangle, or lunacy, I didn't care. I felt intoxicated by our delicious closeness.

8

Shem Tov, Francine, and their little Jacques had come back to New York from their vacation. He anxiously wanted to see me to discuss something. One day in late July, we went to a restaurant near the UN for lunch.

As soon as we settled at a table, Shem Tov said, "I need your help. I want to work in UNRWA. Can you place me there?"

UNRWA stood for the United Nations Relief and Works Agency for Palestine Refugees in the Near East, which was a humanitarian assistance and relief mission for displaced Palestinians in the West Bank and Gaza. It was not one of the peacekeeping missions my department, the Department of Peace-keeping Operations, was responsible for, but we assisted with certain of their administrative tasks like procurement, personnel recruitment, and others. As a Human Resource Management Officer, therefore, I had some relevance to the mission.

"I can understand that you want to work close to home," I said. "But what on earth would you do there?"

"UNRWA is a huge mission," Shem Tov replied without hesitation. "They must have a strong IT infrastructure. As a Systems Management Officer, I can work on all IT issues, like PCs, servers, and the Internet."

"I see; then I may be able to find a vacant post for you," I said. "But the duration of mission assignments is usually at least two years. You can't leave Francine and the baby for two years. Jacques isn't even a year old. He needs his father. Besides, the field missions always involve some risk. The Palestinian issues are politically delicate, and the area is not really safe. I wouldn't recommend it for you."

"I haven't discussed the subject with Francine yet," he confessed. "But if you can find me a post in UNRWA, I'm sure I can persuade her."

We ate our lunch, which we had almost forgotten. Then I found I didn't remember what I had eaten as I gathered my thoughts. It occurred to me that before his vacation, Shem Tov had said he had some personal project there. His desire to go to UNRWA seemed related to that.

"C'mon, Shem Tov," I said. "Tell me what's really on your mind."

"This is strictly confidential," he said with a serious face. "Promise me you'll keep it to yourself." Getting an assurance from me, he continued. "Okay, then … as you well know, the relationship between Israel and the Palestinian Authority has always been tense. Palestinian people want an independent state with its capital in Jerusalem. Israel does not mind giving the Palestinians an autonomous territory in the state of Israel, provided that they live in peace, but we consider Jerusalem our capital."

"Wait a minute," I interrupted. "This is too political. We UN staff members are supposed to follow only the instructions of the Secretary-General, independent of the political views of each country."

"But I can't sit in my office and let the violence continue in Israel. I want to do something." He took a deep breath. "Here are my thoughts. As long as Palestinians want their independent state with its capital in Jerusalem, and as long as Israel never agrees with an idea of creating a hostile state as its neighbor, it won't work. So it's best to have one state in which both Israelis and Palestinians are democratically represented with equal rights. Israel's state capital should be Tel Aviv, while Jerusalem should become an international territory administered by the United Nation, free from politics. The UN has the Trusteeship Council, which administers trust territories, so without reinventing a new wheel, the UN can manage the trust territory of Jerusalem. Then Jerusalem would transform into a peaceful sanctuary where all religions of the world — Judaism, Christianity, Islam, Bahá'í, and others — could co-exist. Then Israelis and Palestinians can live together peacefully in one state. This will work."

"That's quite unrealistic," I said, shaking my head. "Since the Palestinian people want their own state, they would never agree to such a radical idea. I don't know if the Israelis would agree to it, either. Did you discuss this with people there while you were there?"

"Yes, I did," he answered, lowering his voice. "I talked to my people. I also talked to Palestinians who are friendly

to Israelis. Unfortunately I couldn't find anyone who sup-
ports me, either Israeli or Palestinian." He couldn't help hiding
his disappointment.

"That's what I thought," I said with a little grin. "I don't
mean to be cynical. But what you've just described seems to me
a utopian dream."

"It's not a utopian dream," he protested with passion.
"There is a precedent in South Africa. When they dismantled
their apartheid policy, they had two choices. One was to break
up the country into two states: the white state and the black
state. The other was to give equal rights to both white people
and black people, and let them represent themselves democratically in the Parliament. They chose the latter. So now South
Africa is an integrated state with equal rights among its people,
regardless of the color of their skin. This is the one-state solution that has worked. We can do it in Israel, too, between Jews
and Palestinians, regardless of the differences in our ethnic and
religious heritage." He took a moment to breathe. "That's the
reason I want to go to UNWRA. From there I want to undertake the groundwork for persuading people on both sides to
accept this one-state solution."

"No, no, Shem Tov," I said rather strongly. "UNRWA is
not for that kind of political purpose, but a humanitarian mission. If you work like that in UNWRA, you might encounter
some physical danger. It may not be outrageous to envision
that you'll be assassinated by either Israelis or Palestinians."

Shem Tov swigged water from the glass. "You sound
like my father. He served as an Israeli ambassador to several
countries, so he understands delicate diplomacy, particularly
between hostile nations. He strongly opposed my idea."

"See? Your father is right," I said firmly. "Frankly, it's none of my business to meddle with you as you work on such a radical idea. You have the freedom to express and act upon your political belief. My objection is from the point of view of the UN. The Secretary-General is a peace mediator, and we work for him, independent of any government. Do you remember you took the oath as an international civil servant? We solemnly swore our loyalty to the SG. So you can't go to UNRWA to promote such a radical political idea. No, no, Shem Tov, you can't do that."

After a moment of silence, he asked me point blank, "So no chance you can help me?"

"Sorry, I can't," I replied firmly, but with warmth. "I do want to help you, but what you are going to do there is wrong as an international civil servant. You have to understand the purpose of UNRWA. Besides, what about Francine and Jacques? I don't want them to become a widow and a fatherless boy, no matter how slim the chance may be."

That seemed to strike his heart.

"I don't want that either," he said, sighing. "I love them."

"The only way you can achieve what you want to do," I continued, "is to quit the UN, go back to Israel, run for Parliament, and become a political activist. But again, what would you do with Francine and Jacques? Most likely she wouldn't want to live in Israel, because there is not much she can do there as a professional. She would want to remain in New York to work for the UN. She is also a believer in the UN, you know that."

This seemed another blow to him. He just gazed at his hands on the table.

"Don't take me wrong, Shem Tov," I added, softening my voice. "I fully understand your frustration that the UN can't do much to resolve the Israeli-Palestinian conflicts. For example, what am I doing here? Just a Human Resource Management Officer, far from directly resolving these problems. You, too, a Systems Management Officer, working on IT. Our jobs are indirect support functions for the UN to do its job well. But in the end, I always hope that we are contributing to the goals of the UN."

I paused, but decided to go on. "I'm American. You know how the US government treats the UN. As far as the US government is concerned, they want the US to lead the world. They don't want the UN to become strong enough to lead the world. So they don't participate in the UN too much unless the US's interests are threatened. They really don't care what is going on in the UN. As an American who works for the UN, I feel ashamed and frustrated to observe this. But still I am hoping that somehow my small work contributes to the UN achieving its goals."

"You're right there," Shem Tov said earnestly. "You and I share the same frustration. The difference is: I want to act, whereas you hope your contribution at the UN will eventually benefit the world. But I understand what you're saying. I have to give it some thought."

Our discussion ended after I encouraged Shem Tov to think in the light of his family, because now he was not alone, but had his wife and a little child. He consented.

A few days later, when I arrived at my office in the morning, I found Francine waiting for me with a concerned look.

She directly came to the point I was anticipating. "Mark, please persuade Shem Tov not to go to UNRWA. Quitting the UN is out of question. He has a responsibility for his family."

"So he has revealed his plan to you?" I asked.

"Yes," she replied. "But he hasn't made up his mind yet. I understand he talked to you. He seems to have three choices: to go to UNRWA, to quit the UN, or to stay with the UN in New York. I told him he has to stay with the UN in New York and with his family."

"Right now he is going through what all international civil servants go through one way or the other at some point in our career," I said, "when we have to choose our loyalty either to the SG or to our national government, not both. That's the challenge. In my case, since I had worked for the US government before I came to the UN, and since I made a conscious choice to become an international civil servant, I didn't experience that challenge here."

"Growing up in Switzerland," she said, "it seemed natural that I would work toward world peace in the UN. But Shem Tov worked in the private sector for an Israeli IT company before coming to the UN here. So this may be the first time he has had to face that struggle."

"Yes," I said, sighing. "There is not much we can do for now, other than quietly watch him until he comes to a conclusion."

"That's what I think, too," she said, nodding sadly. "But it's painful."

"Of course, it is. Hang on tight now, Francine, all right?" I said with sympathy. Then a great idea flashed inside me. "Why don't you come with Shem Tov to the UN garden after work today? I'll invite Hans. He and I have something to show you both."

Francine agreed and left. I called Hans in his office and explained the situation. I thought that if we showed Shem Tov our blue roses, he might feel some inspiration for the UN. Hans promised to come with Yukari.

Late that afternoon after work, Shem Tov and Francine came to the UN garden. Shem Tov looked pale, probably from sleepless nights. Other than that, I didn't observe any negative sign in his demeanor. Francine was a proud mother, as she held Jacques in a carrier at her chest, having retrieved him from the UN's daycare center. But she couldn't hide her worry from her face. Jacques cooed, healthy and content. I shook his tiny hand gently. With a cute smile, he waved his hands and even his legs in joy, which made me happy.

Hans showed up with Yukari. Both appeared in high spirits. This was the first time Yukari had met Jacques. She hugged Francine and kissed Jacques. As he smiled at her, she crinkled her eyes in delight. I was happy that Yukari liked Jacques, who would have been my son.

Our blue roses were swaying magnificently in the summer breeze. The blooms were near the end of their season, but they still looked beautiful. Hans introduced our blue roses to Shem Tov and Francine, and explained our top-secret endeavor.

"Wow, this is gorgeous!" Shem Tov exclaimed.

"Yes, it's awesome!" Francine cried.

"And you both took such a risk," Shem Tov said in admiration.

"It wasn't easy," I responded with an exaggerated gesture. We all laughed.

"But surely it was worth the risk," I added. "I love our blue roses."

"And now look at that." Hans pointed to a large UN flag waving proudly at the top of a flagpole near the GA building. The light blue color of the flag mirrored the color of our roses. "Whenever I see that flag, I feel I am right to be here, working for the UN. Yes, the UN is not functioning as well as it should be. I know that. But within that reality, I still feel proud to be here." Then he directed his hand to our gardening coup. "Now look at these roses. The color of the UN. Whenever I see our blue roses, it reminds me that I work for the UN, which makes me proud."

I saw in Hans the zest of an ideal international civil servant, who devoted his life to the cause of the UN. I had been like him when I started working for the UN. Although my naïve idealism had faded since then, I still believed in the UN's work and goals. Like Hans, our blue roses made me proud.

"Thank you, Hans and Mark, for bringing me here," Shem Tov said thoughtfully. "This reminds me why I chose to work for the UN. Me too, I believe in the UN."

"I'm happy to hear that, Shem Tov," Francine said. "I want you to know that I'm a UN believer too. Let's work together here and do our best, please." She recovered some lively color in her face as she seemed to find hope.

Shem Tov gazed at our blue roses and the UN flag wafting back and forth. "Yes, this is good. I should stay here. These blue roses convince me." He, too, appeared to recover his spirits.

We didn't get into the discussion of what Shem Tov had been contemplating. But this was enough, I thought. Shem Tov seemed to realize what he truly wanted to do in his life, particularly with Francine and their little Jacques.

Yukari said, "Our blue roses are the symbol of peace mediation. I'm so happy we are all here to admire them."

"Yes," I said. "Remember the pledge we made the evening of the UN concert? Let's renew our pledge."

We embraced each other before our blue roses.

*　*　*

The next morning Francine came to my office. She thanked me and said that Shem Tov had cooled off after seeing our blue roses the day before, and he had decided to stay with the UN in New York, at least for now. I was pleased to see her happy.

Then she said, "You, poor Mark."

"What?" I asked.

"You are in love with Yukari. Not just in love, but deeply in love up to your neck, or even up to the top of your head."

"What are you talking about? Yesterday I didn't do or say anything to imply that."

"Your face tells it all. No women miss it. The complication obviously comes from the triangle situation. In this situation, usually the husband becomes jealous. But Hans seems completely content. Yukari, too, appears very happy. Above all, you are the happiest. I don't understand it. People might think you are crazy."

"Oh, my goodness, do I look that bad?"

We laughed. I thought it was better to keep it light.

"As I said before, I want you to be happy with Yukari," Francine told me. "But in this situation I don't know what to suggest to you to reach that goal."

"As I said before," I replied, "Hans, Yukari, and I are just good friends. Don't worry. I'm not crazy."

Deep down in my mind, however, I began to doubt the words I had just spoken. This was the first time I seriously felt that Francine might be right, that I was in love with Yukari. The implication agonized me, because I was feeling happy at the expense of the matrimony between Yukari and Hans. I thought I was indeed out of mind.

9

One Saturday in August, Hans, Yukari, and I had a picnic in the Conservatory Garden of Central Park. This was to fulfill my long-standing promise to paint the three of us together. We made a deal that Yukari would prepare lunch, Hans would take care of all transportation and logistics, and I would paint us picnicking.

It was a hot but dry and bright day, perfect for painting. I brought a 32"x42" canvas — too big for outdoor painting, but I wanted to create a masterpiece, for which the canvas would have to be this size, I believed. I also brought an easel, my paint box, disposable palette sheets, a portable chair, a small flat table, containers of turpentine and linseed oil, and two empty coffee cans to be used for the oils. Finally came a digital camera, a tripod, and a laptop PC.

Hans helped me to carry it all. He also brought Yukari's violin, a portable CD player, and a large picnic basket with bottles of wine and soft drinks.

Yukari wore a sleeveless white summer dress with a long skirt and a white belt gently delineating her waist. She also wore a matching hat with a light yellow ribbon, and white sandals. Following my suggestion, she wore blush, lipstick, and eyeliner so I could catch her character better. She looked like a shining goddess under the sun.

Hans wore a white shirt and white trousers, the costume, he claimed, of a great tenor. I wore a similar outfit, but I had to wear a blue painting apron to cover my front. At least I looked like a painter, I thought.

We chose a spot with a shaded picnic table and benches amid trees and grasses. The bordering gardens were filled with multicolored flowers: sunflowers, summer lilies, cosmos, gladioli, and geraniums.

Yukari covered the table with a white tablecloth and opened the basket, withdrawing salad, sandwiches, fruits, plastic dishes, and plastic cups. She arranged these on the table, as well as the bottles of wine. The table looked appetizing.

Then we rehearsed our tableau. Hans was to pose as a singer, standing on the left side of the canvas and singing an opera aria. Yukari would sit on a bench in the center of the painting, playing the violin to accompany the singer. I would sit on a portable chair on the right, facing a canvas and easel, painting the singer and the violinist. The background consisted of the picnic table with food and wine, surrounding trees, grasses, and many flowers. At the front left bottom, I was to paint a few blue roses. *A good composition*, I thought, and taped the position of each of us on the ground, which we would require later to recreate the scene.

I installed the easel at a proper spot and set the canvas on it. In front of it, I placed the portable chair. Beside the chair, I set the flat table to hold the paint box and the palette sheets. I poured turpentine into one of the coffee cans and a mixture of turpentine and linseed oil into the other.

"Okay, we are ready," I told Hans and Yukari. "Your positions, please. I have to take several pictures first."

Using the automatic shutter of the camera on the tripod, I took a few pictures of the three of us together. Then, stepping out of the scene, I took several close-ups of Hans, Yukari, and the background. I plugged the camera into my laptop, which displayed color photos of us.

Yukari squealed with pleasure. "You're completely equipped."

"Yes, this is convenient." I patted my camera. "I can refer to these pictures later for an accuracy check, so I can make my painting perfect."

"I see," Yukari said. "You're a real pro."

Now I was ready to begin painting.

"You'll have to pose for five minutes," I told them. "No movement, just frozen. Then you will get a ten-minute rest, during which you can eat and drink."

Hans put a CD into the CD player, a live recording from a chamber concert Yukari had performed. It consisted of Brahms's string quartets, quintets, and sestets. When the music started, Hans made a gesture as if singing, holding his right hand gently in the air, while Yukari held the violin and the bow as if she were playing. They froze.

I began quickly drawing on the canvas to fix the position of the major figures and objects, using a regular brush soaked with paints thinned in a lot of turpentine oil. I could see Hans and Yukari, but naturally I couldn't see myself, so when I drew my figure, I referred to the photo on the laptop.

"Oh, five minutes is too long," Yukari cried. "It hurts my arms."

"Now you understand," I said, "that posing as a model appears easy, but it's actually a tough job."

"Yes, yes, I surrender. May I rest?" Yukari begged.

"Okay, you can rest. Go to the table and eat." I continued sketching.

Hans had a glass of wine and Yukari a cup of gingerale at the table. They came back next to me and watched me still rapidly moving the brush with washy paints, sometimes wiping out an area with a piece of cloth for a correction, then repainting over it. Since the paints were thin, I could make the initial drawing and corrections quickly and easily.

"Interesting." Yukari observed me work with a childlike curiosity. "Is this the way to initially fix the outline of the painting? This canvas is very big, but in this way, you can cover the large area very quickly."

"Yes, that's precisely the point," I said. "See? I've almost finished the outline. Now I need to add more colors. Are you rested? Can you pose for another five minutes?"

We repeated the poses and rests. The music offered relief from the monotonous posing. I gradually added colors, still in washy paints. I used a lot of Permalba white, lemon yellow, Thalo yellow green, flesh, pink madder, and burnt umber. The mixture of these paints with other colors would create a soft, pastel-like effect in the painting, which was a secret technique I had developed. Soon the entire canvas was completely covered with paints in jolly colors.

I now focused on the individual objects, using more paint with less turpentine oil. Since the figures appeared at distance, I could not paint the faces like a portrait. Rather, I tried to catch their characters as a singer, a violinist, and a painter. Three figures in white clothes gradually emerged against the background of a picnic table, and behind it the greenery and flowers.

In the front left bottom, I painted three branches of blue roses with several buds from my imagination. I knew that at home I had the real watercolor paintings of our blue roses in the UN garden, which I could use for the finishing of this painting.

The canvas started looking like "Blue Roses and Three Friends," the title I would use for this painting. I had spent about an hour and half by this stage. Hans and Yukari appeared exhausted.

"Thank you for your patience," I declared. "This is it for today."

Hans and Yukari sighed and stretched. They came to my side and inspected the canvas.

"You've done it, Mark," Hans commented. "This painting reflects the character of each of us at our best."

"I think so, too." I nodded modestly. "Another thing that pleases me in this painting is that I'm getting close to finding my style — the influence of Matisse, Renoir, Degas, and Morandi, but my own taste and sensitivity."

"I like it very much," Yukari said.

Their comments made me feel good.

In the fresh air of the garden, the sandwiches tasted delicious. After such a fruitful collaboration together, we felt very content. While eating and drinking, we surveyed the painting on the easel.

After lunch we relaxed on the benches, stretching our arms and legs, sipping our drinks, and listening to the music. I noticed that Yukari was avoiding wine today. She sipped her gingerale, appearing more thoughtful than usual.

The CD played a new piece, and she brightened.

"Listen," she said. "This is Brahms's *Sestet No. 1 in B flat major*, my favorite. It's usually played by two violins, two violas, and two cellos. But for this performance we added two more violins, like a string octet, in order to heighten the effects of the violin parts. So two musicians are each playing first and second violin. I'm playing the first violin here. We call this arrangement the 'double ensemble.' I think we succeeded in producing a sound Brahms would have approved of. The second movement, the *Andante*, is so beautiful."

We listened to the double ensemble quietly. We were by ourselves, isolated from the rest of the park. All we saw were blue sky, radiant sun, the meadow-like setting, and the painting. The music, mellow and carefree, yet lyrical and touching, sounded as if it had been composed just for us, for this very afternoon.

A little over halfway through the *Andante*, Yukari straightened her posture.

"I have an announcement to make," she said, looking directly at both Hans and me. She hesitated for a few seconds, then continued with a tender smile. "It's joyful news. I'm pregnant, Hans. I'm carrying your child."

Hans, who had been relaxing on the bench, immediately sat up straight. "Oh, Yukari, are you sure?"

"I'm sorry, Hans, I couldn't tell you until now, since I wasn't certain," she went on. "But last week I noticed that I had missed a period. Yesterday I visited my gynecologist for a checkup. The pregnancy test came up positive. According to the doctor, I'm pregnant a little over one month."

She took a deep breath. Her eyes were moist, but her cheeks were flushed with joy. As if blessing her, the sun shone brilliantly in the cloudless blue sky, birds twittered nearby, flowers swayed, and our painting, "Blue Roses and Three Friends," was coming to life.

"Remember, Hans?" she continued. "On the Fourth of July we made love in Mark's bedroom. I felt an indescribable sensation that night. Listening to this music now, I'm absolutely convinced that that was the moment I conceived." Then she gazed at me. "Mark, thank you. I wanted to have a child so much. Now finally I will. You helped us. You are practically the half-father to our child. I'm grateful." Tears streamed down her cheeks, while her face glowed, full of life.

"Oh, Yukari, I'm so proud of you." Hans passionately hugged and kissed her. "Mark, thank you very much. Yes, you helped us." He shook my hand so hard that it almost hurt me.

"This is splendid news indeed," I pronounced. "Yukari and Hans, I'm so delighted. Congratulations!" I gently hugged Yukari, then firmly shook Hans's hand.

Yukari affectionately kissed my cheek. Was it my fantasy that her kiss meant more than a kiss to a friend? I remembered her before me in the morning twilight that day. So it was not a dream after all. She had come to me and had said those words to me, which had now been transformed into — "You are practically the half-father to our child."

I came to myself and realized that I was now in the Conservatory Garden with Yukari and Hans. There was something tenderly exultant on her face that prevented me from uttering any further words; for what could words express? I saw that Hans noticed it as well. Thus, we three just gazed at each other, smiled, and resumed listening to the double ensemble, which soared to a peak and returned to a noble cello solo. Our hearts trembled in rejoicing.

10

In early September the United Nations staff members returned from their summer vacations, and the UN compound came alive again. Late in September the General Assembly began its new session. Hans was all excited about the Secretary-General's report he had drafted during the summer. The formal report came out in print with a long, impressive title: "Implementation of the Declaration on International Economic Cooperation, in particular the Revitalization of Economic Growth and Development of the Developing Countries, and Implementation of the International Development Strategy for the Fourth United Nations Development Decade; Report of the Secretary-General."

The report would be presented to the GA's Second Committee, and the debates would take place in October. Usually if a report was critical in nature, the Under-Secretary-General or Assistant Secretary-General of the authorizing department would present it to the committee. Hans's director, Pierre Skoog, asked Hans to draft the introduction to the report for the USG of the Department of Economic and Social Affairs, who would deliver the report to the committee. Thrilled, Hans immediately started working on it.

On the last Saturday of September, I visited Hans's apartment, bringing flowers for Yukari. I had not seen her for a while. She opened the door. She wore a comfortable short-sleeved one-piece cotton dress of a light peach color, looking as elegant as ever. Seeing the bouquet, her face lit up with a dazzling smile.

"How pretty! I love flowers. Thank you, Mark." She hugged and kissed me.

"You're very welcome. How are you feeling?"

"I'm fine. Occasionally I feel morning sickness, but otherwise I'm all right. I guess my body is preparing for the baby."

Hans appeared behind her. "Yes, her body is really changing. Look, her breasts are much bigger."

She blushed. "Oh, Hans!"

Indeed, her bust was higher. Her waist appeared a little wider, although her abdomen did not show any sign of pregnancy yet.

"You are blooming, Yukari," I told her.

"Thank you, Mark," she said. "You have to come here often to reassure us. We need you. After all, our baby was conceived in your bed."

We laughed heartily.

"If you want another baby," I said, "you're welcome to use my bed again any time."

"Yes, we will," she chirped happily. "But for now we have to attend to this one." She tenderly caressed her tummy.

"It will be a big job," Hans said. "I bought several books on pregnancy, childbirth, and parenthood, which I'm reading now. I'm already overwhelmed. But it's worth the effort."

Yukari arranged the flowers in a vase, which she placed on the dining table. We sat in the living room and talked more about her condition. Being pregnant for the first time at age thirty-nine, she felt concerned, even fearful, particularly for the first few months of pregnancy, when the risk of miscarriage was relatively high. She did not want to take any chances. Hans sat next to her and listened, appearing very protective.

They had stayed in New York all summer, avoiding the hustle of traveling. But she had continued to work as a freelance violinist. Now that the baby was coming, she needed to save as much money as possible while she could still work. Fortunately the summer was over, and she was already busy with the Parnassus Symphony Orchestra for the new season, which included more concerts than usual and many ambitious programs. She seemed content with her situation.

"How is our painting coming?" Yukari asked.

"I've been working on it every weekend since our day in the park," I replied. "It's almost done. All I need now is finishing touches." I showed them a color photo that I'd taken with my digital camera.

"How lovely!" Yukari exclaimed.

"Splendid," Hans said.

"Not bad, don't you think?" I said with a little pride. "I'm waiting for our blue roses to bloom again in late October or early November. I need them to really capture on the roses on the canvas. Then I'll have to ask you to come to my apartment with the same outfits you wore that day for the final pose so I can finish our portraits too."

Hans and I had a few glasses of wine, but Yukari sipped a glass of mineral water with a lemon slice in it.

"By the way, did you notice?" Hans said. "We like it very much."

He pointed to a framed drawing on the wall of the living room — the figure drawing of Yukari I had done that memorable night. She looked very natural, healthy, and pretty.

"When we have guests, we simply say it was a gift from our artist friend. We don't say exactly who she is," said Yukari, giggling. "But I'm going to tell my child that this is me just before conceiving."

I was pleased to see my drawing settled in their home with their blessing.

*　　*　　*

One day in early October, Hans called me at my office and asked me to come to his apartment so he could show me what he was doing. He had just completed the introductory statement to the report he had drafted during the summer, which the USG was to present to the Second Committee.

Yukari was at home, but since my visit was unexpected, she had only prepared dinner for two. I asked her not to bother about it, but she insisted that I take her portion, as she was happy eating only a big salad. After a quick dinner, while we had tea, Hans explained his work at the UN.

According to Hans, the EGlobe was a cooperative, non-governmental, international research activity that integrated independently developed national econometric models into a global econometric model. It was initiated under the leadership of Professor Joshua R. Cohen of Princeton University. It organized two meetings a year to discuss the results of the forecast and impacts of critical economic events in the world. The spring meeting took place at the UN in New York, and the other was usually hosted by one of the countries participating in the research. This year the fall meeting would be held the first week in November in Athens, Greece.

"When I came to the UN and started to working in DESA," Hans explained, "Professor Cohen had been seeking a permanent home for the EGlobe, because he was retiring. My first job at the UN was to transfer the EGlobe system from Princeton to the UN. I was thrilled to work with the professor, who had received the Nobel Prize for his contribution to the EGlobe. I worked hard, visiting Princeton many times. Finally we completed the transfer. Since the UN was seen as the most proper place for the EGlobe to be maintained, the successful transfer was welcomed by economists around the world." Hans beamed with pride.

I could see that the EGlobe's transfer to the UN must have been a critical milestone for economists around the world. I understood why Hans felt so high-spirited.

"On a day-to-day basis, I'm responsible for maintaining the EGlobe system," Hans continued. "The individual country econometric models and regional models are prepared by Professor Cohen's pupils around the world. These are sent to me before the semi-annual meetings, and I am responsible for integrating these individual models and data into the global model and making the forecast. So for the next few weeks, I'll be very busy."

"I'm sorry to ask you a novice question," I said, "but why is the EGlobe so unique?"

"Because we can forecast the global economy and analyze impacts of critical economic events," Hans answered with passion. "For example, late last year there was a financial crisis in Asia. We forecast the impacts of the crisis on the regional economies as well as the global economy, and discussed the implications in the EGlobe meeting in May here at the UN."

In order to understand Hans's explanation, we needed a good knowledge of economics and econometrics. I had some background in these from my business school days. As Hans showed me a few models on his PC, which was connected to the main EGlobe system at the UN over the network, I could see that the equations he used were very complex and advanced. He demonstrated effects of fictional events over the regional and global economy. The graphic presentation of the forecast results in many indices were clear and persuasive.

"I see," I said. "Very impressive. The EGlobe must be especially helpful to the developing countries."

"Precisely," Hans replied. "This is why the semi-annual EGlobe meetings are attended by more than a hundred economists from around the world."

"Are you going to Athens next month?" asked Yukari, frowning. "I know it's an important part of your job, but I hate to have you gone right now."

Hans smiled and shrugged. "I have to, but only for a week. Usually I do some sightseeing in the host country, but this time

I'll come home immediately. I'll bring you some nice souvenirs from Greece." He couldn't help smiling at the prospect. "I hope you understand how honored I feel to be working on this. It's a dream come true for an econometrician specializing in the global economy. I've poured my entire professional life into it. But before the EGlobe meeting in Athens, I have to get through the Second Committee in two weeks."

*   *   *

In mid-October, the Second Committee began its formal session, in which the USG of DESA was to present the SG's report, with its introductory statement, both of which Hans had drafted. I decided to attend the meeting. As a basic rule, the committee meetings were open to UN staff members, unless otherwise noted. I invited Yukari. I also asked Shem Tov and Francine to come, since the occasion would be Hans's shining moment.

I called Ramez Al-Hadidi, a Conference Officer in charge of the Second Committee. He was a Jordanian and a good friend of mine and Francine's. He had been a translator of Arabic, then got bored and switched his career to his present position. I had met him in the French class. He was interested in American literature, and we had talked many times over lunch about the novels of Hemingway and Faulkner. He assured me that bringing Yukari would not be a problem as long as she had a valid visitor's pass.

I met Yukari at the visitor's entrance around ten o'clock and assisted in getting her visitor's pass. Then we went to the large conference room where the committee session was held. Before the door, Shem Tov and Francine were waiting for us. Since we'd met at the UN garden several weeks before, Shem Tov's decision to stay with the UN in New York with Francine and Jacques seemed to be holding. He had told me that he was now extremely busy with Y2K, which was a sensational hype in the IT industry that year. I was pleased to see Francine and Shem Tov together, appearing happy.

Justin Tugutu was also with them, as at Shem Tov and Francine's request, he had made sure that the SG's report Hans drafted went through the Official Document System without any problems. This was important, Hans had told Justin, because through ODS the government officials and economists, particularly in developing countries, could read the report in six official languages right away without waiting for the hard copies of the report to arrive in their countries.

Since this was the first time they'd seen Yukari after her pregnancy, they congratulated her. Yukari radiated, the proverbial expectant mother.

Inside the conference room, Ramez was sitting at the table near the door, handing out copies of the SG's report, or Hans's report as we called it.

The committee was already in session, and all delegates' seats were taken. We went to the left corner of the room, where usually the UN staff members pertinent to the debates sat to wait their turn in case they were summoned. We found vacant seats together. Hans and Mr. Skoog, his director, were sitting in the same row of seats, closer to the podium.

Soon the debate on the present agenda was completed. The chairman took the next agenda. Mr. Skoog and Hans moved up to the podium to sit behind the USG and the chairman. The chairman invited the USG to introduce the report.

"Mr. Chairman and distinguished delegates," the USG began in English, "I am pleased to present to you the report of the Secretary-General ..."

The USG, a Canadian economist and statesman, was renowned for his excellent economic policies for developing countries. He read the statement as written, in a cool scholarly tone, from time to time looking up toward the delegates, emphasizing some sentences. The delegates listened attentively to the address in their preferred official language, using their earphones, sometimes referring to the copy of the report they had on the table.

The address, which highlighted the important points of the report, continued for several minutes, and finally the USG concluded.

"Mr. Chairman and distinguished delegates, in closing, please be assured that the Secretariat is firmly committed to pursuing the implementation of International Economic Cooperation even further in the coming new millennium. Thank you very much."

The delegates warmly applauded the USG. The chairman thanked him and invited delegates to ask questions. The USG answered some questions directly himself, but for others he consulted with Mr. Skoog. Sometimes Mr. Skoog referred him to Hans, who then spoke to the USG from behind. The USG nodded and answered the delegates. With that, the chairman declared the agenda item had been concluded and banged the gavel on the table. Mr. Skoog and Hans shook the USG's hand and left the podium. The chairman took the next agenda item.

We met Hans outside the conference room. His face was still flushing with excitement and shining with sweat.

"It went very well," Hans told us with full satisfaction. "The USG was very pleased, and so was Mr. Skoog."

"The verbatim of the USG's statement should appear soon," Francine said. "Ramez will take care of that."

"When you find out the document number, please let me know," said Justin. "I'll make sure that it goes through ODS quickly and smoothly."

"You'd better," Shem Tov said to Justin. "This is so important."

"Hans, now you're a big shot," I said. "Even the USG has consulted with you. Wow!" I gave a huge thumbs-up.

"The committee session is like a big diplomatic ceremony," Yukari said. "It's fascinating."

"That's right," Hans replied. "The formal session is rather ceremonial. The real questions will come in the informal sessions, which will be held next week. But observing the delegates' responses this morning, the informal sessions should also go without much problem."

"Congratulations!" we cried to Hans, and shook his hands or embraced him.

"Thank you." He shone.

It was Hans's triumph. But then …

A woman in her late forties accosted him. She looked like a Central American. With an exaggerated smile, she said, "Congratulations, Hans. It's an outstanding report, and the USG presented it nicely to the committee." She shook his hand.

"Thank you," Hans said politely.

The woman moved away.

Hans followed her with his eyes. As soon as she disappeared from sight, he said, "Why on earth is she here? I didn't know she was interested in the EGlobe. I don't think she can comprehend any part of the EGlobe. I hope this isn't a bad omen."

*   *   *

The next morning Francine rushed into my office and closed the door. She looked sad.

"Poor Mark, what are you going to do?" she said, gasping in one breath.

I was puzzled by her agitated state. "What's wrong?"

"Yukari is pregnant!" she said as if she were announcing that someone had died.

"So?" I replied, undisturbed.

"This creates more complications, which will diminish your happiness. Yukari is stuck with Hans."

Now I understood what she was thinking. I didn't blame her because I would not have been honest if I had said I had not felt that way too. But I had come to my understanding of the situation in a positive way.

"Francine, I've been thinking of our relationship since Yukari became pregnant," I said. "Actually I think it's a good thing, because it will cement their marriage. I'm very happy for them. In this way I can remain as a good friend to them as I always wanted."

"Poor Mark." She shook her head. "You are forcing yourself to be rational and trying to hide your pain. Why don't you admit you are sad?"

"Because I'm not sad. I'm happy to see them happy."

She widened her eyes. "You're deluded, you know that?"

"On the contrary, I'm quite sane," I assured her.

"I'm afraid that something tragic will happen among you three." She exhaled heavily. "I hope you won't get hurt."

"Don't worry," I said. "I can handle the situation."

No sooner had I said this than I thought that feeling happy in this situation itself might be a sign of delusion. I was grateful to Francine for her concern over me — but she might be right. I felt that I needed to keep my sanity.

11

Around this time a major change occurred in my division, the Administrative Support Division. The director had served six years, during which she had not been able to do much, except to install her friends in the key posts. In the meantime, the work for the UN's peacekeeping missions shot up due to the instability in regional conflicts around the world. Since the director was a politically high-powered person without professional competence, she had no idea how to adjust and redirect the division to face these challenges. Sharp criticism and complaints from missions mounted against the division.

The upper management of the Department of Peacekeeping Operations finally seemed to recognize the cause of the problem. The director was abruptly transferred, and in the beginning of September a new director came to my division.

The new director was a former Austrian diplomat, a woman in her early fifties who had represented Austria in

several countries as well as at the UN. She was quite familiar with the administrative aspects of our department in the
light of critical peacekeeping operations. By the middle of
September, she had completed her review of the division and
started reorganizing. All of the former director's incompetent
friends were removed. Able managers and senior officers were
restored to their former authority. Young, highly motivated
professionals were given broader responsibilities. She issued
her own white paper, a down-to-earth, no-nonsense descrip-
tion of new administrative support services she envisioned
for the peacekeeping missions. She was enthusiastically welcomed by the division staff members after six miserable years
of mismanagement.

One of her first changes affected me. Until then, on paper,
I had been working in the director's office, directly reporting
to the director. I had been on so-called "Special Assignment,"
which really meant a dumping yard. The new director created
a new section, called the Recruitment and Placing Section, and
she appointed me as the chief of the section.

A similar function had existed in the division before. But
the person in charge, a friend of the former director, had del-
egated the authority to individual missions, so in effect each
mission had taken over these activities, while there had been
no centralized recruitment or placement policies because staff
members under her at the UN headquarters practically didn't
do anything. Consequently the quality of the staff recruited had
varied from mission to mission, which was dangerous, particularly when staff members were transferred among missions.

My first task was to establish centralized, cohesive
recruitment and placement policies among the missions and

the UN headquarters in New York. I gave a semi-autonomous authority to the individual missions for recruiting local personnel within the established central guidelines, but my section would take care of placements and transfers of professional staff members from UN offices to the missions, vice versa, and among missions.

I was busy, but I didn't mind. Working hard was never one of my problems. I felt that the worst of my professional career at the UN might be behind me and was glad that now I was doing something positive for the UN, as I had done during my early years.

*   *   *

While I was going through the changes in my office, I was unexpectedly exposed to a new prospect for a love life.

One of my acquaintances, Gerard Clifford, had worked for the Security and Exchange Commission in Washington DC, where he had been a close friend of my father, who had served in the Federal Reserve. After retiring from the SEC, Mr. Clifford moved to New York to become a senior executive in a Wall Street investment bank. When I came to New York to take up a post at the UN, he helped me find the apartment where I still lived.

Mr. Clifford and his wife Elizabeth lived in a two-bedroom co-op apartment on Fifth Avenue in the eighties. As their apartment was close to mine, they occasionally invited me for dinner. They had a daughter, Jane, who had a job as a fundraiser at the Metropolitan Museum of Art. She was married to an investment banker in another Wall Street firm. Sometimes Jane and her husband were also invited to these dinners.

Since the Cliffords were parishioners of the Heavenly Rest, they suggested I come to the church. Although I was not a regular churchgoer, whenever I went to the church, I met Mr. and Mrs. Clifford, sometimes joined by Jane and her husband.

Three years earlier Mr. Clifford had passed away of some illness. Two years later, Jane was divorced from her husband for reasons I did not know. Now Jane had moved into the Cliffords' apartment and lived with her mother. Since then I had started seeing Jane and Mrs. Clifford at church whenever I went there. Soon I observed that Jane was not paying much attention to the service, but instead looking around at the people or flipping pages of a magazine. I guessed that she came to the service only to please her mother, who was a devoted Episcopalian. Mrs. Clifford, Jane, and I occasionally had lunch together after the service at one of the cozy restaurants around Carnegie Hill.

Jane and I shared much in common. She was three years younger than me. She had graduated from Wellesley College, and I from GWU and USC. She was about 5'7", two inches shorter than me. She and I were both slim. She had dark blond hair as I did. Her eyes were gray, as were mine. She had a fine, pale complexion that I shared. She was beautiful; I was presentable. We both liked art and classical music. The Cliffords were an old family, not as old as mine, but old enough for Americans. She and I had played together when we were children. She was my high school sweetheart, and we had pledged to marry. But we went separate ways as we left for college and began working. Years later we met again in New York.

Mrs. Clifford and Jane knew that I was divorced without children. Mrs. Clifford appeared to think that her daughter and I were a good match for remarriage, because she knew that Jane and I had spoken of it as teenagers. So directly and indirectly Mrs. Clifford encouraged me to get closer to Jane. Jane seemed perfectly agreeable to the idea, and whenever she had a chance, she talked to me like an intimate, her face shining.

One Sunday after the service I again joined the women at a neighborhood restaurant. I was already accustomed to these pleasant Sunday lunches with the mother and the daughter of my old family acquaintance. But this time after the meal Mrs. Clifford said, "I have to run to meet my friends. Why don't you two go back to our apartment and have some dessert and tea?"

"That's a good idea," Jane said. "I'll buy some cake on the way back." She turned to me. "I hope you are free this afternoon?"

I didn't have any particular plans, and visiting the Cliffords' apartment was nothing new to me. As I wanted to be polite to Mrs. Clifford, I said, "Sounds nice."

Mrs. Clifford broke into a broad smile. "Have a good time!" She hailed a taxi and drove off toward midtown.

Jane bought some dessert for us at a confectionary, and we walked to their apartment on Fifth Avenue.

It was a fine, cool day in late October. But inside the apartment was warm. From the windows of the twelfth floor, I gazed at Central Park, which was covered with lush foliage ranging from yellow to red. Jane changed to comfortable clothes, appearing at home yet gracious. She set tea and cake on a table before a sofa. We sat on the sofa and relaxed.

"My mom won't come back until this evening, so we have a whole afternoon for ourselves," Jane said, winking. "How is your work at the UN?"

"Busy," I answered. "Recently a new director started revitalizing my division. I was promoted to a section chief. So I have a lot to do."

"That's great," she said. "I'm happy for you."

"How is your work at the Met?" I asked in return, just to keep the conversation going.

"Boring," she replied. "My job is fundraising, so I mostly contact philanthropic organizations to ask for donations. But I'm good at it. I can't complain."

"Good," I said.

There was a pause. Jane seemed to sink into a reverie. This was the first time I had been alone with a woman in a private setting since my divorce. I felt a little odd, even though Jane had been my high school girlfriend and I had occasionally spent time in this apartment with her family present.

"I miss our innocent years in Georgetown." Jane broke the silence in a longing tone. "When I was a little girl, my mother often brought me to your house, and we played together, like hide-and-seek. You were a cute boy then and practically my big brother. I was good at hiding under the table or behind doors. You couldn't find me. Then suddenly I would jump up right in front of you, scaring you. … Do you remember?" She giggled.

"Yes, those were good childhood days," I said, nodding. "I miss it too."

"As we grew up," she continued, "I didn't think of you as a brother anymore. Then when you were a senior in a high school, you said you loved me. I said I loved you too. You proposed to me, and I said yes." Her face grew sentimental.

"I remember that day," I replied, also feeling nostalgic. "But we didn't know anything about marriage then. It was just a silly teenagers' fantasy."

"No," she said firmly. "I may have been only fifteen, but I meant it. I was so happy." She smiled.

"I was a bad boy," I confessed. "When I went to GWU, I forgot about you." I hastily added. "Sorry, I don't mean I wasn't sincere when I said those things. But we were just kids."

"When you left for college, I was sad." She inclined her head. "And since you lived in one of fraternity houses, I couldn't see you. Then I went to Wellesley, and we lost contact." She took a deep breath. "I'm really glad we met again after so many years. Now that we're both divorced I would be happy if we can resume our relationship." She gazed at me with inquisitive eyes.

"Oh, Jane," I uttered, "there was no real relationship between us. We talked about love and marriage, but that was a teenage talk and meant nothing."

"I don't think so," she said, slowly shaking her head. "Yes, we were young, but we knew each other well."

"That I agree," I pronounced. "But we've both changed a great deal since then."

"Now we are more mature and wiser." Her voice became affectionate. "If we resume our relationship now, I think this time we can develop it into full-grown love. Would you think about it, please?"

"Okay, I will think about it," I answered to be polite, but without commitment.

"Thank you." She kissed me on my cheek. "A kiss to you after so many years." She kissed me again, this time on my lips.

I accepted her kisses. I felt good, remembering our kisses so long ago.

"Do you want to know why I got divorced?" she asked.

"I don't want to intrude into your privacy," I answered. "But if you want to tell me, I'll listen. I should know you more as a grown woman."

"Good, that's my man," she said. "Then hear me out."

After gathering her thoughts, she began. "Wall Street is a wild place. Some people, like my ex-husband, can make millions of dollars in one day. Those people believe they can buy anything. Because of that, their material desires are as flagrant as naked lust — and so are their physical desires. Some of their offices were adorned with *Penthouse* centerfolds and outright porn. I can't believe they have the nerve to post these indecent photos in their public offices."

"Yes, I've heard those horrible stories," I said, wondering what she was going to tell.

She sighed. "I didn't know until later, but my ex was one of those."

"Really?" I said. "It's hard to believe. He seemed like a decent businessman."

"I thought so too when I married him. But he turned out to be a monster." She frowned in disgust. "About five years ago my ex started coming home late every day. He claimed he was busy at his office. He traveled often, leaving me alone for several days at a time or entire weekends. He said it was business. He lost interest in making love to me. I became suspicious, so I hired a private detective. What we found —" Her face twisted.

"According to the detective's report, my ex had a pied-à-terre in downtown Manhattan. He was a member of an online sugar-daddy dating service, through which he found several sugar babies, college girls, meaning from age eighteen to twenty-two. He lavished them with cash, tens of thousands of dollars each. In return they came to his apartment and slept with him. Sometimes he took his sugar babies to Florida, the Bahamas, Bermuda, and other resort areas. So I was like a widow, while my ex enjoyed sex with these young girls."

"Oh, no," I said with sympathy. "How awful for you."

"Yes, it was. But more dreadful is that those girls use the money for their living expenses and tuition. Can you imagine, selling sex for college tuition? Sickening! And supposedly they're all the students at prestigious universities in Manhattan!" She exhaled.

I shook my head, appalled. "That must have been devastating."

"Of course it was!" she spat. "I felt furious. But the private detective's report was very candid beyond dispute, with many photos of my ex with these girls in bars, restaurants, at the entrance to his apartment building, and even inside his apartment through the windows, taken with high-powered zoom lenses. Some photos showed my naked ex with naked girls having sex in the sofa or in the bed, or even standing at the windows."

"Good lord," I said. "That's a nightmare."

"Exactly," she said in anger and resignation. "As you can imagine, my marriage was hell."

"I bet it was," I said, gently patting her shoulder.

"My divorce petition, prepared by my attorney, included the detective's report with the photos," she went on. "So it was a clear-cut case of a husband cheating on a wife, and our divorce was settled swiftly, awarding me a huge alimony. I thought justice had been served for his treachery. It was only fair that he had to pay me to compensate for my injury. That was one year ago. Now I'm free from that hell. Thank God. What a relief!"

"I can't imagine this kind of thing really happens in the real world," I remarked. "You must have felt so betrayed."

"Grief is one thing, but rage is a better word to express my feeling at the time," she said.

"I'm sure it was so," I said. "I really sympathize with you."

"Thank you. The shock was enough to wipe out any happy memories of my marriage, so for me, the healing process was relatively speedy. I can live comfortably on the alimony. But I'm working at the Met simply to do something among good people. This keeps me sane. Now I want to move into a new chapter of my life, and I'm ready for another marriage with a better man."

"I'm glad you recovered from the trauma so fast."

Jane took a moment of reflection.

"Mark, I've been thinking about this for the past year," she said tenderly, moving closer to me. "We've known each other for a long time. Why don't we give our old pledge a chance?"

I frowned, confused. "What do you mean?"

"We pledged once to marry. That pledge never materialized. After so many years I think we've been given a renewed opportunity." She carefully searched for words. "What I mean is … we should get married, Mark. We'll make a good couple, and I'll make you very happy." She warmly kissed me on my lips. Her words and gesture reflected honesty.

"Wait, Jane, please," I said, gingerly pressing her back. "This is too sudden. I need time to think about it, because we've been just acquaintances in New York. I've never thought of you as a potential lover or partner for marriage."

"No need to be embarrassed between you and me. After all, we were once engaged."

"You can't think it was a formal engagement! Please don't bring up our childish past as a means to persuade me."

"But we were serious when we pledged our love. That's a fact."

Stunned, I moved away from her on the sofa. "Don't press me too much, I beg you."

At last she yielded. "Ah … I'm disappointed." She exhaled deeply. "All right, then think about it." She sounded reasonable. "But I want you to know this. If we get married, my mom says she doesn't mind moving out of this apartment so you and I can live here. She says she'll be content to live alone near here — may be in your apartment — or even move back to DC, where she has many friends, including your parents. So this apartment will be all ours."

She swept her hand over the living room, which was opulently yet tastefully decorated with paintings, sculptures, oriental rugs, and other luxuries.

"Yes, this is a gorgeous apartment," I said, going along with her, though taken aback that she and her mother seemed to have my future all planned out.

We continued our innocuous conversation for some time as we ate the cake and sipped tea. At one point, while I was trying to scoop up a small piece of cake with a fork, my right hand slipped and my forefinger dipped into the white frosting. I was going to wipe my finger with a paper napkin. Jane moved closer to me, her body pressing against mine. As she wore a thin peach-color silk blouse and a fine black wool skirt, I felt her breast, waist, and thigh directly through the filmy fabrics.

She gently took my hand and said, "Mmm … let me clean it for you."

She inserted my forefinger into her mouth and started licking, pushing my finger into her mouth and pulling back as her warm tongue sensually caressed my finger. I quickly grew aroused. She then dipped her right forefinger into the frosting.

"Now it's your turn," she said, slowly screwing her forefinger into my mouth. "Clean it for me."

She thrust her finger inside my mouth and pulled back in suggestive rhythm. "Mmm … that feels so good."

I felt good in my mouth, too, so I didn't resist her.

Soon her finger was clean. Then she took a piece of cake into her mouth. "Let's eat together," she said. She kissed me, injecting part of the sweet cake into my mouth from her mouth.

We kissed and munched the cake together, our mouths tightly coupled. As her tongue coiled into my mouth and played with my tongue, the cake meshed with our saliva. When the cake melted down into our throats, she scooped up another piece and put into her mouth. We kissed again, sharing the cake in our melded mouths. I had never thought a cake could taste so erotic.

Then suddenly out of blue a name struck me, like huge stone-carved letters falling from the sky and resounding deep in my heart — *Yu-ka-ri*. I immediately pulled myself out of Jane.

"Sorry, I can't do this," I declared. "This isn't a good idea."

"Why?" she protested. "We've played like this many times before. You liked it."

"We were just kids then," I said. "Now we are grownups, and I don't want to lead you on, Jane. I mean no offense to you."

Jane backed off. "I'm sorry." She straightened out her clothes. "I just got carried away."

*   *   *

How could you do it! I said repeatedly in my mind after that Sunday afternoon. Jane was just the daughter of my old family acquaintance. Although we may have promised to marry when we were teenagers, now she was not my girlfriend or my lover. It was not my cup of tea, either, to indulge in an afternoon quickie with a girl to whom I felt no attachment. The incident shamed me.

Then I thought of the situation more carefully. It might make a lot of sense if Jane and I got married. We would be a respectable couple any parents could be proud of. We could still have a child or two if we were blessed. We could raise a happy family. We could be a socially responsible husband and a wife. Most importantly, we could be good friends to Hans and Yukari. — Indeed, this was a positive and healthy prospect.

However, deep down in my heart, that prospect did not attract me at all, because I didn't feel love for Jane, though she was a charming, eligible woman. I tried to persuade myself that love would grow between us over time. Yet somehow I knew that that wouldn't happen anytime soon.

Instead, I still strongly preferred to befriend Hans and Yukari, no matter how outlandish our relationship was. Strangely I felt happier with the idea of whatever I had with Hans and Yukari than the idea of marrying Jane.

I still tried to convince myself that any rational man would embrace the opportunity to marry Jane, such a beautiful woman of substance and status. Obviously she cared for me. Why didn't I feel grateful for her offer? Why did I still prefer the friendship of Hans and Yukari? I thought certainly I must be mad.

*   *   *

In the beginning of November, Hans left for Athens to attend the EGlobe meeting, which was to start on Monday. Hans's director, Mr. Skoog, would also go, as the EGlobe was one of the major mandates of his division. Also the USG of DESA would be co-chairing the general session with Professor Cohen, who had retired from Princeton and moved to Stanford University, but was still active on the EGlobe. This suggested how important the meeting was for the UN, as well as the international economic community.

I received email from Hans every day. The time difference between New York and Athens worked in our favor, as Athens time was seven hours ahead of New York. Hans wrote email each night in his hotel room, summarizing the events of the day, and I received them in the late afternoon when I was still in my office.

Judging from Hans's email, everything seemed to be moving smoothly as planned. The individual country models had been successfully integrated into the global model. There was no error in the global economic forecast made by the EGlobe system. Hans was busily working closely with Professor Cohen and Mr. Skoog. I'd had a nagging worry about his trip, so his frequent communications left me much relieved.

Since Yukari did not operate Hans's PC at home, before he left New York, he had asked me to hand-deliver a printout of his email to her every day. This gave me an excuse to ensure that she was all right. If anything was found wrong, I was supposed to report to him immediately.

Every day after work I stopped at their apartment. A few evenings she was out for performances or rehearsals, so I left the email with the doorman and later called to make sure she had received it and she was all right. On evenings she was there, I would visit. Now in the middle of her second trimester, Yukari had calmly settled into expectant motherhood. Her abdomen was not yet very visible, but she had already began wearing maternity dresses. Fortunately she showed no sign of complication from her pregnancy.

The EGlobe meeting was a great success, and Hans came back to New York late the following Saturday night. He called me after midnight to let me know that everything at home had gone smoothly during his absence. Both he and I were relieved. But probably we'd been overly nervous about Yukari, we agreed.

He had bought two small marble copies of a Nike — a goddess of victory — at the Acropolis Museum in Athens. The fragment of relief decoration showed Nike adjusting her sandal, though her head and part of her hand were missing. In sensual clothes like wet silk, the goddess looked exquisite. He gave me one as a souvenir and kept the other at home.

For Yukari he bought, among other gifts, a dress of ancient Greek style which, according to her, could be worn as an elegant maternity dress.

So much for Hans's trip to Athens. There was nothing to be worried about after all.

*　　*　　*

While Hans was away in Athens, the blue roses in the UN garden bloomed again. I visited the garden during my lunch breaks and painted the blossoms in watercolor. I also took pictures of them with my digital camera. Aided by these, I made final touches to my oil painting of the three of us in Central Park.

I told Yukari and Hans about the blue roses when he returned from Greece. They were eager to see the roses, even impatient. The following Saturday we met at the UN garden.

It was a beautiful autumn afternoon. The sky was pure blue without a single cloud. Only a few tourists strolled in the garden. At the south corner of the garden, we had the flower beds all to ourselves. While most roses in the beds had already faded away, our blue roses were in full bloom with more than a dozen sparkling flowers on the branches. Their delicate petals were very light cerulean blue, close to white, and produced a rich, sweet fragrance.

The UN flag waved slowly at the top of a nearby flagpole. The color of the sky, the UN flag, and our roses were variations of the same sublime blue. While the roses looked pale against the sky, the deeper the interior of the blooms, the deeper the blue color.

We were impressed by the energy of the Blue Earth, able to bloom twice a year, each time so beautifully. No wonder the hybrid perpetual roses were all the rage among rose lovers.

Yukari was almost breathless, admiring the blue roses, sometimes moving her face close to the blossoms to inhale the elegant aroma. She wore the Greek dress Hans had brought from Athens. As she had predicted, it served her as a fashionable maternity dress, showing her slightly high abdomen. The sight of the roses and Yukari in that dress suggested to me a mystical symbolism of fertility, and I felt that the coming baby would be as beautiful and celestial as the blue roses. She faced her abdomen directly toward the blue roses and gently caressed them.

"I have a strange feeling," she murmured, "that my baby is right now gazing at these blue roses from inside me and liking them very much."

"The baby must be happy," Hans said.

"What a beautiful thought, Yukari," I told her. "I feel these blue roses have become part of us, including the baby."

We couldn't stop admiring these pure light blue blossoms — "we" now meant the baby, too.

Soon after, we went to my apartment. Due to the changes in my office, I had found little time to work on the oil painting, but finally I had managed to schedule our session to finish it.

As I had asked, Yukari and Hans had brought the outfits they had worn to Central Park. Yukari had a little difficulty fitting into her summer dress for this occasion, but she managed somehow.

My living room was my studio, where the canvas, easel, and other painting tools were already in place. I positioned extra lamps to make the lighting similar to that day. Yukari's abdomen was slightly bigger, but I could work around it. She brought her violin and sat on my sofa. They assumed their pose, recreating the scene in the park.

I was ready to apply the finishing touches. I used linseed oil, but very little turpentine oil, so the hue of the paints would become thick and powerful. I carefully moved my brushes in deep concentration on their faces and postures. The bright summer sun had to be reflected on the figures so they projected the vigor I wished to capture.

In less than an hour, it was over.

"Thank you. This is it," I announced. "Now relax, please."

They stretched their limbs, alleviated. It was a relief to me too. They came around me and inspected the result.

Yukari sighed deeply. "Beautiful!"

"Excellent!" was Hans's response.

"I'm pleased," I said.

Using a fine brush and mixture of dark paints, I put my initials and the year in the dark area of the greenery at the bottom right corner of the canvas. On the back side of the canvas, I wrote the title, "Blue Roses and Three Friends," my initials, and the date.

Hans helped me to hang the canvas on the wall at the center of the living room. We moved slowly and carefully, because the paint was still wet. Standing before the painting, Yukari and Hans applauded. I acknowledged by bowing ceremoniously to them.

We took a photo with my digital camera, set on auto-shutter, the three of us standing in front of the painting, posing as the singer, the violinist, and the painter, just as in the painting. Immediately, I printed the photo on my color printer. I gave one to Hans and Yukari and kept another for myself.

Then I uncorked a bottle of champagne for Hans and me and poured a glass of gingerale for Yukari. We toasted, shouting in a delighted cry.

"Success!"

The painting, in impressionist style, glowed with soft pure colors, but intense power as well. Its pastel softness was balanced by the bright effect of sunlight reflecting on the three figures and our blue roses. The darker colors of the background pushed the figures and our blue roses forward. The composition was simple and the figures were simplified, yet I felt they expressed a serene joy.

I had finally succeeded in creating my optimum mixture of Matisse, Renoir, Degas, and Morandi in my own style and sensitivity. I felt deeply satisfied. Hans and Yukari congratulated me. I thanked them sincerely, because their enthusiastic moral support had certainly encouraged me to reach my potential.

We viewed our painting from different angles, moving from right to left and from close-up to far away. As we moved, the figures and our blue roses also moved, seeming as lively as we had felt that day in the park, embracing life together in exuberance.

I thought I heard some familiar music that was so intimate to us.

"Listen," I said. "I have a wild feeling that I hear the second movement of Brahms's *Sestet No. 1 in B flat major* in the double ensemble as we heard it in the park."

"Yes, I can hear it, too," Yukari said. "I think it's coming from this painting."

"Yes, me too, I hear it," Hans said.

"Ah! The baby moved!" Yukari cried. "I think the baby loves it."

Without words, we listened to the noble music in our hearts, while gazing at the painting "Blue Roses and Three Friends."

In my mind I kept saying, *This is fine. We are good friends. This is the way it should be. I'm not insane.*

Then the thought of Jane resurfaced again in my mind. If I married her, she and I would be good friends to Hans and Yukari. This would be better than my current peculiar relationship with them. This was still a tempting prospect. I tried to imagine my painting with Jane in the picture. But no … I couldn't see her at our picnic. Even if she brought cake.

12

On the Sunday one week prior to Christmas Day, Yukari organized Christmas caroling at the entrance of the Metropolitan Museum of Art. It was a seasonably cold day but without wind. We gathered just outside the entrance around three o'clock. Many visitors were coming and going. There were about fifteen carolers, all of whom were friends of Yukari and Hans from her Parnassus Symphony Orchestra and his church. At their strong invitation, I, too, participated as a baritone. We wore festive outfits with red hats and scarves. The voices were reasonably mixed, though perhaps a few more women than men. Each of us carried a carol book. One fellow from the orchestra assumed the role of conductor.

We started with "Joy to the World" as the attention catcher. Although the group of carolers was small, our voices were enhanced by the marble walls and glass doors of the museum, creating good acoustics. Quickly a large crowd surrounded us.

We continued singing popular Christmas songs: "We Wish You Merry Christmas;" "Hark! The Herald Angels Sing;" and "Oh, How Joyfully."

This is great. Sing more. Yes, do more. Do you have any requests? Please sing … Any other requests? How about …? Can you do …? Yes, yes, we can sing anything you want. Don't forget …, it's my favorite. You got it. We'll do them all.

So we went on: "Jingle Bells;" "Deck the Hall;" "It Came Upon a Midnight Clear;" "Angels We Have Heard on High;" and "O Holy Night." Then we wound down to a reverent and peaceful mood by singing quieter songs, "O Come, All Ye Faithful" and "The First Noël."

We concluded the caroling with "Silent Night." The chorus sang three verses. Then we sang the first verse again, encouraging the audience to sing as well. Everyone in the surrounding area sang spontaneously.

The visitors smiled at the carolers and applauded.

A little girl came to Yukari, tapped her visible tummy, and asked innocently, "Are you going to have a baby on Christmas Day?"

Yukari gently caressed the girl's head. "I wish. But it will be sometime next April."

"Have a pretty baby then," the girl said.

"Thank you, dear," Yukari answered. "Merry Christmas!" She kissed the child's cheek.

The child responded happily, "Merry Christmas!"

This affected us all. Everyone there greeted everyone else. "Merry Christmas!"

Yukari, Hans, and I went back to their apartment. On the way I bought them a Christmas tree. It was a good size, not too big, but not too small either. With Hans holding the bottom of the tree and me the top, we carried it to their home. Yukari walked beside us, leading with her eminent tummy.

The streets were full of people, busy with their Christmas shopping. They gazed at us curiously. After a while Yukari giggled, then started laughing.

"Look," she said to Hans and me in a low voice. "People are confused. A pregnant Japanese woman is walking beside a Christmas tree which is being carried by two Caucasian men. What's going on here?" She laughed heartily.

I wondered whether it was really so funny. I asked Hans if I should carry the tree alone. He ignored my inquiry and giggled too, holding the tree steadily in his hands. Yukari laughed and laughed.

In the living room of their apartment, we decorated the tree. As I understood it, Germans were known to take Christmas very seriously. Indeed, Hans was passionate, paying attention to every detail. First we secured the tree upright in a metal tree stand and carefully strung the lights around the tree branches. Then we hung twinkling ornaments in various sizes: silver stars, gold stars, and shiny balls, plus a sled with reindeer and a Santa. Yukari further added miniature angels, trumpets, harps, and music sheets. I poured water into the plate on the metal tree stand and sprinkled the white cotton snow on the branches. At the top of the tree, Hans affixed a large silver star. Finally he switched the power on. The tree shone brightly.

The air of the living room was filled with the smell of fresh evergreen, the nostalgic aroma of Christmas. Our tree stood there majestically, beaming with joyful colors. We felt that Christmas had arrived. We beamed as well, and sang:

O Christmas tree, O Christmas tree!
Thou tree most fair and lovely!
The sight of thee at Christmas tide
Spreads hope and gladness far and wide.
O Christmas tree, O Christmas tree!
Thou tree most fair and lovely.

Then, this being a German folk song, Hans sang in German.

O Tannenbaum, O Tannenbaum!
wie treu sind deine Blätter!
Du grünst nicht nur zur Sommerzeit,
nein, auch im Winter, wenn es schneit.
O Tannenbaum, O Tannenbaum!
wie treu sind deine Blätter.

Christmas Eve and Christmas Day came and went. I gave Hans and Yukari the private time together by themselves, in spite of their protest that they wanted to share the occasion with me. We just exchanged our cards, gifts, and "Merry Christmas." But I promised I would spend New Year's Eve with them.

During those days, that simple German folk song we had sung together reverberated in my heart, as if it symbolized our friendship — *most fair and lovely,* that *spreads hope and gladness far and wide.* My heart swelled with gratitude for our friendship over the past several months. Such was my joy of Christmas that year.

*   *   *

Hans had told me that there would be an "Annual New Year's Eve Concert for Peace" at the Cathedral of St. John the Divine at 110th Street and Amsterdam Avenue. It had been his New Year's Eve tradition to attend the concert every year as a member of the volunteer chorus. Since they'd been married, Yukari had been joining him. Particularly this year, what a great way it would be to spend the evening of the last day of 1999 and to welcome a new millennium. He had insisted that I join the volunteer chorus, and I had been easily persuaded.

I had managed to attend all the rehearsals with Hans and Yukari during the past four evenings after work. With their help I had studied the music carefully. The short pieces were relatively easy. But the main program, Beethoven's No. 9, was not an easy piece, even though some melodies were well known. As a native German, Hans coached the chorus members in German diction. I sat next to a good baritone who was a friend of Hans, which helped my singing. By the end of our final rehearsal, I felt able to sing fairly well.

On December 31, after leaving my office, I stopped at my apartment to change to the tuxedo that was the concert dress for men, added a black bowtie, then went to the Cathedral of St. John the Divine. The dress rehearsal was to start at three o'clock. I barely made it. Hans and Yukari were already there. He was in a tuxedo with a red bowtie. She wore a white blouse with long sleeves, a black long skirt, and a red scarf. Something red was encouraged in order to heighten the festive mood. Seeing me without any red, Yukari arranged her red handkerchief in the chest pocket of my jacket.

The dress rehearsal went smoothly. The orchestra was provided by nearby Manhattan School of Music. The conductor was an instructor at the school. The volunteer chorus, named the "New York Festival Singers," sang well. After the rehearsal we had time for a quick dinner in a nearby restaurant.

On our return we saw a long waiting line surrounding the cathedral. It had been estimated that more than ten thousand people would show up, as the cathedral was one of the largest in the world. It seemed true.

At half past seven the concert started. The chorus sat behind the orchestra before the altar. The cathedral, which was larger than a football field, was completely packed with people. As the name "Concert for Peace" suggested, although it was held in the cathedral, it was nondenominational. A master of ceremonies guided the program skillfully. The orchestra performed excellently several pieces by Copland, Mozart, and Haydn, by itself or with solo instrumentalists, solo singers, or chorus. Between the performances, prayers for peace were said by a rabbi, a Muslim clergyman, and the Dean of the Cathedral.

The last piece was the Finale from Beethoven's *Ninth Symphony*, the cantata based on Schiller's poem "*An Die Freude*" (Ode to Joy). The orchestra established the mood and led to the main theme. Then the baritone solo introduced the first words, followed by the chorus.

All chorus members busied ourselves with singing and following the music, which was demanding but enjoyable. There were only few places where the chorus could rest while soloists or orchestra continued. Once it reached *Allegro energico*, the music ran by itself, uniting the orchestra, soloists, and chorus. We became inspired by the spirit of Schiller's poem, calling for the universal fraternity of people. When it reached *Prestissimo*, all singers were ecstatic, almost yelling. At last we burst into "*Freude, schöner Gotterfunken*" (Joy, bright spark of divinity), followed by the orchestra's frantic finale.

When the music ended at the height of the climax, the echo resounded throughout the cathedral for several seconds. Then tidal waves of applause and "Bravo" came from the audience.

The concert concluded with a candlelight ceremony. Each audience and chorus member held a candle and sang "Auld Lang Syne" to bid farewell to the current millennium. I felt an overwhelming serenity watching more than ten thousand candle flames floating in the vast, mysterious cathedral.

After the concert Hans, Yukari, and I strolled around inside the cathedral, wishing people a happy new year. Noticing our concert dress, several people smiled at us and complimented our singing. A tall, beautifully decorated Christmas tree tranquilly pleased us. A postlude from a huge pipe organ peacefully blessed us.

*   *   *

Hans, Yukari, and I came back to their apartment together. It was about eleven o'clock. Yukari prepared some hors d'oeuvres, a bottle of champagne, and a pot of tea for our private celebration.

We watched TV for the new millennium celebrations, which had already taken place in various cities in the world, such as Sydney, Tokyo, Beijing, New Delhi, Jerusalem, Cairo, Moscow, Johannesburg, Athens, Rome, Vienna, Berlin, Paris,

Madrid, London, and so on. We had never seen such storms of celebrations and parties.

Now, it was one minute to midnight. The mayor of New York City pushed the button for an illuminated ball at Times Square. The ball slowly came down. People started counting.

"... Five, four, three, two, one!"

A big bang exploded. Fireworks shot skyward. Torrents of confetti and balloons filled the air. An estimated two million people shouted, hugged, kissed, blew merry noisemakers, and waved shiny hats. "Happy New Year 2000" flashed everywhere.

Yukari poured champagne into three glasses. We toasted. She took one sip as an exception, after which she had a cup of tea. We continued watching TV while eating hors d'oeuvres and drinking champagne and tea.

I called Shem Tov. He was at home with Francine and their little Jacques.

"We've been watching TV. It was a fantastic celebration," Shem Tov said in high spirits. "But as far as Y2K is concerned, it was an extraordinary anticlimax. No catastrophe occurred anywhere in the world. Not that I was hoping, but I'm kind of disappointed — though this is a blessing to humankind. Well, we worked hard to fix Y2K bugs. Probably that helped, so our computer data center at the UN is running as usual. I checked it remotely a few minutes ago. I hope our efforts produced this result; otherwise what a waste of our time and money."

"So much for Y2K, eh?" I said. "Now you can enjoy the New Year celebration."

"Yeah, that's what we're doing here."

Francine took over, and we exchanged "Happy New Year!"

Yukari took the phone from me and cheerfully chatted with Francine until Hans took the phone and chatted with Francine and Shem Tov, wrapping up with "Happy New Year!"

As he hung up the phone, I asked Hans, "Have you fixed Y2K bugs in the EGlobe system?"

"No, I didn't have to do anything," he replied easily. "You see, Y2K bugs occur when we code a four-digit year with the last two digits only, which confuses the computer programs as we enter into the new millennium. But the EGlobe system was designed for long-term economic forecasting, so the system always uses the full four-digit year like 19xx or 20yy. So it didn't have the inherent Y2K issues from the beginning."

Now, completely relaxed, we resumed watching TV for a while. This time the broadcasts showed American cities such as Boston, Philadelphia, Washington DC, Atlanta, and Miami Beach. People were celebrating everywhere endlessly.

It had been a long day for me. While I did not know anything of pregnancy, I was a little concerned for Yukari, who might have had too much activity and excitement.

"Yukari, how are you feeling?" I asked. "Are you tired out?"

"Oh, no, I'm fine," she answered matter-of-factly. "Actually, I'm at the end of the second trimester, which is supposed to be a reasonably stable period of pregnancy. Doctors encourage expectant mothers in this period to have a normal life as much as possible. I try to work normally and to attend social activities as usual. Of course, I shouldn't do too much."

"Yes," Hans added, "her doctor assured us that she would go through a healthy childbirth. It will be exciting."

"That's great," I said.

"Mark, I meant to tell you this," Hans said in a warm voice. "Come close to Yukari and touch her tummy with both hands. You'll feel the baby moving sometimes."

I hesitated because I thought such a gesture might seem immodest to a pregnant woman next to her husband. But Hans appeared to think it a most natural thing to do.

"Go on," he encouraged me.

Yukari, too, appeared to welcome me. "Come, Mark — after all, you are the half-father to the child." She guided my hands to her abdomen and carefully placed them in certain position.

We held our breath for a moment.

"Aha!" Yukari and I cried together at the same time. Yes, the baby moved.

"It's a girl," Hans said with a father's smile. "She is a healthy one. She is already strong and kicking."

"Do you know for sure it's a girl?" I asked.

"Yes," Yukari replied, "two tests showed the same results, and recently it was confirmed by the ultrasound scan. I'm so happy it's a girl. I can teach her the violin. I want her to become better than me." She smiled at the prospect.

Hans added, "I'll teach her economics, so she can become an economist as an alternative career." He grinned.

Yukari met my eyes. "Hans and I have already decided the name of the coming child. It's Anne Kariope Schmidt. Anne, to honor your great-great grandmother, who presumably met my great-grandfather. Kariope is after Calliope, the muse of poetry. Its Greek spelling is Καλλιόπη, which is transformed into Kariope after my name Yukari. Then Schmidt is of course after Hans, whose grandfather presumably met my father. So in this name, the child will represent all three of us."

"It's a good name, isn't it?" Hans said with pride.

"Yes, it's beautiful," I said, feeling deeply touched. "I like it very much."

We dreamed of the coming child — Anne Kariope Schmidt.

"Well," Yukari resumed joyfully, "it's now the first day of the year 2000, the first year of the new millennium. Let's make a New Year's resolution. It's best to make a simple one so we can really keep it."

After some thought, Yukari presented her resolution, tenderly caressing her tummy. "I'll be a good mother."

"And I'll be a good father," Hans promised, showing me his pile of baby and parenthood books.

I offered, "I'll be a good friend to you two and to Anne Kariope Schmidt."

We were content with our resolutions.

"I'm more than convinced," spoke Yukari happily, "that it's going to be a wonderful year."

"Yes," agreed Hans, "it's going to be a prosperous year for all four of us."

"Indeed," seconded I, "I'm sure it will be."

"Let's toast," proposed Hans.

Hans and I raised our champagne glasses and Yukari raised her teacup.

"To a Happy New Year!"

13

It was my custom on New Year's Day to call my parents in Washington DC, unless I could visit them in person. Following the ritual, I telephoned them.

My father, Jonathan Graham Sanders, had retired from the Federal Reserve some years ago. After that he had worked for an international finance consulting firm as a senior advisor, but now had retired from there as well. My mother, Leslie, had devoted herself to a women's charity organization, but had also retired. While they were in their seventies now, fortunately they were in good health and enjoying their retirement life.

My father had been nominated a few times as a vice president of the World Bank or a member of its Board of Governors. Because of that, although he had never gotten a job at the bank, he had many friends there, and he had some influence over there as well. When I decided to work for the United Nations, my father was very pleased with my new career as an international civil servant. He occasionally found a post vacancy at the World Bank for me and encouraged me to apply for it, promising that he would get good recommendations from his friends. During the period of my internal exile in my division (so I called it), on a few occasions I had been tempted to apply for the World Bank post my father suggested. But I had decided to remain at the UN, because I felt my job as a personnel officer in the Department of Peacekeeping Operations was more interesting than a post at the World Bank. Now that my internal exile was over, I was very happy I'd stayed at the UN.

It seemed that Mrs. Clifford had called my mother often and brought up the idea of a marriage between Jane and me. Apparently both my mother and my father liked the idea.

My mother said, full of enthusiasm, "Jane is a lovely lady. She'll make a perfect wife for you." As she talked, from her voice, I could easily visualize her huge smile. "I remember well when you were still in high school you told me that you and Jane planned to marry. Since we knew Jane and her parents well, we approved it on the condition that you wait until after college graduation. I know you've both taken detours, but now you have a second chance. I'll be very happy if you choose to take it."

I sighed quietly, feeling a little annoyed, because my mother still treated me like her baby boy. I simply replied, "Okay, I'll ponder about it."

My father said, "Son, your mother and I are getting old. We want you to come back to Washington DC. Why don't you get a job at the World Bank? You can live in this house. If you are agreeable, I can find a post for you. Jane grew up here in

Georgetown, so she should feel at home settling here with you. Leslie and I can live in a small apartment near here."

In the past my father had respected my independence and did not interfere with my life decisions like my career or my marriage. So this was an unusual suggestion coming from him.

"I'll think about it," I said, uncommitted to the idea.

"Son, your life is your own. I have no wish to intervene," my father continued. "But as I get old, I grow concerned with my legacy. You know our family carries a long heritage. It's my responsibility to make sure the line is carried down to future generations. It's your responsibility too. That's why I feel happy with the idea of your marrying Jane, living here, and working for the World Bank. Jane is still young enough to bear children for you. Then our family heritage can be carried down to your children. I hope you'll consider it seriously."

My mother added, "Elizabeth is completely convinced that this marriage must take place. She won't hear of any other men for Jane's potential husband. I've talked to Jane myself. She loves you very much. She told me so plainly, and I believe her."

"All right, I'll give it more thought," I said.

With that we exchanged well wishes for the new year.

*　*　*

I had not gone to the Heavenly Rest since that late October Sunday, as I felt hesitant to see Jane again. For Thanksgiving Day and Christmas Eve, Mrs. Clifford had called me and invited me for dinner at her place. On both occasions I politely declined the invitation, making up an innocuous excuse. After talking to my parents, however, I felt it would be uncivil to avoid Mrs. Clifford and Jane any longer.

The first Sunday of the new year happened to be January 2. I went to church and found Mrs. Clifford and Jane sitting in their customary pew. Dressed for the first service of the year, both of them looked elegant. They greeted me with amicable nods. No sooner had I sat in a pew a few rows behind them than Jane rose and slid in next to me.

"Merry Christmas and a Happy New Year!" she said, and kissed me on my cheek.

"Merry Christmas and a Happy New Year to you!" I replied in an intentionally warm tone, as a peace offering for that October day.

"I hope you are not angry with me," she said, anxiously staring at me.

"Not at all," I said. "On the contrary, I'm the one who needs to apologize. I offended you. Sorry. It was just so unexpected, and I was unprepared. Forgive me."

"I understand," she said, obviously relieved. "I hope you don't think I'm too aggressive, because I'm not."

"Nothing like that," I answered. "Just give me time, will you?"

"I'm glad," Jane said. "All right. Take time."

During the service Jane held my hand fondly. She looked at me more than at the priest who was officiating the service. I could see she was in love with me. I recalled the conversation with my parents the day prior. Certainly she would make a fine wife. Yet my heart grew heavy.

After the service Mrs. Clifford came to the pew where Jane and I were sitting. Seeing Jane holding my hand, Mrs. Clifford's face lit up.

"Mark, today you must come to our apartment for lunch," she said. "We had ordered a goose for the Christmas Eve feast. But since you couldn't make it, we didn't roast it until New Year's Eve. We have some leftovers. So let's have our feast for Christmas and the new year together this afternoon."

I could not decline her invitation this time. I said, "Thank you. It will be my pleasure."

"Wonderful!" Mrs. Clifford cried.

"That's my man, Mark. Thank you," Jane said and kissed me on my lips.

At the sight of Jane kissing me, Mrs. Clifford gave a satisfied smile.

It was a mild day for January in New York City. We walked to the Cliffords' apartment on Fifth Avenue. Jane clasped my arm and walked closely beside me. I felt her curvaceous body through our coats. Was it my imagination that people gazed at Jane and me and grinned at us as if we were an ideal wife and husband? Jane saw it, and she appeared very pleased, holding my arm tighter.

At their apartment Mrs. Clifford busily prepared our lunch, setting out smoked salmon as an appetizer, salad, roast goose, and red wine. I noticed that the dining table was set for only two.

When the lunch was served, Mrs. Clifford said, "Actually this afternoon I have a New Year tea party at my friend's home. I'm leaving you two alone. So Mark, enjoy the lunch."

In no time Mrs. Clifford had left the apartment. This seemed to have been arranged between Mrs. Clifford and Jane. I suspected that my parents had also played some role in this conspiracy. But I pretended ignorance.

Jane had changed to a chic black cashmere one-piece dress with long sleeves. She looked young and handsome. She uncorked the red wine and poured two glasses.

We raised the glasses and said together, "Happy New Year!"

Jane acted as a splendid hostess, making sure that my glass was always filled with wine and changing the dishes as we finished the appetizer and salad. Then she served the roast goose, which had a special festive flavor. The room was a comfortable temperature; the food and wine further warmed me up. Jane seemed to be enjoying the feast with me as her face grew rosy.

After the meal we sat on the sofa for dessert and tea. *Oh dear*, I thought. *Cake again.* I hoped that we wouldn't get into more cake-play this afternoon. But Jane appeared to consciously behave more ladylike this time. She served tea for me and invited me to take the dessert on the table. We ate the cake and sipped tea. It was a peaceful Sunday afternoon. I felt at home.

"How did you spend Thanksgiving and Christmas?" she asked.

"I didn't do anything particular," I replied. "Since I became the section chief, I've been working very hard. So those holidays were just days of rest for me." This was the fact.

She sighed. "I'm afraid you aren't telling me the truth. Do you have a girlfriend?" She peered at me curiously, as if she had been asking the question for the past entire two months.

"No, I don't," I answered. This was true too … sort of.

"Mark, I love you," she said, moving close to me. "Tell me the truth. Don't keep me in suspense." She held my shoulders with her two hands, facing me directly. "Do you think I'm not attractive enough to be your wife?"

"Not that, please, Jane," I replied, trying not to distress her. "I think you're beautiful. Any eligible man should adore you."

"Then why are you keeping a distance from me?"

"Just that I haven't thought of you as my prospective wife."

"No, that's a lie. You must have a girlfriend." She started sobbing.

I felt sorry for her. All signs showed that she had fallen in love with me — probably long before I had any idea of her feelings. I felt I should not torment her any longer; I needed to tell her my real situation.

"It's difficult for me, because I don't want to hurt you," I said cautiously. "But do you want to hear it?"

"I knew you have a girlfriend," she repeated.

"No, it's a little more complicated."

"All right," she said with resignation. "Tell me."

I explained about my situation since last April: Hans, my close friend and an economist at the UN; Yukari, a professional violinist, his wife, now pregnant with his child; our family heritages; our bond as dear friends; and our joy in sharing time together. I told her all, without hiding anything. What I told her was nothing but truth — we were dear friends, no matter how queer our relationship might appear.

Jane listened to me attentively, occasionally nodding and sometimes shaking her head, yet without interrupting. As I spoke to her, to my surprise, instead of getting upset, her face grew lively and happy.

When I finished my story, she said, "Thank you for telling me all this. I really appreciate it." She straightened her clothes. "I've been depressed since that October day until today. But now I feel I have hope." She took a sip of tea. "Mark," she continued, "I have absolutely no problem with befriending Hans and Yukari. They seem to be a nice couple. Most of all they are your best friends. Actually I can't wait to meet them. I'm sure I would like them."

She moved closer to me, our bodies tightly touching each other. She kissed me affectionately on my lips. Her face flashed full of love.

"As far as I can see," she went on, "keeping your friendship with Hans and Yukari will not prevent us from getting married — in fact, I think it's perfect. As a married couple, we can be close friends to Hans and Yukari, who are also a married couple after all. They are going to have a child soon. I'll bear a child for you. Then our child and their child will be good playmates. We'll be two mutual families, more than just good friends. So much the better, don't you think?" She showered me with kisses.

I hadn't anticipated this. I thought Jane would get upset when she heard my story. Instead, my story only reinforced her love for me. However, somehow she didn't convince me. I still felt happier to remain alone, keeping my friendship with Hans and Yukari, than to marry Jane and then, as husband and wife, befriend Hans and Yukari.

In the meantime Jane stood up.

"Remember how we used to dance while we were engaged?" she said nostalgically. "You didn't like dancing, except for the waltz. So we waltzed a lot. Our favorite was Johann Strauss's *The Blue Danube*. Come. Let's dance."

She pulled me up and led me to dance, humming the familiar melody. This was unexpected, but I remembered our dancing days. I went along with her.

"It's just like old times," she said, whirling, her face radiant.

"Yes, this is nice," I seconded, swinging.

She had been a terrific dancer when she was a teenager. Even now she danced gracefully. I, too, in no time, recalled the waltz steps. As we danced, our body touched. I felt her soft feminine body through her dress. Our breath grew shorter; our bodies grew warmer; and our intimacy grew stronger. I felt like our youth had returned. Her longing eyes suggested she was feeling the same.

Oh, that music — *The Blue Danube* — the sound of our adolescent love. How happy we were then. We had dreamed of our marriage. But it was a long time ago. It had gone forever. We could never retrieve it now.

She stopped and started unzipping her dress.

"W-w-what are you doing?" I asked.

"When we were teenagers we never had sex, but we had a lot of fun with risqué play, particularly after dancing, remember? You saw me half-naked. You liked it. So let's play for old time's sake."

The one-piece dress easily dropped to the floor, exposing her copious body covered with only a white lace bra and a minuscule white bikini panty, both of which were diaphanous, hinting at the sensual skin, nipples, and hair underneath.

"Am I beautiful enough for you?" She smiled at me. "Watch."

She took the waltz steps alone, humming *The Blue Danube*. She turned around and around. Her breasts bounced, her butt swung, and her dark blond hair curled. I'd never seen her semi-nude as an adult until now. It was a splendid sight, like a muse dancing. I felt aroused. We were no longer innocent, but we might be able to foster our mature love as divorced adults. This was certainly a possibility. I began to understand how she was feeling toward me. As if she had read my mind, she abruptly stopped dancing and faced me directly.

"We should make love today," she said, embracing me and kissing me passionately. "I've been dreaming of this every night since that October Sunday. We should become real lovers that will lead us into marriage. Then as a couple, we can befriend Hans and Yukari. ... Let's go to my bedroom, or do you want to do it here?"

She started removing my jacket and unbuttoning my shirt. But the names of Hans and Yukari brought me back to this world again. I gingerly pushed her back. She resisted me, clinging onto me.

"Jane," I said with determination, "my problem is that right now I have no space for marriage in my mind. I'm perfectly happy as a single man to continue my friendship with Hans and Yukari." This was my honest feeling and wish.

Jane drew back and stared at me, her eyes bewildered. Then they flashed with understanding.

"You love Yukari!" she exclaimed. "Oh, poor Mark! You're in love with Yukari! And you are hiding your true feeling, justifying it as a friendship. What an excruciating conflict — it must be hell. But oddly you're completely happy with this situation. I don't understand you. You're crazy, you know that?" Tears started streaming from her eyes.

"Yes," I admitted, "sometimes I think so too. But I can't help it."

"Mark," she said, gently pressing my lips with her fingers, "you've been a divorcé too long. Your inhibited male desire has accumulated inside you so much that it has coerced you into going along with this weird relationship. I think you should release this suppressed libido from your system."

She hesitated for a moment. But she swallowed and took a deep breath, as if she were about to jump from a steep cliff. Then she said decidedly, "Sweetie, take off your clothes. Then let's make love. Remember last October? We were almost there. C'mon, make me pregnant. I'll give you a beautiful child. Then you'll be a normal man, and we'll be a happy husband and wife. All will end in happiness. So let's do it."

She drew close and tightly hugged me. I felt her soft breasts and abdomen. She began to kiss me with ardent craving, pleading, "I love you, Mark … Take me … Make me pregnant … I want your child."

I was moved. If I married her, she would be my beautiful wife, and we would be an enviable couple. I would be happy with her and proud of her. She would give me a child. And best of all, she and I would be good friends to Hans and Yukari as married couples. How could I expect more than this? But, but … did I love Jane?

Then that name struck my heart again with full force, this time repeatedly, like echoes never ceasing — *Yukari ... Yukari ... Yukari ... Yukari ...*

"Forgive me," I said, disentangling from Jane. "It's not you. But I just can't do this."

I scooped up her one-piece dress and covered her. She clung to me tightly and wept.

Jane, Jane, you are a beautiful lady. Why can't I accept your love? All is favorable for our marriage. Why can't I embrace the thought of it? I'm helpless. Forgive me. But I just cherish the friendship with Hans and Yukari more than your love. Yes, I must be crazy!

14

I reflected on the situation I was in with Jane. I had to concede that my marriage to her made a lot of sense. I could clearly see it by myself, without being told by my parents or Jane herself. I felt grateful to and honored by her unshakable love for me. But what I had felt and said to her on that Sunday was the truth: I was happy as I was. I did not want to distress her any more. I decided not to see her until something changed in my heart, if that ever happened.

In the beginning of January, as the United Nations resumed its normal business, I was busily involved in my new function, working late every day. Two weeks passed quickly this way. I had not had a chance to see or talk to Hans or Yukari. I thought that they needed to be alone, to prepare for the coming baby. I assumed that they were enjoying the early days of the new millennium.

One evening I was still working at my office when the telephone rang. It was Yukari, which alarmed me, because it was unusual for her to call me at my office. She sounded very agitated, almost crying.

"Mark, please come to our apartment," she begged. "Hans is so upset. He is saying that he will quit or sue the UN. It's something related to his promotion. Since I don't know how the UN administration works, I can't help or understand him. Right now he's shut himself in the bedroom and doesn't want to talk."

I took a taxi and found Hans visibly shaken, though he had emerged from the bedroom. He, Yukari, and I sat together around the dining table. I asked him what had happened.

"Mark, I'm sorry to involve you in this," Hans answered. "But I'm so upset and angry that I don't trust my judgment. I need a third person's opinion. I'm glad Yukari called you and you came for me. Please hear me out."

According to Hans, about six months earlier there had been a vacancy announcement in his office for the post of Senior Economic Affairs Officer who would oversee technical administration of the EGlobe system. Since he had been First Economic Affairs Officer for six years, he met the seniority requirement and naturally applied for it. Considering that he had been in charge of the EGlobe system since he had come to the UN, this seemed a promotion opportunity almost guaranteed for him.

In October he was interviewed by the management of the Department of Social and Economic Affairs as one of several short-listed candidates. A few days ago, however, the Appointment and Promotion Board had approved the recommendation made by the department that a woman from DESA be promoted to the post.

This woman, a Guatemalan, according to Hans, had only a BA degree in social science. She was not an economist. She did not have a Masters or a Ph.D. degree in economics, nor did she know anything about the EGlobe. In contrast, Hans had a Ph.D. in economics from Berkeley, specializing in econometrics and global economy. He had been instrumental in maintaining the EGlobe global model, being the right hand to Professor Cohen in the EGlobe meetings.

"When I came to the UN eleven years ago as Associate Economic Affairs Officer," explained Hans discontentedly, "she was just a secretary and studying for an undergraduate degree in social science at a small community college in the evenings. I even helped her with her homework in economics and statistics. Later, when she received her BA, she passed an examination from the General Service category to the Professional category, and she has worked up the ranks to my level, at which she has been for two years. She does not even satisfy the minimum seniority requirement of three years. Does she deserve an accelerated promotion? Now she is going to be Senior Economic Affairs Officer in charge of the EGlobe over me? I can't accept that. I'm far better qualified for the post. Her only qualification I can think of is her gender."

I nodded. He was referring to the promise made by the Secretary-General to promote women to senior posts so the gender balance at that level would become even. While the SG himself did not declare this official policy, he and his predecessor had been forced to make the promise under heavy pressure from the women's group in the UN, my former director being one of the high officials in the group. Since the gender balance was not yet even, the senior management was strongly pressured to promote women, irrespective of their professional capability. In order to press further, the Gender Equality Group sent their representatives to every case of promotion process and intervened.

"Hans," I said, "according to UN regulations, the decision of the APB is final, and you have no recourse. The only way you can fight officially against this decision is to appeal to the Joint Appeals Board, and only if there were technical or procedural errors in the vacancy-filling process. May I ask if the vacancy announcement was officially made public for this post? If so, were the short-listed candidates officially interviewed by a formal interview panel?"

His reply was affirmative to both.

"Then the vacant post was filled in accordance with official procedure," I said. "I'm sorry. You have no grounds for appeal."

Hans pounded the dining table with his fists and stomped his feet on the floor.

"This woman doesn't know anything about the EGlobe except its name," he shouted. "How can the management justify that she is more qualified than me? It doesn't make sense. I can't accept it."

I remembered something and asked, "Is this the woman you met outside the conference room of the Second Committee meeting last October?"

"Yes, that's her. Her name is Luisa Rodriguez. She works in a different division, one floor below," he said. "Hmm, I see ... she must have already set her eyes on the post of senior officer in charge of the EGlobe. So she read my report — mind you, *my* report — then attended the Second Committee meeting and heard the debate I participated in with my director, Mr. Skoog, and the USG. Now she claims she is an expert on the EGlobe? Baaah! Bullshit! Fuck her!" He hammered the dining table again with his fists, his face red with rage.

He shuffled some papers in his briefcase and presented a document of three pages, his hands trembling.

"Look at this. This just came out today. It's a General Assembly Resolution."

I read it. It was indeed the GA resolution entitled, "Implementation of the commitments and policies agreed upon in the Declaration on International Economic Cooperation ..." The document referred to the SG's report Hans had drafted.

Hans continued his argument rapidly, pointing to a paragraph, his tone indignant and frustrated. "Here, it says, 'The General Assembly takes note of the report of the Secretary-General.' That's my report. The EGlobe provided the supporting figures used in the report, and I'm the one who manages the EGlobe system. When the USG delivered the report to the Second Committee, I drafted his introductory statement and participated in the debates. I did all of these things with Mr. Skoog and the USG. She can't do any of them. So why was she promoted instead of me? No, no, no, I can't accept it!" He sank back into his chair, clasped his arms over his chest, and glared at the ceiling, pursing his lips tight.

I had never seen Hans in such an emotional state before, as he was usually a calm, intelligent gentleman. I fully understood how deeply hurt and outraged he felt. I wanted to help him. But there was not much I could do.

"Hans," I said with a deep sigh, "I sympathize with you from the bottom of my heart. But the management can creatively justify the promotion of this woman by saying that promoting women is more important than promoting the right person for the post."

"Do you believe that? Is it good for the organization?" Hans shot back.

"No, I don't believe it a bit. It's wrong. But that's the way it is right now. Face the reality. Until the organization realizes that it's gone too far, we can't do anything about it."

"It's injustice. Are you saying that we have to live with injustice in the United Nations? I can't believe that. The UN must be better than this."

"Hans, I'm sorry to be blunt. There is absolutely nothing you can do about it. You have only two choices here. Either you accept it, or you resign from the UN."

I described my similar experience. The past director had brought her friends, all women, of course, and promoted four of them to the senior posts in my division, at least one of which had been meant for me. What happened then? Due to her incompetence, in six years of her regime, her division had in effect disintegrated. Because of the inability of the four female senior officers she promoted, their groups had become dysfunctional. The new director was now trying to repair the damages to the division. In Hans's case, I could foresee that the EGlobe would be heading toward a collision course. The UN would be embarrassed before the world if the EGlobe failed in even one of two meetings a year.

I told Hans all this. But I couldn't tell him how hard it was to endure the harassment, intimidation, and humiliation from the incompetent management that I had swallowed for six years in my division as a *persona non grata*. It was just miserable. Hans did not deserve this kind of brutal treatment from the UN, because he had always believed in the UN and devoted himself to it. I couldn't find a single word of consolation for him.

"As a woman," Yukari joined in, "I am naturally supportive of the women's movement and gender equality. But in my humble opinion, gender equality doesn't necessarily mean fifty-fifty. In the job market, for one reason or other, the population of women is generally less than that of men, depending on the nature of the work. The gender equality in the workplace must reflect this ratio. It's wrong to simply declare that the number of women in management must be literally equal to the number of men in management."

Hans grumbled an assent, but didn't interrupt.

"In addition, promoting incompetent women over competent men is preposterous," Yukari went on, "because it sets up the women to fail. Then everyone suffers. The policy should firmly remain to promote the competent professionals, regardless of the gender. Only where the qualifications of a male candidate and a female candidate are equal should the preference be given to the woman. Even as a woman, I feel that the UN's gender policy is too extreme."

"Thank you, Yukari," I said. "I fully agree with you. But unfortunately in the UN, our view is not accepted, and incompetent women take advantage of the situation."

Hans seemed a little calmer. "I don't even mind this fifty-fifty gender policy, if that's what has to be done in the UN. But how can they promote incompetent women over competent men based on this policy? That, I can't accept. Never, never! It's simply wrong."

I nodded, agreeing with him. "Hans, if you insist, there is actually one thing you could do in this situation. You could appeal to JAB on the basis of reverse gender discrimination. However, it will be hard to make a case. You'll have to spend hundreds of hours in preparation, and you'll have to hire a professional lawyer at your own expense if you really want to win. The review of your case by JAB will take several months, and it may take a few years for JAB to come to a decision."

I stopped in order to refresh my memory on something with which I was familiar as a senior personnel officer. Then I continued. "You may win the case with a compensation of one dollar. I'm not joking; it happened before; just one dollar. With this compensation to you, all will remain the same: that is, Luisa will stay in her current senior officer's post, and you will continue working under her."

Hans ground his teeth and grumbled, "One dollar? That's all?"

"Yes, it's absurd," I replied. "I know a similar verdict by JAB took place in the past, so it could happen again in your case. And that's if you win the case. Or worse, you may lose the case. Then you'll gain absolutely nothing, after so much time, effort, and money of your own."

"Oh, God!" Hans moaned.

"In the meantime," I moved on, "you'll face retaliation from the management. Your professional career at the UN would be practically finished. Is it worth pursuing?"

My cruel statement of reality pushed Hans to the corner.

"Then what am I to do?" he spewed. "Sit in my office and bite my nails? Work on the EGlobe under Luisa, who doesn't know anything? I can't do that. I refuse that. Maybe I should quit and go back to academia. I could be an associate professor in economics, teaching in Berkeley or even at Berlin University. I'm not afraid of that."

Yukari's eyes widened in alarm. "Hans, I understand that you are going through a difficult time. I fully sympathize with you, and I wish I could help you more. But please try to remain calm and rational. Don't do anything so drastic. Our child is coming in April. You can't leave New York now." She broke into tears.

I sadly remembered my divorce case, which was certainly affected by the aggravation in my office when the past director came to my division. I wouldn't let the same thing happen to the marriage of Hans and Yukari. But how could I help him? I didn't have an answer.

We were all distressed and couldn't find any good solution. But at least I managed to get a promise from Hans that he would not do anything without discussing it with Yukari and me.

*　*　*

A few days passed. I hoped that Hans would bite the bullet no matter how painful it was for him. However, it did not turn out that way. One evening I received another anguished call from Yukari, this time at home.

"Mark, please come over. It's getting worse. Hans is going to go to a peacekeeping mission in Sarajevo. It's a war zone there. I don't want him to go. Please come talk to him."

I hurried to their apartment, where I found that Hans had changed from a handsome, smart, and bright professional to a tired and stressed-out middle-aged man. His face looked sickly pale, and the skin surrounding his eyes was dark blue. He moved slowly.

According to Hans he had gone to Mr. Skoog and demanded an explanation. Hans had been very close to Mr. Skoog because the EGlobe was critical to his division's mandates. Mr. Skoog knew Hans's qualifications and merit. But Mr. Skoog merely mumbled that he was under tremendous pressure to promote women in his division and that the decision was irreversible. Hans challenged him by saying that if he, Hans, left the division, the EGlobe would fail. Mr. Skoog was well aware of that, but he couldn't do anything about it. Hans pressed Mr. Skoog further by asking whether promoting women was more important than the EGlobe. Mr. Skoog asked Hans to be fair, since the UN was a political organization, and as such even a director couldn't do anything about certain matters, particularly the women's issues, which were considered untouchable at the UN.

Because of Yukari and the coming child, Hans ruled out the option of resigning and the option of appealing to JAB. But then he found no strong reason to work for the UN any more. Until now his professional life had been entirely dedicated to the EGlobe. He might want to seek a transfer to another function. Where? He didn't know.

Therefore, he decided to join a peacekeeping mission. He learned there was an opening for a Civil Affairs Officer in the United Nations Mission in Bosnia and Herzegovina. He wanted to apply for the post. But knowing I was the chief of the Recruitment and Placement Section of the Department of Peacekeeping Operations, he wanted to consult with me first.

Personnel placement for UNMIBH, along with other missions, was now under my responsibility, so I knew it well. UNMIBH had been established in 1995 in order to implement the Peace Agreement on Bosnia and Herzegovina, signed in Paris by the Republic of Bosnia and Herzegovina, the Republic of Croatia, and the Federal Republic of Yugoslavia. Its head-quarters was located in Sarajevo, Bosnia and Herzegovina. Its main tasks included: monitoring, observing, and inspecting law enforcement activities and facilities; advising and train-ing law enforcement personnel; and assessing threats to public order and advising on the capability of law enforcement agen-cies to deal with such threats; among others.

UNMIBH was headed by the Special Representative of the Secretary-General who exercised authority over the International Police Task Force and coordinated other UN activities in Bosnia and Herzegovina relating to humanitarian relief, refugees, de-mining, human rights, elections, rehabilita-tion of infrastructure, and economic reconstruction.

The Civil Affairs Unit of UNMIBH was responsible for providing expert advice and assistance to all UNMIBH units on policy development, strategic analysis, and program imple-mentation. The Civil Affairs Officers maintained liaisons with local authorities and international organizations, and they sought to build confidence among all citizens and to ensure that the strategic vision, policy, and guidelines for UNMIBH were implemented effectively.

I knew that there was no post for economists in UNMIBH, so the Civil Affairs Officer was the closest post an economist like Hans could get for his profession.

When UNMIBH was established, there had been many civil disturbances in the region, and the region was considered dangerous. But by now, January 2000, the public order had been well restored and the region was considered reasonably safe. He would be living in a hotel or an apartment building in Sarajevo, where UN staff members and international correspondents lived.

When I explained this, Hans had known most of what I told him. He seemed to have done good research on UNMIBH, and I could see his mind was made up to go there.

"Yukari and Mark," he said, "I've decided to stay with the UN in New York. But for that, I need to see myself and the UN from a distance. I need to find a reason to work for the UN. Please let me go."

His plea was hard to reject. But Yukari and I were both very anxious. We looked at each other with knit brows.

He continued. "There are currently two peacekeeping missions in former Yugoslavia. One is in Bosnia and Herzegovina and the other is in Kosovo. The situation in Kosovo is still dangerous and very fluid. Catastrophic events could erupt any time. But I'm going to Sarajevo, a peaceful city at this time. You don't have to worry."

Hans seemed so determined that I saw no way to change his mind. But at least I didn't see any negative or self-destructive sign in him. He was just trying to gain some perspective. Probably it was best to let him go. Yet there remained a big obstacle.

"Wait a minute, Hans," I said. "The duration of a mission assignment is at least two years. How long is your assignment?"

"Three years," Hans reluctantly replied.

"TH-RE-E years! That's crazy!" Yukari cried. "No, no, you can't leave me and our baby daughter for three years. That's out of the question."

"Yes, that worries me, too," Hans confessed. "But I'll take short vacations often and visit here, including the time of your childbirth. So I think it'll work out."

"Oh, Hans, please stop this nonsense." Yukari broke down into miserable sobs.

There was a deep silence for a few minutes.

Then I talked about the similar case when Shem Tov had wanted to go to UNRWA. At the time Jacques was about six months old. After I had talked with Shem Tov about his plan, he must have noticed how distressed Francine was. He seemed to have weighed his priorities between his family and his radical political agenda. In the end he decided to stay in New York with Francine and Jacques. I urged Hans to do the same for the sake of Yukari and the coming child.

"I didn't know Shem Tov went through this," Hans said. "But the difference is I don't have that kind of political agenda. My objective is purely to see with my own eyes how the UN is working. I need to see it in order to remain in the UN. So please let me go."

Another prolonged silence. Hans seemed really undeterred.

"Okay, then, let me try this," I said at last. "Since I am responsible for the placement of the mission personnel, let me negotiate the duration of your assignment to UNMIBH for a short-term assignment of, say, two months. I know someone in the mission. It might work out."

Hans thanked me, though Yukari was still apprehensive.

The next day I called Antonio Kendall in UNMIBH, an Argentinian who was a good friend of mine. He used to be a personnel officer in the Executive Office of DESA and now served in UNMIBH as the leader of the personnel placement group in the Administration Unit. I explained Hans's situation and asked for a short-term assignment of two months. Initially Antonio was reluctant, but since he was desperate to hire more Civil Affairs Officers, he agreed to my request, hoping that Hans would change his mind by the end of a two-month period and stay there longer. Hans was supposed to leave New York in the beginning of February and come back at the end of March. This would allow him to be present for the birth of his child.

I met Hans and Yukari again that evening and explained what I had achieved on Hans's behalf. Hans was happy. Yukari remained anxious, but even to her, this must have looked like the best we could get under the circumstances.

"Hold on, Hans," I said, remembering something important. "If my memory is correct, the next EGlobe meeting will be held in New York in mid-April. If you go to Sarajevo, who is going to update the EGlobe system and make the forecast for the meeting?"

Hans shrugged bitterly. "Ha! That's no longer my problem. Let Luisa deal with it if she can. We'll see how well she can do. I'll let my management worry about it. After all, they are the ones who promoted her. If the EGlobe global model can't be updated by the time of the meeting, the department can explain it to the world — a consequence of the gender equality policy. That will be a farce on the world stage. Shame on the UN!"

Hans gave another sarcastic laugh. Then, changing the tone of his voice to that of resignation, he said, "Even after all this I'm still attached to the EGlobe. It's my professional life. Actually, I have a contingency plan. If Luisa cannot update the model, let her management worry. When I come back at the end of March, I'll still have about two weeks to prepare. It will be tough, but I'll do it. I'll do the global economic forecast as I used to do. The EGlobe meeting will go on as usual. I wouldn't let the UN down."

It seemed that Hans had planned carefully and considered all aspects. There was not much left for Yukari or me to object to.

Yukari appreciated that Hans had decided to remain at the UN without appealing to JAB. But she didn't want him to be depressed and unhappy at the office for the rest of his professional career there. While she felt insecure at the thought of living without him for such a critical time of her pregnancy, she wanted him to be happy no matter how difficult it was. She was brave and inclined to let him go.

"Hans, please promise to come back safely by the end of March." She shed tears.

"Yukari, it's very important for me to be here to help you when you deliver our child. I'll come back safely by the end of March. I promise."

Yukari and I reluctantly agreed.

Hans spent several extremely busy days. He completed the paperwork for the mission assignment and had a medical examination and immunizations. He received his UN *Laissez-passer*, a UN passport, which could be indispensable, even life-saving, in dangerous war zones, as it proved that he represented the UN for official work. He arranged reservations for his flight and hotel. He undertook a quick session in his office with Luisa Rodriguez, passing to her all information related to the EGlobe system.

According to Hans, Mr. Skoog had asked him not to go because they knew that without Hans they would not be able to prepare for the EGlobe meeting in April. But Mr. Skoog couldn't change Hans's mind, as he couldn't offer any incentive for Hans to stay in New York. Besides, Hans's mind was firmly made up. He didn't tell Mr. Skoog of his contingency plan.

The date of departure was set for February 3. Hans would fly to Berlin first to visit his parents. He would spend one day there, then fly to Sarajevo and report for duty at UNMIBH headquarters.

I kept a respectful distance from Hans and Yukari so they could spend the last few days together by themselves. The day before his departure, Hans called me at my office and asked me to accompany him for dinner after work. We met at a restaurant in German Town, which was close to both his apartment and mine.

"Before our marriage, Yukari and I used to come here often," Hans said. "This is a typical German restaurant with excellent German cuisine. On Fridays and Saturdays, they provide live music, too." He smiled.

I had not seen his smile for a while, and I was glad that the mission assignment had boosted his spirits. Indeed, he looked better, and the brightness had come back to his face.

We ordered a sausage salad for two as an appetizer, a pot of lamb stew for two as the entrée, and two large glasses of warm house beer. I had not known that warm beer meant beer at room temperature. According to Hans, this was the way to drink beer in Northern Germany. Actually, it went along very well with the hot sausages and the lamb stew.

"This is our 'Last Supper' before my mission," Hans said casually, laughing.

I tried to laugh too, but I felt a pang in my heart and a clamp at my throat. We ate and drank for a while in silence. Then, slowly, we started talking.

"Tomorrow late afternoon," Hans said, "I'll leave New York for Berlin."

"I know," I said. "Are you ready?"

"Yes. There was not much to prepare. All I need are clothes, a digital camera, and a laptop. I'm ready."

"You have to email me often. I will bring it to Yukari as I did while you were in Athens."

"Yes, I will."

I felt a little awkward, and I could see Hans did as well. We wanted to say something important, but we also wanted to avoid it. Little by little, we broke the ice.

"Mark, while I'm away, would you take care of Yukari? You are the only one I can trust."

"You don't have to worry. I'll do my best. You know that."

We were still being too polite with each other. We ate and drank in silence again for a while.

Then Hans informed me thoughtfully, "As most people do in my situation, just in case, I made a will. Yukari knows how to contact my lawyer. It's a simple document. Basically, all of my savings and benefits such as life insurance and pension will go to Yukari."

Hans paused, then shrugged off some hesitation.

"I haven't told Yukari about this. But I'd like you to remember that if I die, I don't want her to see my body. It would be too much for her. Therefore, my body would be cremated and the ashes would be sent to my parents in Berlin. I'm going to tell this to my parents. This is one of the reasons I'm stopping in Berlin."

"I hope it will never happen."

"Yes, I don't think it will happen. Remember, Sarajevo is a safe city now. This is just a precaution."

He paused again. Then he moved his face close to me.

"And one more thing." He cleared his throat, then spoke slowly with a sincere but determined expression. "If I die, Mark, you should marry Yukari."

"Oh, Hans, you can't be serious," I protested. "I don't want to hear it."

"Mark, please hear me out. I'm serious. I'm so worried about Yukari. If I die, she can't be left alone. You must take care of her childbirth and her recovery afterwards. I really ask you to marry her and take care of her and my child. If you propose marriage, she will accept. This I know. And this is what I want too. I'll be very happy. Please consider this as my wish. I mean it." He nodded earnestly.

We again fell into a deep silence. He didn't talk, and I couldn't talk. Finally Hans spoke.

"I have a confession to make," he said with a repentant face. "I had an affair after I married Yukari. It was a deliberate seduction by our housekeeper, but I went along with her. Shame on me. Yukari discovered it. As you can imagine, we had a fight. Yukari wanted a divorce. I begged her for forgiveness. Around this time we met you at the Metropolitan Museum of Art. Somehow Yukari sensed that the chemistry blended well between her and you. She backed off a little from our divorce talk. After the discovery of our family heritages over our dinner, she changed her mind and gave me another chance. Do you remember a Filipino woman we met at the UN after the June concert? That was her. But by then I'd had nothing to do with her. … So Mark, you kept our marriage together, for which I'm grateful."

Now I had heard the story of his affair in his own words. What Yukari had told me was all true. This made me better understand why Hans had been so open to my enjoying our life together with Yukari and him. What did this mean to me then? Did this make any difference at this point? I found no answer. All I knew was that Hans, Yukari, the coming child, and I were bound together. Nothing could break our bond.

Hans resumed with a sincere face. "Yukari loves you. This is why I'm saying if I die, you should marry her."

"Hans, stop it! Don't say 'if I die.' You are going to come back safely. You must. Yukari will need you for the childbirth. It's your child. You are going to be a father. Don't you feel the responsibility?"

I raised my voice, trying to make him come to his senses. Suddenly, a suspicion struck me like a sharp knife at my heart, and I stared at Hans. My eyes were probably wet. Several seconds passed in silence.

Then he responded, "What? Do you think I would commit suicide? … Oh, no. You are mistaken. I'm not that weak. Look at me."

I met his gaze. He was no longer the tired stressed-out middle-aged man he had appeared a few weeks before. He had regained his vigorous intelligence in the past several days. He was again a smart and handsome professional. My suspicion faded away slowly.

"I'm really looking forward to being in UNMIBH," Hans said with enthusiasm. "I want to know what the UN really means. I want to discover myself in the UN again. Going to a mission is the only way." His statement had the ring of honesty in it.

"Hans, take good care of yourself. I'll do my best for Yukari. I promise."

We shook hands firmly.

"Mark, thank you. I'll see you in two months."

15

Yukari kept me informed about Hans. He arrived in Berlin as scheduled and stayed at his parents' home. He called her from there in good spirits. He spent the next day there, then traveled to Sarajevo, where he settled into a hotel. The next day he reported for duty at the headquarters of the UNMIBH.

Between the United Nations New York Headquarters and UNMIBH, there was a direct satellite telecommunications link, operated by the UN. The UNMIBH staff used this link for telephone calls, email, Internet, and videoconferences. Therefore, Hans was able to call Yukari at home in Manhattan from his office in Sarajevo, and he also sent me email frequently, which I passed on to Yukari. Considering that Sarajevo was still a war-wearied city, where the telecommunication infrastructure was just being rebuilt after severe damages, we were able to communicate well between Sarajevo and New York, which greatly eased Yukari's anxiety.

I learned from Yukari that Hans had actually bought a
new laptop PC for her so they could directly communicate
with each other by email. However, at the time, while the tech-
nologies of Internet and email were readily available in large
organizations, as far as ordinary households were concerned,
people had to use one of the limited number of Internet portal
companies with a slow-speed telephone line. Internet security
software that cleaned viruses was complicated to operate for
non-technical people. Although Hans set up all the hardware
and software for her, Yukari just hated to operate the computer
and soon gave up using it. Then he had to rely on me as we
had done during his trip to Greece previous year. I wishfully
speculated that she had deliberately refused to use the laptop
so I could come to her apartment to bring email. I was happy
to be helpful to her.

For strictly personal matters, Hans and Yukari used the
telephone, so the emails I carried to her contained general
news that described his life in the field. He wanted us to share
these, and I was able to do so without intruding on their privacy. I vowed to myself not to cross the line of friendship by
invading the marriage of Hans and Yukari and resolved to keep
my sanity for that purpose during his absence.

To Yukari and me, Hans's email served like his diary. The
first several emails explained orientations he was getting about
UNMIBH, his job, the region, the war, and its aftermath, which
obviously he had to know in order to do his job effectively.

My first day in UNMIBH. After the paperwork to reg-
ister myself here as a Civil Affairs Officer, I was briefed
as to my responsibilities and current conditions. I am to

accompany local police officers with the members of the International Police Task Force.

After the terrible war, due to the multiethnic nature of the region, there still exists strong mistrust among locals of one ethnic group toward local police of other ethnic groups, and there have been allegations of human rights abuses by the local police. My job as the Civil Affairs Officer is to monitor just law enforcement by the multiethnic local police under the supervision of IPTF.

I was given a pocket radio communications device. We are to go out and patrol the city and suburbs in vans. I really feel that I am now in the center of a peacekeeping mission.

They gave me a lecture on Bosnia. Historically, the region has been located in a crossroad of empires, religions, and cultures. It stood in the middle of the Roman Empire and the Byzantine Empire. Croats settled in the west and became Roman Catholic, while Serbs settled in the east and became Greek Orthodox. Then the region was conquered by the Ottoman Empire, and Muslims settled in. Eventually the region became part of the Austro-Hungarian Empire.

The region, mixed with Croats, Serbs, and Muslims, is prone to be unstable. It is no coincidence that one of most bloody historic events occurred at the center of the region: the 1914 assassination in Sarajevo of Archduke Francis Ferdinand, heir to the Austro-Hungarian Empire, and his wife Sofia, which precipitated World War I.

During World War II, the region was occupied by the Nazis. After the war, Tito formed the Federal Republic of Yugoslavia. With his exceptional charisma, Tito held the region together for over thirty years, during which the region developed rapidly and flourished. Unfortunately, when Tito died in 1980, the region started breaking up.

I cannot believe that the 14th Winter Olympic Games took place in Sarajevo in February 1984. The city hosted athletes and winter sports enthusiasts from all over the world. The Olympic Games set a record, at the time, for the number of countries and athletes participating in the games. I was at Berkeley then. I watched the Olympics on TV. I still remember well that the city was affluent, beautiful, and peaceful. People were multiethnic but mingling easily and enjoying life. I saw absolutely no ethnic tension then.

In 1992, the brutal war started in Bosnia. Uncontrollable hatred erupted among ethnic groups. Serbs and Muslims killed each other. Croats and Muslims killed each other. Serbs and Croats killed each other. They called it "Ethnic Cleansing." Madness!

Sarajevo was taken under siege and bombarded from the misty peaks around the city. Machine-gun fire, artillery fire, and mortar fire raged. The beautiful city was destroyed. People fled or were killed. Madness!

Eventually the United States and its allies intervened, which brought three groups of combatants, the Bosnian Muslims, the Croats, and the Bosnian Serbs, to the negotiation table in Dayton, Ohio. In December 1995, the Dayton Peace Agreement was signed in Paris. Peace at last. But it has been a long hard road to recovery. The UN Security Council authorized the establishment of UNMIBH. Slowly the civil order was restored and industrial infrastructure was rebuilt.

Today we patrolled Sarajevo and its suburbs as a group of multiethnic local police officers, IPTF officers, and UN Civil Affairs Officers. Driving through the areas, I still saw the devastation of the war. A local police officer pointed out sites to me, saying that this used to be an oil refinery, that a TV station, and so on. Many of these buildings are still skeletons. While some buildings and houses have escaped total destruction, they still have bullet holes in the walls. However, there are signs of recovery. Everywhere are "Sarajevo roses," which are the shell craters gouged in the sidewalks and building walls and now filled with red rubber. They are a sad reminder of the war, but they are a sign of the recovery, too.

Hans seemed to be settling down well at UNMIBH in Sarajevo, leaving behind what had happened to him at the UN Headquarters in New York. Probably he was right. The new post might be the best way for him to cope with the trauma.

While he remained reflective, from the third week onward of his term in Sarajevo, his email started sounding more positive and energetic. As he began to work as the Civil Affairs Officer, he appeared to observe the uneasy reality of mistrust among ethnic groups.

This is my third week in UNMIBH. The jetlag is gone from my body. I'm now quite familiar with my work. It's not too complicated, but it requires a lot of attention, sensitivity, compassion, impartiality, and sense of fairness. As I'm getting along well with my colleagues, I'm beginning to enjoy my role here.

There are still hundreds of thousands of Bosnian refugees who are slowly returning to the city and suburbs. Some find their homes have been occupied by another ethnic group. One of my jobs as a Civil Affairs Officer is to monitor the eviction of wrongful occupants and the return of the house to the legal original owners without violence. Some returning refugees cannot find their houses, which have been destroyed by shells or burned down by fire. For those, we built a camp consisting of several tents. There are numerous such camps near Sarajevo, and we monitor the civil order there.

Fights and intimidation are still continuing among different ethnic groups. But the presence of multiethnic local police officers, IPTF officers, UN Civil Affairs Officers, and Humanitarian Affairs Officers in the community certainly improves the harmonious coexistence of different ethnic groups. Before the war, Sarajevo was a multiethnic city. They can do it. But I understand that healing the destroyed trust caused by the war will take some time.

Usually we cruise around Sarajevo and its suburbs in a van. But sometimes we use a helicopter for long excursions. I had not ridden in one before. The first time it was a little scary — bouncy and loud. But now I'm used to it. The civil order in the areas far away from the city is still fluid, and sometimes we feel a strong tension surrounding us. But this is precisely why we need to be here.

Yesterday three children were killed in a mine explosion while trying to enter an abandoned dugout on Mt. Trebevic near Sarajevo. The rescue team had to spend five hours to recover the bodies because the area is believed to be still heavily mined. This was a tragic event nobody wanted to happen.

Today we visited one of the de-mining sites in the city. A map showed locations of the mines that had been defused. I was surprised to see how densely all of Sarajevo had been mined. Most of the mines near the city have been removed. But we suspect that some undetected mines are still there, for which we have to make clear warning signs. Then we visited local elementary schools, distributed the mine awareness materials to the children, and explained the danger to them. Poor children. We want them to study and play safely. We must prevent them from getting hurt by the mines.

In the next few emails, Hans seemed to discover dedicated UN staff members in the mission, which must have begun restoring his enthusiasm for the UN. I thought this was positive for him, because he was able to see it with his own eyes. Working in the mission appeared to be nicely paying off for him, which made me happy.

By now I have realized that UNMIBH is a large mission. While I belong to the Civil Affairs Unit, there are many other UN staff members working in the different organizational units. They are dedicated to the work in their own areas. This is refreshing. At UNHQ, I felt sick to observe the many parasites and dead-woods doing nothing but sucking their salary from the UN. Here in the field, however, it's different. Here the work is directly related to the local people whose lives literally depend on the UN. Therefore, virtually all of the UN staff members here are motivated by the cause of the UN, and they work hard.

Today I met Jan van Daalen, a Public Affairs Officer from the Netherlands, who had originally worked in the Department of Public Information at UNHQ. He is about my age but still a second officer. According to him, he has been this level for eleven years, because DPI is notorious for irrelevance between promotion and a staff member's professional achievement. He was disgusted at UNHQ and came to UNMIBH three years ago.

Jan writes press releases about major events at the mission. They are not only provided to the press, but also posted on the UNMIBH Website, which can be read by anyone in the world. Here, he says, he sees the UN in action. The UN is helping the people who would otherwise be living a miserable life or worse, be killed. Here, he is literally the originator of the press releases to the world. He is part of the UN.

Today I met another dedicated staff member, Robert Anderson, a Financial Affairs Officer and American, who had originally worked in the Accounts Division at UNHQ. He was also stuck at the second officer level for twelve years, as the Accounts Division has a limited number of Professional posts, while it has many General Service posts. Frustrated in New York, he came to UNMIBH four years ago as one of the first UN staff members. He is overseeing book-keeping and payroll.

Robert, too, is enthusiastic about the UN. His job here is not directly active with UNMIBH. However, he feels very close to his colleagues here, who are working hard for the local people who need the UN. He is supporting his colleagues. He too is part of the mission. He too is part of the UN.

Today I had lunch with Antonio Kendall, an Argentinian and the group leader of personnel administration in UNMIBH. I met him first on the day I came here, as he briefed me on my job in this mission. Since then we have talked often. I understand you, Mark, negotiated the duration of my assignment with him. An interesting fellow. He had a green card, working for a private company in Manhattan. But he wanted to work on the world peace and prosperity, so he joined the UN. But he was quickly disillusioned by so many people at UNHQ who were working for their personal economic necessity and who had nothing to do with the goals of the UN. So he came to UNMIBH. Here he manages personnel administration. He is an exemplar of how an international civil servant should be. He tries to recruit the best people for this mission. He redresses any problems among mission staff. He liaises between the mission personnel and the local community if a tension arises. He is tireless. I felt inspired to see such a dedicated UN staff member.

We went to a Muslim-run restaurant in the downtown. Yes, restaurants are open for business in Sarajevo. Other stores are open for business as well. We can stroll there safely. I had *trahana*, which is a traditional sourdough soup, and *janjetina*, roasted lamb, which is a Bosnian culinary specialty. They tasted pretty good. Also I tried Bosnian coffee, a kind of Turkish coffee. It's very strong. They don't serve any alcohol. Weird!

Over the course of the meal, Antonio invited me to stay in this mission beyond my assignment of two months, citing that people here like me because of my enthusiasm and dedication to the UN. I felt flattered, but grateful that they perceived me that way, because that is exactly how I try to be. I was almost persuaded by him to extend my assignment. If I were not married, I would certainly stay longer, because like him, here in this mission I can feel to my core the UN's objectives being carried out.

Shortly after the last email, Hans sent me a personal email with the subject line "Strictly Confidential." I wondered what it was, and opened it.

Dear Mark, I need to discuss an important matter with you in confidence. Please don't tell this to Yukari, at least not yet.

I am enjoying my work here in UNMIBH so much. My colleagues like me and I also like them. I feel I'm really doing something for the UN's cause. Since my career at UNHQ is practically over, I'm contemplating staying here for several years until the mission is dissolved. It pains me, but in order to do it, I have to divorce Yukari and set her free from me. I know she loves you, and I know you love her too. You have my blessing to marry her and have children as many as you wish. As long as you look after my coming daughter as your daughter, I'll be happy with your marriage to Yukari.

In short, I'm not coming back to UNHQ. I'm considering this very seriously. What do you think? If you agree, I'll proceed immediately. Please let me know your opinion.

Hans has lost his mind! This is madness! — was my first reaction. I was angry with him for sending this kind of absurd email. *I'll never agree with him,* I shouted in my mind. *Plus Yukari is not just a piece of property Hans can hand over to me. What would she say?* Then I thought of Francine. This might be what she had been hoping to happen so I would be happy with Yukari. Immediately I shrugged off that selfish thought, which was simply not right. I felt ashamed of myself. Reflecting, I replied to Hans that he was insane to come up with such a ridiculous fantasy. I reminded him in the strongest terms that he had made a commitment as Yukari's husband and was responsible, as the father, for their coming daughter.

A few days later Hans replied.

Dear Mark, I'm so sorry. Since I'm far away from New York and Yukari, I was somehow persuaded by Antonio's invitation to extend my stay here longer, and was carried away by the wild idea. You reminded me of my responsibility. You are right. If I turn myself away from the responsibility, I'll be a coward. Besides, I realize how much I love Yukari and coming Annie. I miss them — I'm saying "them," because Annie is already part of my family, though she is not born yet. So be assured that I'm now cooled off. I'll keep my short-term assignment here. Don't worry about me anymore.

Send my love to Yukari and Annie.

I took a deep breath; the worst seemed averted. I sympathized with Hans, fathoming how deeply his experience at UNHQ had hurt him and how vulnerable he had been to any idea that allowed him to get away from UNHQ. I only hoped that this crazy fantasy wouldn't resurface in his mind. Of course, I didn't mention any of these email conversations to Yukari. But did I also feel a slight disappointment? I pushed the thought from my mind.

In the meantime Yukari had been seeing her doctors regularly — though what kind of doctors she was seeing or what kind of treatment she was getting, I had absolutely no idea. Her abdomen was very visible in her maternity dress, but she looked all right, at least to me. Whenever I brought Hans's email to her apartment, she was calm. Except for her concern over Hans, she never showed any sign of stress. I thought that she was very brave. I was glad that so far, no problem had arisen for her.

In another email addressed personally to me, Hans asked me to take Yukari out for dinner or some entertainment. Probably he was feeling guilty for his wild idea. I would have enjoyed his request, but I was not sure whether it was proper for me to do. To my relief, however, Yukari never showed the necessity for it.

As February went by, Hans grew more involved with the civil affairs of UNMIBH. Some of his email seemed rather tense as he described the crude situation there. He was sensing physically what it was to be a UN staff member. Reading these emails, even I felt inspired by the vision of the UN peacekeeping mission in action. Yukari, too, appeared to understand why Hans had wanted to go to the field to see this with his own eyes.

> There are two hot spots right now from my job's perspective. One is Kopaci (Serb Gorazde), about 30 miles southeast of Sarajevo, and the other is Prnjavor, about 80 miles northwest of Sarajevo. Incidents in both locations occurred about the same time and are still continuing.
>
> The Kopaci case is as follows: 50 Kopaci refugees agreed to return to Kopaci from the Gorazde border, where they had been living in tents. They were to stay in three houses near Kopaci until the renovation of their own houses is completed. One afternoon one of the houses was bombed. There were no injuries, but two cars were damaged. It was rumored that the local police were not impartial in handling the situation.
>
> Two other UN officers, several IPTF officers, and I rushed to Kopaci in a convoy of vans. We started supervising the local police officers to secure the area. Four

local police officers were reprimanded. An investigation was started to find the perpetrator of the attack and a group of radicals who supported such an attack. One suspect was questioned. We advised that the returnees enter Kopaci in smaller groups of two to three families.

A few days later a group of extremists stoned one of houses occupied by the returnees. A drinking fountain of a returnee family's house was ruined. The walls of another returnee family's house were pulled down. We rushed to Kopaci again and patrolled the area with IPTF officers and local police officers.

We were concerned that these incidents might slow down the return process of refugees. However, in spite of the incident, the Kopaci refugees decided to remain there. It shows the returners' confidence in the UNMIBH to secure the area and enforce fair treatment of the refugees. We were very pleased. But we felt heavy responsibility, too.

The Prnjavor case is as follows: One day in Prnjavor a butcher shop was bombed, completely damaging the building, though causing no injuries. Ten days later a hand grenade was thrown on a returnee family's house, causing an explosion and fire, injuring two. Another ten days later, a hand grenade exploded in a local community near Prnjavor, killing one and seriously injuring others. These three incidents in twenty days indicated an organized campaign of violence and intimidation, aiming to instill fear among the returnees and to obstruct returns.

Since the third incident was serious, I and two other UN officers with IPTF officers flew to Prnjavor via helicopter. We reviewed the current security plan, which was not adequate. We developed a new plan that required intensified patrols by IPTF and local police, accompanied by UN Civil Affairs Officers and Humanitarian Affairs Officers. To my gratification, I am needed on this mission.

The attack prompted twenty-five returnees to ask UNIMBH for protection. We are making sure that the renovation of the houses of the returnees continues without delay, so the returnees can live safely and comfortably in their homes. In the meantime, we are carefully monitoring construction of the housing units so there is no illegal construction for those who were required to leave the region.

Usually, IPTF officers and the UN officers go back to UNMIBH headquarters in Sarajevo at the end of a working day. But since Prnjavor is a little far from Sarajevo, and since the situation was tense, we stayed a few days at a local police station there. After our intensified patrol, the situation started to calm and stabilize.

I'm in action, covering a wide geographical area. I feel I'm really in the field. It's a nice feeling, because local people's lives literally depend on UNMIBH, which means my colleagues and me. This firsthand experience and feeling can be understood only by those in the field. I'm glad I came here. I would have never experienced this if I had stayed in UNHQ. Oh, how I love it!

I've been taking many pictures with my digital camera. It's very useful for recording incidents. I'm attaching
one picture of me in this email. It was taken with my colleagues in front of the helicopter that flew us to Prnjavor. I
look very good, don't I? Please don't worry about me. I'm
perfectly all right here.

Whenever I received email from Hans, I printed it and
brought it to Yukari after work. We were glad that he felt valu-
able and busy, forgetting the aggravation and disappointment
of his failed promotion. The photo he sent showed Hans looking
like an experienced field officer in the peacekeeping mission.

By the beginning of March, his email started showing
the signs of the competent, confident, enthusiastic professional
Hans used to be.

Today an interesting thing happened. Mr. Skoog
called me from UNHQ by telephone. He sounded desperate. According to him, Luisa Rodriguez cannot do anything on the EGlobe system. She can't understand the
EGlobe econometric model and how to update it. It's simply beyond her comprehension. Since I left UNHQ, therefore, nothing has been done on the EGlobe system. What
did I tell you, eh? I knew this would happen.

The next EGlobe meeting is only one month away. Mr.
Skoog is scared to death. He begged me to come back.
He told me that he was on his knees right that moment.
He promised that I would be considered for a promotion
to Senior Economic Affairs Officer as soon as the next
vacancy comes up in the division. He emphasized that he

had spoken to the USG of DESA and received a verbal consent on this matter. I said that I would think about it. He is going to call me again in a few days. Since the USG co-chairs the EGlobe meetings with Prof. Cohen, he knows me well. If Mr. Skoog had to speak to the USG about me, he must have been really desperate. Maybe it's about time to tell him of my contingency plan.

I've been thinking. There are UN staff members who really believe in the UN. They may not be rewarded by the organization as much as they deserve, but they maintain their enthusiasm and loyalty and work hard. They may be the minority in the UN, but they do exist — like Jan van Daalen, Robert Anderson, and Antonio Kendall here in UNMIBH I told you about. Virtually all of my colleagues here who work as Civil Affairs Officers and Humanitarian Affairs Officers are like them.

To think of it, Mark, you are one of them, too. You must have been so distressed when your previous director removed all your authority, although you had the professional competence. But you stayed in the division, enduring the harassment, ridicule, and humiliation, biding your time until you could again serve the division and the UN.

You are brave. I should be one of you, who dedicate your lives to the cause of the UN. I'm ashamed that I didn't have enough courage. But now I'm stronger and tougher. I'm going to be one of you.

I've made up my mind. I'll complete my assignment here at the end of March and I'll go back to UNHQ. I'm no longer bitter. I may have lost the promotion, but so what? The promotion is not the only thing in life. My life is the EGlobe, for which the UN provides a home. EGlobe helps economists around the world, who in turn direct the economy of their own countries and regions. They need EGlobe. Hence, the EGlobe system must be maintained. I'm going to work hard again on the EGlobe system, and I'm going to serve the UN again.

If Mr. Skoog calls me back, I'm going tell him of my contingency plan. No need to worry. I'll update the EGlobe system and undertake the forecasting. It'll be ready by the EGlobe meeting in April. I wouldn't let the UN down. Never!

What good timing. Mr. Skoog called me again. I told him of my decision and my contingency plan. He repeated "Thank you" "Thank you" many times. He was almost in tears. He said that he was going to report this good news to the USG immediately — "The EGlobe has been saved." He was ecstatic. I'm glad I told him about this. I realized how much I miss the EGlobe.

I'm so happy to rediscover myself. I'll come back to New York in three weeks and dedicate myself to the UN again.

Hans had found what he had been looking for. Yukari's painful decision to let him go to the mission was handsomely bearing fruit. I too was glad that Hans's mission assignment, even though it was only for two months, was working as well for him as I had hoped. After reading Hans's emails, particularly the last one, Yukari and I looked each other and smiled. This was the first time she and I had really smiled heartily since he had left for UNMIBH.

16

The morning of Tuesday, March 14, started like any other normal working day in my office. There were no major problems in my section, but I had to read many emails and reply to them. Some inquiries or requests required a little research on my part. In addition, I had to prepare for a weekly section meeting that afternoon to discuss the state of my section with my staff. So I was busy in my office.

I heard that there was a helicopter crash in one of missions, and they were investigating casualties and the cause of the crash. Since this was not so unusual in the peacekeeping operations, it did not occur to me to connect it to UNMIBH.

Around ten o'clock I received a telephone call from Yukari. She was sobbing. I could not understand her. I thought that she might have become ill, or she might have had some problem at the Parnassus Symphony Orchestra. I asked what had happened, expecting to hear a minor problem, or hoping so.

Yukari composed herself and managed, "Hans was killed in a helicopter crash in Sarajevo."

All I heard next was her helpless cry. Little by little she told me that about half an hour before, she had received a call from a personnel officer at the headquarters of UNMIBH in Sarajevo, informing her of the sad news with deep regret. The cause of the crash was still under investigation.

"What am I to do?" Yukari broke down into piteous weeping.

I felt stunned, barely able to speak. So the crash I had heard about was actually in UNMIBH? And Hans was one of the fatalities? There must be some mistake. I didn't want to believe it. I needed to know more about exactly what had happened. I promised her I would get detailed information on the incident directly from UNMIBH and would visit her apartment as soon as possible.

In disbelief, or refusing to believe, I immediately called Antonio Kendall at UNMIBH. Antonio confirmed the crash, but was reluctant to give me the details, citing confidentiality because the crash was still under formal investigation. Mentioning Hans's name, I said to Antonio that his wife was pregnant, and I had to take care of her. Antonio remembered that he and I had negotiated the duration of Hans's assignment there. He became more open.

"Is Hans Schmidt among the casualties?" I pressed.

Antonio shuffled papers — I heard the noise — and confirmed that Hans's name was on the list of casualties. I sank into my chair. Antonio explained the situation known to them so far.

The UNMIBH helicopter had taken off from Sarajevo in the late morning for a routine patrol. On board were four local police officers, four IPTF officers, two Civil Affairs Officers, one Public Affairs Officer, one Humanitarian Affairs Officer, two local interpreters, and two pilots. Shortly after the takeoff, the helicopter crashed on Mt. Igman near the city. Rescue teams were sent immediately to the crash site by air and by land, but the rescue operation went very slowly because the areas were still suspected to hold live mines. It took hours for them to formally assess the situation. Unfortunately it turned out that they could not do much, except to confirm there had been no survivors. Subsequently all bodies of the victims had been recovered and identified. As to the cause of the crash, initially sabotage or a missile attack was suspected. But after a preliminary investigation of the crash site, the cause was now considered to be a mechanical failure. These facts had become known to them only less than an hour before. The entire UNMIBH was in shock, regret, sorrow, and mourning.

"I'm so sorry," Antonio said. "I knew Hans well. We often spoke with each other, and I even had lunch with him. A good fellow. He was a model international civil servant. Please send my sincere condolences to his wife, whom he frequently talked of."

I cleaned up my office and informed my director that I was taking the rest of the day off for a personal matter. Having canceled my weekly section meeting, I took a taxi to Yukari's apartment. She looked like a lost soul. Tears had left blotches on her pale face and her eyes were red and swollen. She said that she had a rehearsal that afternoon but had asked her colleague to take her place.

According to her, several minutes ago she had received a telephone call from Hans's parents in Berlin, informing her of the sad news that she'd already known. They said how much Hans had loved her and how happy he had been with her. They also informed her that following his wish, his body would be cremated in Sarajevo and his ashes would be sent to them in Berlin. They would take care of the rest. They wished they could help her more with the coming child who would be their granddaughter. Yukari wept again.

I told her what I had heard from Antonio in UNMIBH. While listening she slowly shook her head. This was so unexpected that neither she nor I was prepared for it. But it was a fact we had to face. Our only comfort was that Hans did not suffer much, as all aboard had died instantly. But this was hardly a comfort. Some time passed in silence

After a while my eyes rested upon Yukari's heavily pregnant abdomen. She was just about one month from the expected due date. Suddenly I realized that I had to look after her. Her life had to go on. I felt heavy responsibility.

I prepared supper for her and was going to leave.

Yukari panicked. "Mark, please, please don't leave me. I don't want to be left alone. I'm afraid. Without you, I can't go through the night."

She wept helplessly. Her sorrow tore my heart. I couldn't leave her alone either.

When she regained a little composure, we had supper together, though neither of us could eat much. I tried to talk about casual topics, such as her coming concert, my office work, flowers in the UN garden, signs of awakening spring, things like that. Naturally she was in no mood for talking. I was not able to talk well either.

She retired to her bedroom early. I rested on the sofa in the living room. I heard her crying in the bed, but soon after she became quiet, falling into sleep, completely exhausted.

It was a long night. I occasionally heard her crying, moaning, or talking. Probably she was going through a sad dream.

*   *   *

By the middle of the next day, the news of the crash had spread throughout UNHQ. The total number of casualties was sixteen, which was considered very high for one incident in a UN peacekeeping mission. As such the news drew a lot of attention, and a notice was posted on the bulletin board of all floors of the UN buildings, and also broadcast to all UNHQ staff members through email:

Memorial Service

for

the Casualties of the UNMIBH Helicopter Crash

Friday, 17 March 2000

11:00 A.M.

Conference Room 4

The conference room was a large room, but on Friday it was crowded with UN officials and staff members who wished to pay their last respects to their fallen colleagues. The family members of the victims were also invited, Yukari being one of them. She wore a black mourning dress, her pregnancy

obvious. I escorted her to a seat in the front row, which was
reserved for the family members of the victims. About twenty
people were there. I sat one row behind Yukari with Hans' parents, who had flown to New York from Berlin to attend this
service. Shem Tov, Francine, Justin, and Ramez also sat near
us. Yukari told me that she had not informed her own parents
of Hans's death, so they were not present.

The news of the accident and casualties in UNMIBH had
reached all peacekeeping missions and humanitarian missions
around the globe. Every staff member in the missions expressed
their concern and sympathy. The memorial service was to be
simulcast through the UN satellite telecommunications link,
so the mission staff could watch the service at UNHQ from
the field.

The Secretary-General, the president of the Security
Council, and the president of the Staff Committee sat at the
podium. The memorial service was opened by the president
of the Staff Committee, who recited the names of the sixteen
casualties, their function, and their nationality, followed by
one minute of silence.

Then the SG made his speech. He expressed his profound
sorrow about the tragic accident and offered his sincere condolences to the family members of those who had died in the
course of discharging their official duties in UNMIBH. He also
pledged his commitment to safeguarding the UN staff members in the peacekeeping missions.

Next the president of the Security Council spoke. He
stressed the need for the peacekeeping missions in this con-
flicted world. He praised the dedicated international civil
servants who risked their lives for the cause of the missions.

Regrettably, sometimes casualties were unavoidable. He offered his condolences to the family members of the victims.

After these statements the SG stepped down from the podium to the floor for the ceremony of presenting the UN flag to the family members of the deceased. He was joined by his wife, who was fondly known for her warm affection to staff members. One by one, he and his wife shook the hands of the family members, said a few words of consolation, and presented the UN flag.

The SG and his wife reached Yukari and recognized her pregnancy. Their faces twisted with pain, particularly that of his wife. Expressing fatherly compassion, the SG said a few words, gently hugged Yukari, and handed her the flag. His wife also said a few tender words of sympathy for the deceased husband and encouragement for the coming baby. Then she kissed Yukari's cheek and hugged her as if Yukari were her own daughter.

Following the move of the SG and his wife, all of the staff members saw pregnant Yukari courageously trying to suppress her tears. Murmurs of pity and sympathy audibly stirred the atmosphere of the room.

After the service I escorted Yukari out of the room with Hans's parents, Shem Tov, Francine, Justin, and Ramez. Many staff members came to her to express their sympathies and well-wishes.

My heart almost stopped when I saw that Filipino woman exiting the conference room with her friends. I grabbed Shem Tov, Justine, and Ramez, and shoved them close to me to obstruct the sight of the Filipina from Yukari's eyes. The Filipina, too, appeared to be avoiding Yukari and disappeared quickly. Yukari was still receiving the condolences from Hans's friends and colleagues, so she did not notice the Filipina. I felt safe. Though, to my surprise, I saw the Filipina dabbing her eyes. I wondered if she had loved Hans. If so, the affair might not have been a simple seduction by her. I felt a little sympathy for her. But the affair should not have occurred in the first place. Today marked its complete closure, I hoped.

Then, as if that were not enough, I sensed a keen gaze from someone at me and Yukari. I turned to find the Guatemalan woman, Luisa Rodriguez. She appeared to be trying to repress her triumphant grin from her face. Probably she felt, I guessed, that by Hans's death, the threat to her post had been eliminated. My face must have shown my indignant emotion, which I couldn't hide. She made such a face — *What? I didn't kill Hans. Don't look at me like that.* I stepped ahead to block Luisa's presence from Yukari. Fortunately, I thought, Yukari did not seem to notice Luisa.

One gentleman came forward and spoke to Yukari in a choking voice. "Mrs. Schmidt, I'm Pierre Skoog, your husband's director. Please accept my deepest sympathy and sincere condolence. Probably I'm one of the people who spoke to him last. I needed him here. I was looking forward to seeing him again here. I'm so sorry." Mr. Skoog gently squeezed Yukari's hand.

"Thank you, sir," Yukari replied. "Hans loved the EGlobe. He wanted to come back to New York to work on the system again."

Yukari broke into sobs. Mr. Skoog bit his lips. His eyes were wet.

* * *

As Yukari insisted, since the previous Tuesday night I had been sleeping on the sofa in her apartment every night. Her request was one thing, but at the same time I myself didn't want leave her alone, because I feared that something dreadful might happen to her. So when Hans's parents visited Yukari's apartment from their hotel on the following Saturday, I was there.

Mr. Schmidt appeared a typical academician in his late sixties, and Mrs. Schmidt a stern woman in her mid-sixties. They packed a few of Hans's personal belongings and made an arrangement that those be sent to their home in Berlin.

When all was done, Mr. Schmidt said to me, "Hans told me that he had an absolute trust in you, Mr. Sanders, and that since you would look after Yukari, my wife and I must not interfere with you. I'd like to respect my son's wish. But please forgive us. As his parents, my wife and I would like to help our daughter-in-law as much as we can. Please tell us if there is anything we can do for her and the coming child, who will be our first granddaughter."

Before I said anything, Yukari answered, "Thank you, Mr. Schmidt. I'm grateful to you for your offer. But Hans had told me before he left for Sarajevo that he wanted Mark to look after me during my childbirth, if anything happened to him. It was his strong wish that I feel I must respect. Please don't worry about me. I am a strong person. I'll go through my childbirth with Mark's help. That's Hans's wish, as well as mine."

"I'm honored to know," Mr. Schmidt said to Yukari, "that as Hans told me, my father met your father in Berlin before the war. That brought my memory back to my childhood. I remember that a Japanese gentleman indeed visited our home a few times. That was your father. And Hans married you without knowing it. What a destiny between your family and my family. Respecting Hans's wish and your wish, we will return to Berlin. But please feel free to visit us often with your child — our granddaughter. We'll welcome you."

"As your mother-in-law," Mrs. Schmidt added, "I feel I should help you to go through the childbirth and the aftercare as much as possible. I can come back when your due date nears. I really want to do that. Are you sure you don't need me?"

"Thank you, Mrs. Schmidt," Yukari replied. "I'm grateful to you for your thought. But please don't worry. I can manage it with Mark's help. And please don't take this personally. Even my own mother is not coming."

"Mr. and Mrs. Schmidt," I assured them, "Hans, Yukari, and I are bonded together. Even though Hans is gone now, our bond will never be broken. I'll do my best for Yukari so she will have a healthy daughter — Hans's daughter, your granddaughter."

Probably this was not what Hans's parents wished. I was sure that they wanted to help Yukari. But they appeared to concede that there was not much space for them to intrude into the bond among Hans, Yukari, and me. They reluctantly decided to return to Berlin.

Then Mr. Schmidt presented Yukari with the Japanese lacquer box Hans had once held. "Please keep this, which belongs to your family after all, and explain to our granddaughter how this box came into the possession of her father."

Yukari received it with reverence.

The next day, Sunday afternoon, we had a private memorial service for Hans at Church of the Heavenly Rest. At my request the rector himself administered the service at the chapel. There were only Yukari, Hans's parents, Shem Tov, Francine, Justin, Ramez, me, and the rector. I had arranged two baskets of flowers containing white lilies, white roses, and white carnations, which I set at the base of the altar. Hans would have liked them.

Throughout the service Yukari was composed. But from time to time, she could not help from sobbing quietly. I stayed right next to her. We said the prayers together from the Book of Common Prayer. We took the Eucharist, wishing for the peaceful rest of Hans.

At the end of the service, with the permission of the rector, I played a CD of Brahms's *German Requiem* that Hans had loved so dearly. For time's sake, I played only the fourth and fifth movements, both of which sounded soul-comforting.

I remembered the many times Hans, Yukari, and I were together. How happy we were then. It was not so long ago. But it seemed far distant now. My grief at his loss welled like an ocean.

17

The week after the service for Hans, Yukari resumed her work at the Parnassus Symphony Orchestra. Her colleagues showed deep compassion toward the young pregnant widow and provided the best support they could. She was also encouraged by the overwhelming sympathy expressed at the memorial service at the United Nations. Slowly she was recovering from the devastating shock.

The loss of Hans naturally depressed me. Strangely, however, I detected a warm feeling burgeoning inside my heart. I tried to suppress it. But it persisted and even grew — *Now Yukari and I can be lovers*. I felt embarrassed and ashamed. If I was not mistaken, Yukari appeared to feel the same way, in spite of her grief over Hans's death. We were both afraid of directly discussing our sorrow. So we focused on the coming baby.

Now her life had to go on. She had only five weeks left until her due date. She had stubbornly insisted that I help her as her partner for childbirth. I was more than willing to a certain point, but gently reminded her that I was not her husband or a female, and that it would not be proper for me to be in the birthing room with her. As anyone would have done in my situation, I suggested she ask her mother to help.

"Yes, I thought of that," she calmly replied. "But this is a very personal matter. I would like to go through it with my husband, but Hans is no more. Next to Hans is you. Please help me. I prefer it this way."

Then she told me what had happened when she informed her parents of Hans's death. After the initial shock, her parents naturally suggested she come back to Tokyo, at least for childbirth, so they could assist her. After her baby was born, she could go back to the US with the baby if she wanted — this they agreed, because by now they respected her independence as a grown woman. But Yukari declined their suggestion. Then her mother suggested that she come to New York to help Yukari during childbirth and aftercare. Even her father wanted to come with her mother. But this too Yukari declined. She told them that she would go through the childbirth with my help. Since she insisted so strongly, her parents had no choice but to reluctantly consent, on the condition that she would ask their assistance if the situation became too serious — a condition to which she had agreed.

I was astonished by Yukari's determination. But I had absolutely no experience in the area of childbirth, I reminded her. She didn't want to hear it. She just implored me with tears.

"Mark, you are the only person I can trust. Hans would have wanted it this way. To me, you are part of my family. You say you have no experience. Neither do I. I'm so scared. I need your support. We can learn together. Please."

I could no longer refuse her. I also remembered the promise I had made to Hans. I borrowed the books on pregnancy, childbirth, and parenthood that Hans had bought. The more I read, the more complicated it looked. I felt completely overwhelmed. But now it was my responsibility. I had to do it.

Being German, Hans had prepared very well for their coming child before he left for Sarajevo. Their bedroom was already ready as a nursery, with a crib, a rocking chair, a door gate, a baby bathtub, baby clothes, bottles, diapers, a stroller, and toys, all of which he had bought.

I was still anxious, but I felt fatherhood awakening inside me.

*   *   *

One morning while I was working in my office, Francine walked in and closed the door. She looked happy.

"What a tragedy about Hans!" she said, contrary to her appearance. "I knew something like this would happen. Poor Yukari. How is she doing?"

"She is recovering from the trauma of mourning," I replied. "She is a strong person. She is now focusing on her childbirth. I can't believe it's only one month away."

"I'm glad. Would you tell her if she needs my help, she can count on me? We can talk woman to woman."

"That's great! I'll tell her. She'll be happy. Right now she needs as much emotional support as she can get. Since you and she are already good friends, she'll feel secure if she knows you are behind her."

"Uh, huh ... My pediatrician is excellent. I can make referrals to him if Yukari wants."

"Okay, I'll tell her."

I waited. It seemed that these were just innocuous ice-breaking remarks before Francine could say what she had on her mind. At last she came to the point.

"Mark, you should marry Yukari. In that way Hans's tragic death will allow something positive between Yukari and you. I don't mean I hoped for Hans's death. But I see this as a good opportunity for your happiness. Yukari loves you, and you love her. So marriage would be natural for you two." She smiled at me and nodded.

"Oh, Francine," I said with a heavy heart, "we are still in mourning for Hans. I don't think this kind of talk is proper at this time."

"It's true," she admitted. "But I really want you to be happy with Yukari, as I've been saying for some time. Think about it, all right? You have my full support."

She left my office with her pleasant countenance.

I remembered Hans's words before he left for Sarajevo, as well as his email suggesting I marry Yukari. I felt again that familiar warm emotion springing up in my heart. Immediately, though, I forcefully repressed it.

*   *   *

Yukari's obstetrician, Dr. Talmor, had his office at Park Avenue and 83rd Street, close to her apartment. He was affiliated with Lenox Hill Hospital at Park Avenue and 77th Street, and she would be admitted there when the time came. The hospital was only twelve blocks down from her apartment.

Yukari had informed Dr. Talmor that her husband had passed away suddenly in an accident, and the doctor was very concerned for her. She explained she had asked me to be her partner. The doctor approved her decision wholeheartedly. He knew of a few cases where women had to go through childbirth alone for one reason or another. Psychologically, it was hell. Therefore, he was glad that Yukari had someone she could trust, and he encouraged her to bring me to his office with her.

At Dr. Talmor's recommendation, Yukari enrolled us in a four-week childbirth class offered at Lenox Hill Hospital, taught by a Certified Nurse-Midwife. There were about ten couples in the class, and we met once a week for two hours.

The class was very informative. In the first session the couples introduced themselves, describing their background, their experience with childbirth, their due date, and their wishes and anxieties. Since all couples were nervous, mutual support was needed, encouraged, and welcomed. The expectant mothers' ages ranged from the late twenties to early forties. As such, Yukari was not the oldest in the class, which made her breathe a little easier. She introduced me to the class simply as her partner, and to my surprise, I was accepted without the slightest fuss.

In the class we learned how to relax, how to breathe, and how to push. The role of the husband or the partner was extremely important. Yukari relaxed in various positions, and I massaged her back or simply held her hand. She sometimes stood, facing me, leaning on my shoulders and embracing my neck with her arms, while I massaged her back, which helped her really relax. Breathing exercises were relatively easy for her because she knew good breathing techniques from singing. I had to learn well so I could coach her when she needed her calm and steady breathing. Facing each other, she and I practiced breathing, synchronizing our moves.

We were also taught various birth exercises, such as sitting cross-legged, squatting, pelvic tilt, buttocks curl, and more. Many of these were variations of exercises for backache that I did every day, so I was able to learn quickly and coach Yukari well as she practiced. One exercise I could not coach was the Kegel exercise, which she practiced alone, giggling.

One evening, using a big illustrated chart, the instructor explained the details of anatomy and process of a baby coming from the uterus through the birth canal to the outside world. Various delivery positions were described and demonstrated. Using a doll, a delivery was practiced by all couples. Yukari settled in the regular semi-sitting position, the one she preferred, and I supported her back. The instructor explained the way the baby would come out between Yukari's legs. After that she passed the doll to Yukari as if the baby had just been born. Yukari hugged the doll on her upper chest close to her breasts.

Another evening, the instructor explained birth problems, such as placenta previa, shoulder dystocia, prolapsed cord, cephalopelvic disproportion, and others. Most of these problems sounded gruesome to me. For example, prolapsed cord meant, I learned, that the umbilical cord got squeezed between baby's head and the pelvic bones, decreasing the oxygen supply to the baby, and in the worst case, suffocating the baby.

Yukari's face became pale. She raised her hand and said, "I can't take these; I'm so scared. I don't want my baby to suffer from these problems." She gripped my hand.

I was scared too, so I held Yukari's hand tightly. Several participants murmured in assent. It seemed that these possibilities made us all fearful.

The instructor grinned and said, "Don't worry. These birth problems occur less than one percent of the time, or even much less. The huge majority of babies go through a normal birth."

"But, but," Yukari said, agitated, "what if my baby falls into that less than one percent?" She was almost crying.

The instructor coolly told all participants, "Relax. Today I'm explaining these so you're aware that these problems exist and can take every precaution to prevent them. This is why it is extremely important for you to have regular checkups with your obstetricians. If there is any problem, he or she will detect it before it gets serious and take appropriate remedial measures."

Not only Yukari and me, but also other participants breathed easier.

By the end of the course, Yukari and I had learned a lot, and our anxiety level receded. We felt we could do it.

While the childbirth class was going on, Yukari and I visited Dr. Talmor for a regular checkup, the importance of which

I now understood to my core. He welcomed me and thanked me for helping. He reminded me that it would be a heavy responsibility, but it would be worth the effort. I agreed and told him that I was prepared.

Dr. Talmor pressed gently on her abdomen and checked the position of the baby. He attached the heartbeat amplifier on her belly to check the baby's heartbeat, which even I was able to hear. Finally he used the ultrasound scan, and while he was examining her, Yukari and I saw the baby moving on the screen.

Dr. Talmor smiled and said, "All looks good. The baby's heartbeat is strong and regular. She has already settled in the normal head-down position in the pelvis, and the 'engagement' has been completed. I expect the due date to be April 18, or thereabout."

"Thank you," Yukari said happily, but immediately turned anxious. "As I have mentioned to you already, I have a history of leukemia. Because of that, I'm afraid I don't have the vigorous strength to go through a difficult labor, which can take more than ten hours in some cases. Even just the thought of it makes me nervous. Also, I'm thirty-nine, which I think is very late for a first childbirth. I think this raises the possibility of complications."

I implored, "Doctor, I do not wish she suffer from pain too much and too long."

Yukari added, "I'd like to maintain my consciousness while delivering the baby."

Dr. Talmor waved his hands gently with a grin. "Calm down. I have a solution to satisfy both of you." Then he explained. "I will wait for normal signs of imminent delivery, such as regular contractions at short intervals, the ruptured membrane — we call this 'water break' — and a 'show' of mucus sometimes mixed with blood. When these occur I'll advise you, Ms. Asaka, to go to the hospital. Once you are settled in the hospital room, I'll induce the delivery to speed up the labor. Then, when the baby is ready to come out, I'll use a continuous epidural, which will lightly numb the lower half of your body while allowing you to maintain consciousness. In this way you can experience the sensation of natural birth with full consciousness but without suffering from pain."

Yukari and I immediately said at the same time, "I like that."

The matter was settled, and we were no longer fearful.

Dr. Talmor advised us to consider four things. The first was a pediatrician who would take care of the newborn. Dr. Talmor recommended a few of his colleagues. As Francine's pediatrician practiced in midtown, and since Yukari wanted hers close to her apartment, we ruled out Francine's doctor. We made appointments with the pediatricians Dr. Talmor recommended, visited them, asked questions, and observed their offices. We chose a woman in her early forties who was affiliated with Lenox Hill Hospital. She was very warm, sensitive, and sympathetic with Yukari's situation as a young widow. Her office was full of children's books and toys. We saw a few mothers and children, all of whom appeared happy. Yukari was very pleased.

The second was a Professional Labor Assistant, a professional woman to care for the mother's needs before, during, and after the delivery. A PLA would be of invaluable help to both Yukari and me, since both of us were inexperienced with childbirth. Based on Dr. Talmor's referrals, we interviewed a few PLAs and hired one, Lucy, in her late fifties with years of experience in this profession, but of quiet, mild, and warm personality. This helped Yukari relax.

The third was a birth plan. Taking into account Dr. Talmor's several suggestions, Yukari and I together prepared our plan. In essence, it requested an LDR — Labor, Delivery, and Recovery — room; the partner (me) and our PLA to be present all the time; the semi-sitting delivery position; the induced labor and continuous epidural at the doctor's discretion; and so on. We carefully planned every detail. Then we signed the plan and brought it to Dr. Talmor on our next visit. He reviewed it, agreed, and signed. We submitted it to the hospital.

Our last task was advance packing for the hospital stay. We packed Yukari's suitcase. Included were her personal toiletries, clothing for her and the baby, books, and my digital camera.

Yukari intended to work until the day she was to go to the hospital, after which she would take her maternity leave of twelve weeks. This had been agreed with the Parnassus Symphony Orchestra.

"Mark, I'm so grateful to you for doing all this for me," said Yukari with her most earnest face.

"You are welcome. I'm glad I can be of help."

"But I have one more favor to ask. When I come home from the hospital, I would like to ask you to stay with me until I recover my strength enough to take care of my child by myself. Of course you'll have to work. But after work, please come stay with me. Initially, I'm afraid that I won't have enough strength.

I won't bother you too much since Lucy, my PLA, will help me. But I need your emotional support. Please say yes."

I had already agreed to support her during the childbirth. If she needed me for the aftercare also, I would do it as well. Her well-being as the mother was most important now. I agreed.

While Yukari and I learned about childbirth and how the expectant mother and her husband or partner had to deal with it, the process drew us emotionally together. She and I had been close before, but now our intimacy was much deeper.

One evening after the childbirth class, we came back to Yukari's apartment. By then we had learned a lot and our confidence had been built up high. We were content. We sat on the sofa and relaxed. Since both of us had finished supper, we just had tea. Its warmth made us feel mellow. Yukari guided my hands to her abdomen. We were already accustomed to this. Our four hands rested there, and we enjoyed feeling the baby moving.

I felt happy and kissed her cheek. She smiled and kissed me back on my lips. We kissed each other for a long time. My tongue slipped into her mouth, and her tongue coiled with mine. We swallowed each other's saliva as if it were sweet wine.

"Do you remember the night when Hans and I slept in your bed?" Yukari asked.

"Of course I do," I replied. "That's when you became pregnant."

"Did you know I came to you in the living room at dawn?"

"Did you? … I mean, actually?" I said. "I saw you, but I thought I was dreaming. You looked very pretty. I must have been in love with you."

"I said then that when I was making love to Hans, I was actually making love to you. It was true. So this child is emotionally half yours."

"It sounds so serene, Yukari. I like that."

"I also said that I was glad you saw me naked. That was true too."

"I was glad my drawing came out so well."

"No, no, that's not the point. I wanted you to see me entirely. This might sound crazy, but I want you to see me now as a pregnant woman, I mean entirely. … Help me undress."

I gazed at her, but she was earnest, her face shining. She started unzipping her dress. I went along with her as if I were hypnotized. Piece by piece, we removed her clothes. When I unhooked her bra, her swollen breasts plumped out. We carefully took off her one-piece maternity dress and underwear. She stood before me completely naked. This was my first time to see a pregnant woman fully nude. Her belly was so big that she almost needed to support it with her hands. She looked like a goddess of fertility and motherhood.

"Beautiful, Yukari," I said.

"Thank you," Yukari said proudly. "Now kiss my child at my tummy."

I kissed her round tummy. She clasped my head tenderly and pushed it to her abdomen. I kissed all over her belly. I felt the baby moving. She felt it too.

"I think we should make the child really half yours," Yukari said.

"What do you mean?"

"We should consummate."

"But Hans —"

She interrupted, "He wanted this, because he asked me to marry you if he died."

I admitted that Hans had said the same to me. He had told both of us the same thing. So this must have been his true wish.

"Now you should be the father to this child too," she said.

She held my hand and led me into the bedroom. I followed her willingly.

"Dr. Talmor told me that lovemaking during pregnancy, even at this stage, would be all right, as long as we don't put weight on the belly," she said before the bed.

I still felt as if I were hypnotized. But this time I felt that Hans had originated that hypnosis over me, as if he were blessing me to do it. So I didn't resist Yukari's invitation, or to be more precise, Hans's invitation.

We lay naked on our sides in the bed, and I held her from behind, so her abdomen was left free from any weight. In that position we made love. I moved my body gently and slowly in rhythm and penetrated her as she received me with full trust and openness. She and I moaned in pleasure. How sweet it was.

When it was over, she turned to face me.

"That was nice," Yukari said dreamingly, her eyes shining.

"It was wonderful," I said tenderly, still breathing heavily.

"Now you are the real half-father to this child," she said. "Touch me here."

She guided my hands to her bare abdomen. We held our four hands there for a while.

"Ahaa!" Yukari and I cried.

The baby moved as if she were applauding us.

"She loves us," Yukari said.

"I believe so too," I said.

18

On April 18, Yukari's due date, I called her from my office in the morning. She coolly told me that nothing was happening, except occasional mild discomfort in the lower abdomen. She did not have a rehearsal or a performance to attend, and she promised to call me as soon as contractions became noticeable.

I went to see my director. By now I had developed a close working relationship with her. I explained to her about Hans and told her that I had to attend Yukari's childbirth, so I would need a few days off. She said that she had been at the memorial service for the UNMIBH casualties and seen me escorting pregnant Yukari. As a woman, the director sympathized, encouraged me to help Yukari, and approved my leave request.

After lunch I called Yukari again. She said that something was going on in her lower abdomen, but she did not feel pain, just some discomfort, which seemed to be increasing. She was resting a lot or walking around her apartment.

After work I went to her apartment. She was in good spirits but a little disappointed that nothing particular was happening on her due date. Since we did not have much else to do other than just wait, we decided to make a practice run to the hospital. She and I walked across 89th Street to Park Avenue, caught a taxi, and drove down to Lenox Hill Hospital at 77th Street. It took less than ten minutes. No big deal, we felt. We came back to her apartment and had dinner.

We spent the evening watching TV and doing light exercises. I coached her while she exercised. I massaged her back and legs. She took a long hot bath, which relaxed her.

We checked the contents of her suitcase against the checklist and made sure that all was packed neatly. I examined the battery of my digital camera. Everything was all right. No need to panic. We were prepared.

Yukari went to bed early to rest and build her energy. I slept beside her in the bed, as this had become our custom since our lovemaking. Tonight I just caressed her entire body for relaxation, and she dozed off easily.

*   *   *

The next morning, light noise and commotion awoke me around six o'clock. Yukari was moving between the bedroom and the bathroom. She told me that the contractions were becoming regular and stronger, but not too painful yet. She paced between the living room and the bedroom. During the contractions she hung over my shoulders and stretched her back muscles while I massaged her back, which made the contractions easier to bear.

We had breakfast, though Yukari could not eat much because she was so preoccupied with the contractions. They became definitely regular and the intensity increased. By nine o'clock they were four to five minutes apart, lasting about one minute, and had continued consistently in this mode for over one hour. Her water broke. She called Dr. Talmor, who advised her that the time had come to go to the hospital.

She called Lucy, her PLA, took a shower, and wore a comfortable maternity dress. I suggested she wear her usual makeup, which she greatly appreciated later. We left the apartment building with merry well-wishes from the doorman and the concierge. I carried her suitcase in one hand and escorted her with the other. Slowly but steadily she walked. At Park Avenue we had to wait for several minutes to find a taxi, due to late morning rush hour. But once we caught a cab we arrived at Lenox Hill Hospital in ten minutes. Yukari showed no sign of nervousness.

Lucy had already informed the hospital and was waiting for us, so we were admitted quickly. By ten o'clock Yukari and I settled into our LDR room. Yukari changed into a hospital gown, and the nurse checked her. She was not yet fully ready for delivery.

About 10:30 Dr. Talmor arrived, pleasantly greeting us all. He examined Yukari.

"Everything is fine, I assure you," he said. "Now it's time to induce your labor."

Pitocin was added to her IV. The duration of contractions became longer and more intense while the interval became shorter. Soon she was fully ready for delivery. The pain increased, which she reported to the doctor. About 11:15, an anesthesiologist arrived and administered the epidural. The pain faded away. As her lower half became lightly numb, Lucy and I assisted Yukari to settle in the semi-sitting position on the birthing bed. I massaged her forehead to relieve the tension.

About 11:45 the baby's head became visible. Yukari started pushing. I coached her breathing, holding her hands. She clung to me as Lucy and nurses encouraged her. She breathed deeply in the rhythm we had practiced, repeating the breathing and pushing with all her energy. Slowly the baby's head emerged. Yukari saw it, and her energy surged. She continued pushing. Lucy led me in the way to catch the baby.

At 12:15 the baby was born. I held her up to show her to Yukari, saying loudly and happily, "It's a girl!" It was all over. Yukari was euphoric. I felt ecstatic myself.

Dr. Talmor checked the baby, clearing her mouth and nose. With a little helpful tap, the baby started breathing with a big healthy cry. The doctor placed the baby on Yukari's upper stomach. Yukari hugged the baby gently with adoring eyes and a mother's smile. The baby opened her brown eyes, one by one. They met with Yukari's.

"Hello, little Annie," Yukari whispered.

I was asked to cut the umbilical cord. I was nervous, but Lucy guided me and assured me that it would not hurt either the mother or the baby. I positioned the scissors gingerly and cut. The mother and the baby were separated. Then Dr. Talmor massaged Yukari's abdomen gently, and the placenta was expelled.

In the meantime, the baby saw her mother's breast and nipple, and started slowly nuzzling up toward it. The baby reached and sucked the nipple. A cry of pleasure came from Yukari. At this point I removed my medical gloves and started taking pictures. Both Yukari and Baby Anne looked beautiful.

Dr. Talmor examined Yukari and the baby. All was normal. Finally, Yukari and Baby Anne were tidied up, relieving us physically and psychologically from the tension of the day.

All things considered, it had gone very well. I was particularly glad that Yukari did not suffer too much while she experienced the most miraculous moment of childbirth with full consciousness. I exhaled a deep breath. After all the preparations, it was finally over. What a relief! I saw in Yukari the mother's pride and happiness. I felt fatherhood myself inside me. I was the proud father. What joy!

During the emotional and hectic process, Lucy helped Yukari with serenity and sensitivity. I had to admit that without her, an experienced PLA, we could not have gotten through the ordeal. Lucy prepared glasses of lemon juice, sandwiches, and cups of tea. Now that both Yukari and I were relaxed, these were most welcome.

"Yukari, you were brave. You've done it. What a beautiful baby girl you have! I'm proud of you." This was the first time I had spoken to her in a placid tone all day.

"Thank you, Mark," Yukari said. "Yes, she is beautiful, isn't she? I couldn't have done it without you. I'm very grateful." Her eyes were wet.

Yukari needed a well-deserved rest. Lucy relieved me for a while. I went out with my camera. First I stopped at a florist, ordered a huge colorful bouquet for Yukari and Baby Annie, and had it sent to our LDR room in the hospital.

Then I walked to my apartment only a few blocks away and printed the pictures on my PC color printer. They came out very well. Since Yukari had put her makeup on in the morning, even after the exhausting childbirth she looked pretty. Particularly, the picture of Yukari breastfeeding the newborn baby was adorable.

This short sojourn gave me an opportunity to reflect upon the situation.

So the baby had been born. What did the child mean to me now? Strictly speaking, I knew too well, Annie's biological parents were Hans and Yukari. But thinking of the unbreakable bond among Hans, Yukari, and me, I felt I was part of the child's parenthood. Not only emotionally, but also physically, as Yukari and I had made love during her pregnancy. Was it a betrayal of Hans? I didn't think so. Hans wanted it. Yukari wanted it. Of course, I wanted it too. Was I mad enough to believe that Hans had blessed me to do it? It might sound insane, but indeed I did believe so. The child was *ours* — Hans's, Yukari's, and mine. Hans was gone. So I should be Hans for Yukari as well as for Baby Anne. Nothing was wrong with it. I would be a good father to our newborn daughter. Then at a proper moment, I would propose marriage to Yukari. I was sure she would accept. This was what Hans wanted too. Then our marriage would settle everything, as Yukari would be my legal wife and Baby Anne my legal daughter. — Yes, this was what I was going to do.

I bought some snacks, fruit, and fresh juice, and went back to the hospital. Yukari was still sleeping. Beside her bed, the baby was also sleeping in her hospital crib. Lucy was resting too, but when I entered the room, she woke up. We talked for a while. She showed me how to diaper the baby and how to give her a sponge bath.

The flowers had been placed in a glass vase on the side table next to Yukari, brightening the room. Soon the baby awoke and demanded milk. Yukari awoke and breastfed her child. I showed her the pictures I had printed, which pleased her.

It was an excellent idea to have requested, in the birth plan, the hospital stay with full services for at least forty-eight hours after the birth. In this way both Yukari and the baby would receive professional medical care and attention as required, and I could learn how to take care of an infant and how to support Yukari. Lucy was to be with Yukari for two weeks. Since I had taken the rest of the week off, I had a plenty of time to learn from the doctor, nurses, and Lucy.

Before five o'clock, Dr. Talmor and nurses visited and checked both Yukari and Annie.

"Everything is fine for both you and the baby," Dr. Talmor told Yukari. "Congratulations. Have a good rest tonight. I'll come back tomorrow morning." Then he turned to me and said, "Thank you for your support, Mr. Sanders. You did a terrific job."

Dr. Talmor and nurses left. Yukari was content; so was I. Soon Lucy left. Yukari, Baby Anne, and I were alone. We felt we were a happy family.

Throughout the night, every two hours or so, the nurse on duty visited and made sure that both the mother and the newborn were all right. Every two to three hours, the baby woke up and cried for milk. This was taxing to Yukari, but she endured the feedings willingly.

The next morning Lucy showed up promptly at nine o'clock. Soon after, Dr. Talmor and nurses visited to check Yukari and Baby Annie. All was normal. Yukari was given proper medication to speed up her recovery. She tidied herself, wore her elegant nightgown, and applied her makeup. In the meantime, the bed was made up with fresh sheets. She was ready to receive her friends from the Parnassus Symphony Orchestra.

Lucy gave the baby a sponge bath. It made Anne happy, and her gentle smile was so cute. Lucy then put a fresh diaper on her. I watched these activities intently so I would be able to do them by myself.

In the early afternoon, several women from the orchestra visited. I recognized some faces who had participated in our Christmas caroling. Our LDR room suddenly became a merry party room, celebrating the newborn. Yukari was a proud mother showing off her pretty Baby Anne.

After that Yukari and I visited the hospital nursery. I held the baby in my arms so Yukari could walk without strain. We met several mothers with their babies and husbands. We exchanged our experiences. Some had gone through a very difficult birth that had taken many hours. A few had had a medication-free natural birth, enduring prolonged severe pains. One woman had had a cesarean section. Another woman had had a premature baby. Yukari and I sighed with relief that her experience had been relatively straightforward and painless. We could not have appreciated more Dr. Talmor's medical advice, which was just right for Yukari.

When we came back to our LDR room, we found Shem Tov and Francine waiting for us with their little Jacques.

"Congratulations, Yukari!" Shem Tov and Francine cried simultaneously and hugged and kissed Yukari.

"Thank you," Yukari said beaming. "Everything went normally, so the baby is fine and me too. I now understand why they call the childbirth 'labor.' It's hard work, but in the end a joyful one."

"I'm so glad everything went all right," Francine said. "In our case, Jacques was born a few days ahead of the estimated due date. So we were quite uneasy. But fortunately our delivery was also normal."

By now Jacques could stand and walk by himself, though still unsteadily. He stood beside Francine and cuddled her skirt. She gently caressed his head.

"My goodness, he can walk!" Yukari kissed Jacques, crinkling her eyes in delight. Then she said to Francine, "So you don't need the carrier for Jacques anymore. That's something I have to get for Annie."

"You should get one like I had," Francine replied. "I could use it as a front carrier as well as a back carrier, though I usually carried Jacques at the front so I was able to see his face."

"I see. I'll follow your suggestion." Yukari replied.

"Yukari, nursing and raising a baby is a lot of work and a heavy responsibility. Sometimes you might feel overwhelmed. I know what you'll be going through. Call me anytime if you feel anxious or if you have any questions. We can talk as working mothers."

"Thank you, Francine. I'll do that."

Francine scooped up Jacques and brought him close to Baby Anne where I held her at my chest. "See, Jacques? Now you have a little sister, Annie, you can play with."

Jacques gazed curiously at the newborn girl and smiled, mumbling something and waving his hands in glee. Yukari and Francine exchanged motherly grins.

"It's true," I said. "They will be good playmates."

"This is great," Shem Tov said. "We'll be two happy families." We all laughed heartily.

*   *   *

Yukari recovered well enough to walk around and take care of her baby. She was discharged from the hospital after three days.

It took only several minutes by taxi to reach Yukari's apartment building. We emerged slowly from the car. Yukari held the baby in her arms, escorted by Lucy. I carried the suitcase and the flower bouquet. Anne was wrapped in a blanket, wearing baby clothes and a hat that Hans had bought. He would have been a proud father. I choked up at the thought. But now I was Annie's father, I said in my mind, so everything would work out all right.

The doorman and the concierge congratulated Yukari, and exclaimed over the infant.

We came home.

19

A young widow Yukari may have been, but the baby girl gave her peace, comfort, and joy. She focused on nursing the child and her own recovery, assisted by Lucy. Annie was healthy and cried a lot for milk, but once her hunger was satisfied, she slept quietly. According to Lucy, the baby was one of most well-behaved she had ever cared for, which pleased Yukari.

Privately, I praised Hans, who had prepared all practical matters so well in case of the worst. Yukari would receive his life insurance benefit and the widow's entitlement of his pension, in addition to his savings and investments. While Yukari and I had been preparing for the childbirth, I had undertaken all paperwork for her, since she was in no state of mind to deal with such matters. When I explained the forms to her, she had glanced at them and just signed, trusting my work. The payments from these were now coming to her. Therefore, financially, she was well provided for, and she had no need to worry.

During the maternity leave of twelve weeks, the Parnassus Symphony Orchestra would not pay Yukari's salary, but she was guaranteed her position after the leave. Once she emerged from her postpartum recovery, she would be able to resume a normal professional musician's life — except that now she would be a single working mother with an infant daughter. This, she resolved to go through with a firm determination.

Lucy came to Yukari's apartment at nine o'clock in the morning for five hours every day for two weeks to take care of the baby and Yukari. Lucy even tidied up the apartment, grocery shopped, did laundry, and cooked. She also kept Yukari company and explained baby care. Since Lucy was medically trained, if anything went wrong with Annie or Yukari, Lucy would give first aid and liaise with the doctors. This was a superb arrangement for a young widow living alone with her first infant child. Yukari relaxed and was able to indulge in a leisurely recovery without physically and psychologically being overwhelmed. Since the arrangement worked so well, after the initial two weeks Yukari extended Lucy's service for another month with a reduced length of three hours per day. Lucy gladly accepted.

The most difficult thing for Yukari was to breastfeed every two to three hours, regardless of the time of the day. At midnight or three o'clock in the morning, the baby did not care; she simply demanded the milk. Yukari was tired and had to take many catnaps. While she was sleeping, if Annie was awake I played with her, talked to her, and even sang a few songs to her. Sometimes I carried her far above my head with my two hands, playing an airplane in a very slow motion. She liked it and made a delightful laughing sound. The baby's adorable reaction was a cherished pleasure to me.

Soon it became my job to bathe Annie. For the first two weeks I gave her a sponge bath. After the baby's umbilical cord fell off, I started giving her a warm bath. In the baby bathtub, I placed two small plastic yellow ducks, which floated on the water. When they were squeezed, they quacked. Annie happily splashed in the water, getting me wet and soapy. Yukari sat beside me and gleefully watched.

When Annie became tired of playing in her crib, Yukari played the violin to her, which was supposed to be good for intelligence development. This was my favorite time, as I was able to listen to Yukari's private concert right next to me. Usually she played violin sonatas of Mozart, Beethoven, and Brahms. The baby listened quietly, sometimes moving her fingers like those of her mother, which convinced Yukari that Annie would become a great violinist.

Every evening after dinner I relaxed at the dining table, reading, while Yukari nursed the baby, sitting on the rocking chair beside the dining table, gently swaying the chair. Quite often I put the book aside and watched them.

Yukari secured two bed pillows on her lap and held Annie atop the pillows, so the baby was at the level of her breasts. Annie took the nipple into her mouth and started sucking vigorously. The baby's ears moved in the same rhythm as the muscle action of her jaws and cheeks. Yukari told me that this was called latching on.

According to Yukari, the rhythmical sucking of her breast by the baby was so pleasurable that she simply resigned herself to do nothing else but quietly enjoy it with her eyes half-closed.

I clearly heard the sound of the baby swallowing the milk. To me, the scene was so irresistibly picturesque that I could not help proposing that I draw her nursing the baby. Yukari pleasantly accepted my proposition.

One evening I brought from my apartment a drawing board, a few sheets of rough pastel drawing paper, a set of pastels, pastel pencils, a putty rubber, a few torchons, and fixative. I set the drawing board on the dining table and stretched the drawing paper. Then I brought a few additional lamps to the table and directed them to the rocking chair.

We kept the living room warm for the drawing session. Yukari wore a loose white nightgown with a pretty floral pattern of light peach and pink. She sat on the rocking chair comfortably, supported by a cushion at her back. On her lap she placed two pillows, covered with a large white towel. For the drawing, she decided to hold the baby without clothes, which turned out to be an excellent idea.

The regular nursing process started. Yukari watched the baby with her eyes half closed while the baby sucked her breast. One breast was exposed fully for the baby while the other was partly covered by the nightgown.

I started drawing swiftly with pastels. I had only a little over ten minutes for one pose, during which I fixed the main composition of the two figures on the 18"x24" paper, before Annie would deplete the breast. The baby was entirely included, while I showed Yukari's head and torso.

I repeated the sessions on a few consecutive evenings, gradually adding colors. On the fourth evening I added several final touches and signed the bottom right corner of the drawing. On the back I wrote the title, "Yukari Nursing Anne."

Finally, I framed the drawing and hung it on the wall next to the drawing of Yukari dancing in the nude and the photo of us in front of my painting "Blue Roses and Three Friends."

Yukari was very pleased with the new drawing. I too was content with it, since I thought it caught the warm feeling of a mother nursing her baby daughter. I carried Annie to the wall and showed her the drawing. The baby gazed at the drawing full of joy, I thought, waving her hands and kicking her legs.

I pointed at the three artworks one by one. "This was just before the conception; this during the pregnancy; and this after the childbirth. It's a beautiful story of a motherhood in art."

"Yes, it's marvelous, isn't it?" Yukari murmured.

Yukari took out one wine glass from the china cabinet. I wondered what she was going to do. To my surprise, she expressed one of her breasts into the wine glass, filling one quarter of the glass with her milk. She brought it to me and smiled.

"Thank you, Mark. I like the drawing. This is a token of my gratitude. Please drink it."

"Are you serious?"

I looked at her, hesitating a little, but her face was sincere, shining with happiness and intimacy. Holding the baby in one hand, I raised the wine glass with the other hand and swallowed her milk. The taste was hard to describe: rich, creamy, milky, and motherly. I felt it boosted my energy.

"Did you like it?" asked Yukari, curiously watching me.

"Yes, it was excellent. I'm now full of energy and spirit."

Yukari and I giggled a little.

I brought the baby up close to my face and whispered, "Hi, Annie! Now you and I are more closely related than ever by your mother's milk."

The baby smiled and cooed something like "Aye." Yukari and I heartily laughed.

As I had promised, since we came back from the hospital, I had stayed overnight in Yukari's apartment. Following our new custom, I slept with her in her bed. But because Dr. Talmor suggested that we wait for four to six weeks after the childbirth to engage in lovemaking, we just hugged, kissed, and caressed each other. I felt it deeply intimate and pleasurable.

That night in the bed, I brought up the issue I had resolved to talk to her about for some time. I thought at this point we didn't need any flashy ceremonial talk, so I came to the point directly.

"Yukari," I said, "I've been thinking. I'm worried about you and Annie. I want to help you both. The only way to do it right, it seems to me, is to get married. This way you'll be my wife, and Anne will be my daughter — I mean, legally. Hans wanted it this way. Besides, I love you and Annie. I would like to continue my life with you and Annie this way. ... What do you think?"

She kissed me, held me tight, and said, "I have a confession to make." She kissed me again. "When I saw you for the first time in the Metropolitan Museum Art last year, I fell in love with you. I felt instinctively our chemistry blended perfectly. As you know, I had been thinking of divorce from Hans then. I thought that God had sent you to rescue me from my miserable marriage. But it was a struggle. I'm a very conservative person as far as marriage is concerned, and divorce was even then the last resort I would take, and if possible I would want to avoid it. Soon we discovered our family heritage among you, Hans, and me. I felt that this was not a coincidence — that we were destined to meet. I thought that friendship among us three might be possible, while maintaining the marriage with Hans. So I gave him another chance. But my love for you remained inside me. Many times I wanted to tell you this. But I couldn't. Forgive me. The only exception was at the dawn after our memorable July Fourth night in your apartment, when I came to you in the living room and finally said 'I love you.' But while your eyes were open, they were quite blank, so I thought you were still asleep." She kissed me again.

"Thank you for telling me this," I said, kissing her. "I too have a confession." I kissed her again. "When I saw you in the museum last year, I also fell in love with you. But I denied that feeling, because Hans was my close friend, and I thought I must not betray our friendship. For me too it was a struggle. Francine caught it and plainly told me that I was in love with you. But even then I couldn't admit it to her, because I was forcing myself to suppress the feeling. Let me show you something."

I got up from the bed and went to the living room to fetch my sketchbook from my briefcase.

"Take a look," I said, presenting the sketchbook to Yukari in the bed.

She opened and gazed at it, flipping page by page. Every page contained a sketch of Yukari on various occasions: her playing the violin, her performing in the orchestra, her strolling the park, her leaning toward flowers, her standing with the Statue of Liberty in the background, her smiling before our blue roses, her caroling Christmas songs, her in front of the huge Christmas tree at the Cathedral of St. John the Divine, and on and on.

"My goodness! It's beautiful!" she exclaimed. "When did you sketch these?"

"I always carry my sketchbook. You inspired me so much, and I couldn't resist sketching from my memory right after these scenes." I caressed her. "These pages tell my feeling, even though I couldn't admit it openly. Now Hans is gone, so I can show this to you, and I can tell you I loved you, I love you, and I'll love you forever. I hope Hans wouldn't mind."

"He wanted it this way," she said.

"Then will you accept my marriage proposal?"

"Yes, of course. That will be wonderful. My mind has been made up already. Thank you. I'll be happy, and Annie too." She showered me with kisses.

I had expected her affirmative answer, but hearing it directly in her words, I felt overjoyed. "Good," I said. "So it's settled. Only question is when. I think we should give a three-month mourning period for Hans. Then sometime in late June we should get married. By that time Annie will be easier to nurse. During the summer we can go on our honeymoon."

"That's lovely," she said. "I like it."

* * *

Yukari raised the question of baptizing the baby. The sooner, the better. It was her belief that Anne herself should choose her own faith as an adult. But as her mother, Yukari wanted to help Anne now, when she needed her protection

most, even though the baby might not understand the baptis-
mal blessing. Later in her life Anne might confirm the same
faith, change to another, or leave it completely. It would then
be Anne's choice.

Yukari insisted on this because her faith had helped her
while she suffered from leukemia. She told me that without that
faith, she would have committed suicide. She also said her faith
was sustaining her in the wake of Hans's death. I was surprised
to hear this from her, since she was not a regular churchgoer.
But I respected her intention.

There was one problem. Fewer than two months had
passed since Hans died. Strictly speaking, Yukari was still in
mourning. In the old days, the mourning period had lasted one
year or even more. Now, one returned to normal life shortly
after a funeral, as it was one's responsibility to make the most
of the gift of life while one had it. Even so, one needed to discretely avoid an active social life too soon. Yukari and I were
not sure whether the baptism might be considered part of an
active social life.

There was another problem. That was, the baptism
required sponsors, a designated godfather and godmother
who ideally shared the same faith and would be responsible for overseeing the spiritual education and growth of the
child. Godparents were customarily close friends of the parents. Yukari insisted that I and no other serve as the godfather
to her child, because I was an Episcopalian, while she was a
Methodist, both denominations closely related. She hoped that
I could find a church friend who would be willing to serve as
a godmother.

Yukari and I consulted with the rector of the Church of the Heavenly Rest, who remembered the memorial service he had administered for Hans. According to the rector, it would be nice to have the baptism for the child now. But considering Yukari's mourning, there would be no need to rush. The baptism could be done when the lives of Yukari and the child were more settled psychologically as well as in terms of practical day-to-day living.

The rector suggested that a thanksgiving ceremony for the birth of the child be held before the congregation at a regular Sunday service as soon as would be convenient to Yukari. During the ceremony the child would receive the blessing from the church, as well as from the congregation. This was almost the same as a baptism without being so formal.

Yukari happily consented to the rector's suggestion. I thought it sounded most sensible and practical under the circumstances.

One Sunday morning Yukari and I dressed Annie in a pretty all-white dress and brought her to the Heavenly Rest for the service. We sat in the first row. Shem Tov and Francine sat next to us with their little Jacques. After the sermon by the rector, the Prayer of the People was said. Usually the announcements to the congregation would follow. This morning, however, the rector invited Yukari and the baby before the altar. Yukari presented the baby to the associate to the rector, who was an ordained woman. She was quite used to handling infants. She amused the baby in her hands. Annie smiled.

The rector addressed the congregation. "Dear friends, the birth of a child is a joyous and solemn occasion in the life of a family …"

The rector introduced Yukari and Baby Anne to the congregation. He explained that Yukari's husband, Hans, had died in an accident a little less than two months before, and one month later Anne was born. As it was difficult for Yukari, the rector asked the congregation to give support to Yukari and Anne as much as possible.

The prayer for Anne was said. Anne was blessed. Prayers were also said for Yukari as the mother and for Hans as the deceased husband. Yukari received Anne back from the associate.

Francine, Shem Tov, and I went up to Yukari near the altar. Shem Tov held Jacques's hand as he toddled along. We hugged Yukari and kissed Anne on her cheek. Shem Tov brought Jacques up close to Annie. Jacques smiled and touched his little sister with his tiny hand. The congregation applauded Yukari, who bowed her head, then showed Anne to the congregation. Yukari looked happy and proud. Annie remained quiet, as if she had understood the solemnity of the ceremony.

After the service, Yukari and I were leaving the church. I carried Annie in my arms, followed by Francine and Shem Tov, who again held the hand of Jacques unsteadily walking. People smiled at us and offered well wishes. Among the congregation, I sensed a keen stare at me. I turned my head toward it and froze. Jane was gazing at me, Annie, and Yukari. Tears were streaming down her cheeks. Mrs. Clifford too was observing us in wonder.

For the last Easter Sunday, Mrs. Clifford had invited me for lunch at her apartment after the service at this church. I had politely declined, making an innocent excuse. I had not attended the Easter service, although in the past I had always

attended the service on Easter. So this was the first time we had
seen each other since the first Sunday of this year.

I had no wish to make a scene. I politely bowed to them
and walked out of the church. Yukari did not see any of this. I
remembered Jane's sad face and tears. But there was nothing I
could do, because my mind was completely preoccupied with
the wellbeing of Yukari and Annie.

*   *   *

That afternoon Yukari had organized a tea party in honor
of Anne's receiving the blessing. She had invited her close
friends from the Parnassus Symphony Orchestra and her other
church. Since Yukari was conscious of the limitation of social
activities in her situation, she called the occasion an informal
afternoon concert as an innocuous excuse.

I wanted Yukari to enjoy the role of hostess without being
overwhelmed by the preparation and serving. Therefore, I
insisted that I do all the work, and that all Yukari had to do was
to tend to her guests. She would also perform a string quartet
with her colleagues in the Parnassus, the official main event of
the afternoon.

Finger sandwiches were essential to an afternoon tea. But
since I did not know how to make them, I had them catered
from a nearby French restaurant that also sold confections.
They promptly delivered the finger sandwiches, pastries, and
a big white cake bearing "Annie" in pink, one hour prior to the
party. I arranged them on the dining table.

Shem Tov, Francine, and I prepared for tea and coffee, and set the table with cups and champagne glasses. We peeled, cut, and attractively arranged apples, pears, nectarines, and grapes, on a large plate. We also set out small plates, forks, and napkins.

Not least important, we arranged a lot of flowers in blissful colors, which I had bought in advance and put in many vases. These we placed on the dining table, tea table, and side-tables. The apartment became festive.

Yukari and Francine had fed Anne and Jacques and put them down for a nap after we came back from the church. When we were ready to receive the guests, the babies were awake and full of energy. I moved the crib from the bedroom to the living room so Annie too was ready to receive the guests. Jacques sat near or trundled around the crib, as if keeping company with his little sister.

About ten people showed up. They were mostly women, with a few men who were husbands of Yukari's friends. Shem Tov and I stayed busy serving tea or coffee, and making sure that all guests had plates and napkins for finger sandwiches, pastries, and fruits. The guests started mingling, talking, and eating. This was the first time we had had a pleasant gathering in Yukari's apartment since Hans was gone. Yukari was busy with her guests, chatting about her baby and her experience of childbirth and nursing.

When all the guests were settled, Shem Tov and I filled the glasses with champagne. Yukari held Anne in her arms.

Francine joyfully announced, "This morning Anne was blessed before the congregation of the Church of the Heavenly

Rest. This was equivalent to a baptism. I'd like to toast to Annie." She raised her glass.

"Congratulations, Annie!" cried all, raising the glasses.

This was followed by Yukari's toast to her daughter. That was followed by other friends' toasts to Annie. All attention and admiration was on Annie, who remained calm and cheerful despite all these guests.

Then Yukari and her colleagues formed a string quartet group. They had chosen Brahms's *String Quartet No. 3, B flat major, op. 67*, which was considered his best string quartet.

The group performed exquisitely. As Brahms had intended, two violins, a viola, and a cello played together in pure harmony, without any particular instrument standing unduly in the spotlight so as to overshadow the other instruments. Yukari played the second violin part, citing that her energy level was not yet fully recovered.

We all listened to the music, enchanted. While each of the four movements had its own character, as a whole, the quartet was relaxed, intricate, and lyrical.

By now Annie was very familiar with classical music, particularly the violin, as Yukari played often for her. She too listened, moving her arms and fingers as if she were playing the violin. The guests noticed it and nodded with smiles.

After the performance Yukari cut the cake, surrounded by her guests. The decorative "Annie" in pink script on the white frosting was pretty. Shem Tov, Francine, and I served, making sure that everyone had a large slice. We ate the delicious cake with relish. Francine gave a small piece to Jacques, who ate it with delight, seemingly happy to be treated as an adult.

Annie was too young to eat cake, but Yukari gave her a tiny piece of white frosting to suck from her finger. It must have been very sweet even to the baby. She made a lot of cooing sounds of approval and satisfaction, moving her hands and legs joyfully in the crib and inducing smiles from everybody.

*   *   *

Since Yukari needed exercise and fresh air, she and I went out together often, securing the baby in a carriage. At first we just circled the block of her apartment building and Park Avenue. Then gradually we walked further to Fifth Avenue. We were very careful not to expose the baby to direct sunlight, as her skin was still too delicate. We chose the shade under the poplar trees lining Fifth Avenue and walked leisurely.

Although Yukari had learned baby-nursing technique from Lucy, her pediatrician, and books, her ability to take care of Annie seemed as natural and instinctive as if she had been born an experienced mother. While walking, Yukari talked to the baby softly and caressingly with her warm bell-like voice, pointing at anything we saw along the way and patiently waiting for Annie's responses. In this manner, Annie was introduced to the world and to nature.

"Look, that's a doggy. How pretty! Do you want it? We'll get one for you when you get bigger. That's a bus. A huge car, isn't it? Many people can ride together inside. Look, this is a bicycle. It's a lot of fun to ride on it. You'll have one soon. That's a tree. I don't know the name. But it's okay, right? The green leaves are as gentle as your skin. Oh, hi, another doggy. It's a puppy! Bow, wow, wow. Aha, he likes you. He's coming to you. Can you see?"

As Yukari talked, the baby turned her head to her, watched her, and listened to her attentively and solemnly, although I wondered how much she understood of what Yukari said. But Annie reacted with pleasure at being part of the conversation, sometimes waving her tiny arms or mumbling her cooing sounds.

Even at this stage, the baby girl already showed the character of her gender. Loud noises, strong colors, and sharp moves frightened her, and she turned her eyes away from them. Instead, she preferred soft sounds, gentle colors, and slow movements, and she showed her pleasure toward them. Yukari and I quickly learned this and adjusted our way of introducing the world accordingly.

Soon we were able to walk farther and longer. Eventually we were able to reach the Conservatory Garden of Central Park, where we'd had our painting session with Hans. We showed the place to the baby. Since it was early May, the garden was full of flowers.

Yukari pointed out the flowers, naming each. "Look, these are daffodils, and those, roses. See? Here are lilies, there, irises; over there, hyacinths, and under there, tulips. Oh, so many pretty flowers. Do you like flowers? Aren't they beautiful?"

The baby cooed in delight.

We wanted to show Annie the blue roses at the UN garden, but they had not bloomed yet this year. This was our disappointment, but we looked forward to the time they would blossom. It should be only one month away.

Our favorite place was the statue of Alice in Wonderland in Central Park. The large bronze statue of Alice was attended by the creatures of Wonderland, such as the March Hare, the Mad Hatter, the Mouse, the Puppy, and the Cheshire Cat, all surrounded by giant mushrooms. Many children were clambering over the statue. Yukari carried Annie and showed her each creature as the baby made happy cries and laughing sounds. I took a picture of Yukari sitting on a mushroom, holding Annie in front of Alice.

We circled the pond, called "Conservatory Water," which was crowded with remote-controlled model sailboats. We stopped at the bronze statue of Hans Christian Andersen, the Ugly Duckling at his feet. Occasionally volunteers read children's books, surrounded by young listeners. We listened to a story.

The pond was encircled by a wide path with many benches along the side. People strolled or sat on the benches, conversing or watching the people, dogs, sailboats, and ducks. Street musicians sang or played instruments. Some painted the landscape. We walked around, mingling with the crowd.

We went to nearby Bethesda Fountain too. The large fountain commemorated soldiers of the Civil War atop a rising angel, with four figures at the bottom, symbolizing temperance, purity, health, and peace. The water fell from the top. Behind the fountain stretched another large pond crowded with rowboats and drifting swans, surrounded by green willow trees. We strolled on the large terrace, circling the fountain. The baby gazed at the magnificent romantic scene, gurgling sounds of pleasure.

While we were walking, I pushed the carriage and Yukari walked next to me, attentively watching the baby. Many people smiled at the pretty baby girl with brown hair and brown eyes, and said "Hello, dear!" or "Hi, cutie!" The baby charmingly responded, and Yukari greeted them proudly, beaming with joy.

During these walks Yukari had to rest often. We sat on benches here and there in the park. Sometimes Yukari breastfed the baby, who vigorously sucked the nipple. Yukari's face was ecstatic. When the baby was satisfied with the milk, Yukari softly sang her children's songs, sometimes gently clapping her hands in rhythm.

Annie sometimes took short naps, after which she was lively, ready to face the new world again.

During one such rest, holding the baby in her arms, Yukari slightly leaned toward me. People were walking on nearby paths. She did not care. She seemed absorbed deep into herself, cherishing her motherhood, as if the outside world had disappeared. A few minutes passed that way without a word.

May was everywhere in the park, the month of sprouting, growing, and blooming. The surrounding grass and tree leaves were young, delicate, fresh, and green. Some flowers had buds ready to open, while others were fully blossoming. Petals were red, pink, white, yellow, blue, and mixtures of these, but all were simple, soft, and pure. Frolicking aromas of flowers, grass, and trees wafted and mingled in the warm fresh air. The sky was mild blue mixed with light green, reflecting the young grass and leaves.

I took out a Tiffany box and presented it to Yukari. "Please open it," I said. "It's an engagement ring for you."

Yukari opened it and saw a platinum ring with a shiny diamond. She gasped. "Oh, it's beautiful. Thank you, Mark." She kissed me.

"Let me place it in your finger," I said.

She tried to remove from her left ring finger a diamond ring and a wedding band, both the relics of Hans.

"No, no," I said. "Please keep them as they are. Our engagement ring will go with these rings. So Hans will stay with us."

"That's a splendid idea," Yukari said.

I slid the new ring onto her finger next to the existing two rings. I thought they stayed together well.

"Now we are officially engaged," I said. "I love you and Annie with my whole heart."

"I'm so happy," Yukari said. "I love you too, Mark."

Yukari and I embraced and kissed each other for a long time, holding the baby between us. We were surrounded by the spirit of May. Annie made merry noises as if she were congratulating us.

20

Our lives took on a pleasant rhythm for a while. In the middle of May, however, four weeks after her childbirth, Yukari started complaining of physical weakness, fatigue, and some mild pain in her joints and bones. Her rosy face grew pale. We thought that this was a post-childbirth symptom and would go away soon. Lucy, our PLA, showed some concern, but Yukari and I were more optimistic and continued our daily routines. We did not mind the work involved in raising an infant because it gave us such joy to watch her grow healthy and adorable.

Two weeks passed. But against our hopes the symptoms not only persisted, but grew worse. At the end of May, Yukari went to see Dr. Talmor, who referred her to a cancer specialist. After a series of tests and an anxious waiting period, she was diagnosed with leukemia and immediately admitted to the Memorial Sloan-Kettering Cancer Center.

I knew that Yukari had suffered from leukemia before. But for the entire time I had known her, she had shown no sign of its symptoms. Even Yukari seemed to have almost forgotten about it. Therefore, this was a complete blow to Yukari as well as to me.

This time Yukari called her parents in Tokyo and asked them to come to New York and take care of her baby. Since her parents were old, Yukari retained the services of Lucy. Her parents came immediately, and I went back to my apartment.

Yukari's doctor in the Cancer Center explained her case to me. She had suffered from leukemia about ten years earlier. She had recovered from it and returned to her normal life. But her leukemia had not been completely cured. It had only been in "remission" — that is, cancerous blood cells had still existed in her system, but they had been inactive and dormant. This was why she had not had full physical strength while working as a violinist in the Parnassus Symphony Orchestra. She had visited the doctor twice a year for a check-up and continued the required medication, which I had not been aware of.

During her pregnancy, her body and the baby had been protected by hormones, and her immune system had functioned on the highest alert. After the childbirth, however, her hormone level had come down and the immune system had settled back to normal. Then the dormant cells had sprung into action, and the leukemia had relapsed.

The type of leukemia Yukari suffered this time was called "acute myelogenous leukemia," which was reasonably common in adults. It affected white blood cells and progressed very fast. Hence, it was notorious for causing the death of the patient within a few weeks of the relapse unless the right treatment

was immediately provided. The treatment consisted of chemotherapy and bone marrow transplants. Radiation therapy was
not effective for this. In spite of advances in leukemia treatment with the cutting-edge medical technology of our age, the
cure rate of acute myelogenous leukemia was said to be sadly
no more than fifty percent.

During a course of chemotherapy, Yukari received mas-
sive doses of a combination of chemicals in order to kill the
abnormal blood cells. Unfortunately, her body did not respond
well to the therapy. The combination and amounts of chemicals
and medication were changed. But the results were more or
less the same. The therapy only slowed down the rapid increase
of abnormal blood cells a little.

The doctors considered a bone marrow transplant. These
were effective only if the bone marrow of the donor matched
that of the patient. Otherwise it would be dangerous, since the
donor's healthy bone marrow cells might attack the patient's
own cells as a foreign body. Unfortunately, the doctors could
not find a matching donor for Yukari. Her parents were deemed
too old for the procedure, and the baby was too young for it.
I volunteered, but it was found that my bone marrow did not
match hers.

The speed of the treatment was vital. But since the chemotherapy was ineffective and a bone marrow transplant was
not possible, Yukari had no other options. The situation agonized her parents and me, as well as the doctors and the staff
of the Cancer Center, which was renowned as one of the most
sophisticated cancer hospitals in the world. We could not do
much but helplessly observe the progress of her illness.

One day in the middle of June, I visited the Cancer Center with a huge bouquet. Since they considered me a part of Yukari's family, they allowed me to go to the intensive care unit where she was being treated. A nurse escorted me into the ICU room.

Yukari was resting. Her eyes were closed. No matter how often I visited, I was always shocked to see what the chemotherapy had done to her. She had lost her hair completely. She had lost weight. She was skinny and pale and totally worn out. Since she was too weak to eat, she was being fed intravenously. The IV tube in her arm and oxygen tube at her nose looked pitiful. The nurse instructed me to spend only up to fifteen minutes with Yukari, as she was too weak to receive a visitor for longer than that.

At the sound of our entry, Yukari opened her eyes. The nurse announced my visit in an intentionally chipper tone. Then she left the room to give us privacy.

"Hi, Yukari, how are you? I brought you flowers."

I tried to sound casual and cheerful, but my throat choked and my voice trembled. I placed the bouquet on the bed, next to her pillow.

"Thank you, Mark. It's beautiful. I love flowers," she said slowly in a weak and hoarse voice. "I'm sorry for my appearance. I feel so nauseous."

I tried to focus on a pleasant topic. "Annie is just fine. Your parents are taking care of her very well with Lucy's help. You have nothing to worry about."

Yukari' face slightly brightened. "I'm glad. Tell me more."

"She is healthy and getting bigger day by day. She misses you a lot."

"That's nice. I miss her too, very much."

"I brought photos. Look." I showed her several photos I had taken with my digital camera.

Her face broke into a smile. "My goodness! She's grown big. She is pretty, isn't she?"

"Yes, she is beautiful and growing fast. Soon you'll have to start teaching her how to play the violin. I understand that violins smaller than the standard size are available for children so they can start learning at a very early ages. I wonder how early it can be."

"Oh dear, she was just born. It's too early for her. But I have a feeling that she likes violin very much."

"Certainly. No doubt about it. Remember? Whenever you play the violin, she always listens quietly, moving her arms and fingers as if she were playing the instrument. It may be a sign of a prodigy. She might become a great violinist."

Yukari's face showed a faint touch of happiness.

I continued to encourage her. "In order to teach her the violin, you have to recover quickly. Remember, you won the battle the last time. You did recover from it. So this time, too, I'm sure you'll win. For your baby's sake, you must."

"I wish I could."

"No, no, you must," I said. "Besides, remember? We're going to get married soon. Then everything will be all right. You'll be my wife, and Annie will be my daughter. We'll be a happy family. For the honeymoon I'm thinking we should go to Colorado Springs. The climate is cool and fresh, and they organize many music festivals during the summer. So both you and Annie will enjoy it. Would you like that?"

Yukari slowly shook her head and sighed. Heavy clouds came back to her face.

"Dear, that sounds lovely. ... But this time, I know I can't make it. ... I'm going to join Hans soon. Hans and I will be watching Annie and you from above." Streams of tears flowed from her eyes.

"Oh, no. You have to fight back. What happened to your motto? 'Move forward.' So you have to fight on, and please don't give up."

I knew these words did not mean much at this point. I did not sound too convincing either. I observed Yukari trying to gather strength with difficulty, as if she could not rest in peace without telling me something.

"Dear Mark, please remember this. I made a will, in which I entrust the custody of Annie to you. So please, look after my child, my precious daughter. ... Please promise me."

"Yes, I will. I promise."

"Thank you. That's my only concern. I'm glad I can count on you."

There was a little silence. Her eyes searched something in the air, as if dreaming of the past. A slight color returned to her face.

"Dear, we had one lovely year. ... You, Hans, me, our blue roses, together ... and later our little Annie. ... I was very happy. I'd like you to know that."

Her voice was fading.

"Yukari, Yukari, please don't give up. I love you."

I could no longer restrain myself. I let tears flow from my eyes. Streams of tears ran down her face too. She and I watched each other for a while in silence.

Her faint voice came back. "Dear, I love you, too. ... Please hold me."

In a slow motion she extended toward me her left hand, which was free from the IV. The three rings on her finger shone. I gingerly clasped her hand with both of mine. Her hand was cold. I massaged her hand with tender care, as if it would revive her spirit.

"Thank you. ... Please keep holding. ... I feel peaceful."

She sighed deeply, but her breath was steady. I kept caressing her hand. After a while she made one more effort to speak.

"Dear ... please look after our Annie."

Every word echoed in my ears as if it had been a sacred request. Particularly the word *our* struck deep into my heart. I squeezed her hand in a gentle touch.

"Yes, upon my life."

She smiled with relief.

The nurse came back and gestured that my time was up. I carefully placed Yukari's hand back on her chest. Then I kissed her lips and left the room.

Outside, I sank heavily on a chair nearby and wept. From the closed ICU room behind me, I heard her uncontrollable sob, which tore my heart. Probably she heard mine as well.

One week later, she passed away.

21

Within three months I had lost my two best friends one by one. I felt my soul had gone with them too. I sank into sorrow, depression, and emptiness. In my living room I covered my painting "Blue Roses and Three Friends" with a large piece of black drapery, as it was simply too painful to look at.

I did not want to think. I did not want to feel. I did not want to speak of personal matters, but I did not want to be alone either. In order to kill my senses, I went to my office early in the morning every day and worked until nine o'clock in the evening or even later. There was plenty of work. It kept me busy. At home, exhausted, I collapsed on the bed just to sleep. All I wanted was to slip into the abyss of unconsciousness.

Yukari's parents stayed in her apartment to take care of residual business after their daughter's death. They looked after Annie with the PLA's help. I visited the apartment occasionally and saw the baby, who I thought was well taken care of. I spoke to Yukari's parents casually, but we engaged in no formal talk about her death and what to do with Annie.

Yukari's friends in the Parnassus Symphony Orchestra organized a memorial service at the Church of the Heavenly Rest. I attended with Shem Tov, Francine, Justin, and Ramez. Yukari's parents also went. Many members of the orchestra participated. Some of Yukari's friends from the other church came too. The rector of the church led the service. Between prayers, the string members of the orchestra played hymns and excerpts from requiems. At the conclusion they played Mozart's *Ave verum Corpus*, and all of us sang. It gave me a little comfort.

The Fourth of July went by. This year the fireworks sounded sad. I walked around in Central Park and visited places where Hans, Yukari, the baby, and I had spent pleasant time together. The places now appeared deserted and sorrowful. At home I played the CD of Brahms's string sestet, the double ensemble as Yukari called it, which made me remember our painting session in Central Park, where Yukari had announced her pregnancy. The music brought tears to my eyes.

I missed them. Why did it have to be this way? Life without them meant nothing to me anymore. I felt I had lost any reason to live. I wished I could go back to the past and stay there forever with Hans and Yukari. But I knew it could not happen. Life had to move forward. I had to live. But how?

Hans had battled against his crisis. I remembered his words before his departure to Sarajevo: "What? Do you think I would commit suicide? Oh, no. You are mistaken. I am not that weak. Look at me." I believed that he meant it. He struggled to find the meaning of working for the UN in Sarajevo and subsequently found it. He had won the battle. He never gave up.

Yukari, too, had fought against her crisis in her own way. She had recovered once from leukemia, and she had resumed her professional life as a violinist. It must have been a great challenge to her, but she had made it. She had married a caring husband, while continuing her career. She even gave birth to a beautiful baby daughter, overcoming Hans's death. Yukari never gave up either.

I had dealt with crises in my life before. It was not easy, but I survived. I thought I was tough enough. This time, though, I was not sure whether I could get through this. No, I was not going to be defeated, I vowed. I was not done yet. Not yet. I was going to fight on. I was going to come out of this.

I needed courage. I needed strength. I asked Hans and Yukari to give me these. Then I realized that they were gone. It hit me hard, like a physical blow.

My thoughts and emotions circled inside me, around and around. I knew I had to move on. But I was going nowhere.

*   *   *

One day an impending issue brought me back to the real world. A Mr. Edward Cooper called me at my office, introducing himself as an attorney representing the late Ms. Yukari Asaka. He wished me to attend the reading of Yukari's will. Her parents would attend as well.

A few days later at the appointed time, I visited the lawyer's office on Fifth Avenue, in the neighborhood of the public library. In the conference room Mr. Cooper and Mr. and Mrs. Asaka were already waiting for me. Except for the memorial service, this was the first time I had sat close to Yukari's parents on a formal occasion. Medium built, white-haired Mr. Asaka, though in his eighties, looked vigorous and intelligent, with a high forehead and sharp eyes. He had the bearing of a distinguished former diplomat. Mrs. Asaka, in her sixties, was slender, a little small-built, but elegant. Mr. Cooper was tall and heavy, intellectual brightness illuminating his face.

After unsealing the document, Mr. Cooper read Yukari's will, sometimes stopping and explaining the contents in layman's terms. It was relatively simple: she wanted her body to be cremated and the ashes to be scattered in the Atlantic Ocean near Manhattan; her three violins to be given to her daughter Anne; artworks to go to Mr. Mark Graham Sanders; all valuables and financial assets to be liquidated and put in trust for Anne; the full custody of Anne to be given to Mr. Sanders as her guardian; and lastly, for Mr. Sanders to be appointed as the executor of her will.

When Mr. Cooper finished reading, a silence enveloped the room.

Mr. Cooper broke the silence. "First of all, Mr. Sanders, do you agree to serve as Ms. Asaka's executor?"

"Certainly, yes," I said without the slightest hesitation. "That was her wish. I respect it, and I feel honored to serve."

"That's good," Mr. Cooper said with satisfaction. "It's not an easy task, but I'll help you, if you need me. You should get started, the sooner the better."

Another silence.

This time Mr. Asaka broke the silence. "Is this all?" At the affirmative reply from Mr. Cooper, Mr. Asaka continued, "I may have misunderstood, but I see that my wife and I have nothing to do with this document. I don't mean money. But we'd like to bring our daughter's ashes to Japan for burial in our family grave, and most importantly, we'd like to bring our granddaughter back to Tokyo to look after her. I don't see any such provisions in this document. Has our daughter simply left us out?"

Mr. Asaka spoke good English, and his face flashed in dismay and dissatisfaction. Mrs. Asaka quietly nodded.

"Mr. and Mrs. Asaka, I understand your feeling," Mr. Cooper said. "But this is a legally executed document, so the content legally represents what your daughter wished."

"Sorry," Mr. Asaka said, "with due respect, Mr. Cooper, I cannot agree to this document. With due respect, Mr. Sanders, you are just a single gentleman. Raising a baby is a woman's job. You can't take our granddaughter away from us." He shook his head a few times with indignation, then turned to the attorney. "Am I entitled to contest her will, sir?"

"Yes, you can contest her will in court," Mr. Cooper replied. "But only if you believe that Ms. Asaka was mentally incapable of writing this will. It will be hard for you to prove that. As a matter of fact, I was with her when she told me her wishes. I was also with her when she read the final draft, approved it, and signed it. We have two witnesses, my legal practice partner and my secretary, who signed the document too. At Ms. Asaka's request, we did all this in her hospital room. Nobody pressured her. We can testify to that."

"But I am her father. And this is her mother," Mr. Asaka said, pointing to his wife. Then he shouted, "You mean we cannot do anything for our daughter and granddaughter? That's cruel!" His face grew red and his voice began trembling. "We raised our daughter. Now we have lost her, and you tell us there's nothing we can do for her? This is outrageous! You don't understand how we feel!"

Mr. Asaka wiped his eyes with his hand, as Mrs. Asaka burst into tears.

"Mr. Asaka, I fully sympathize with you," Mr. Cooper said. "I am a lawyer, so I can speak only from a legal point of view. But between you and Mr. Sanders, who has full legal authority to execute her will, perhaps you could work out something mutually satisfactory."

"I can't believe this," Mr. Asaka said, his voice still shaking. "I hope you don't mind if I consult with my own attorney?"

"It's up to you, sir," Mr. Cooper said.

"Then I'll get back to you shortly, Mr. Cooper. Good day." Then Mr. Asaka glared at me and said, "Good day, Mr. Sanders." He stormed out of the room, groaning, "I can't believe this!"

Mrs. Asaka bowed politely and said "Please excuse us," then scurried away after her husband.

An awkward pause ensued.

Finally Mr. Cooper cleared his throat and said, "I perfectly understand their feeling. This kind of reaction is fairly common among some relatives of the deceased when a will is unsealed and read. One way or the other, some people are not happy."

I didn't know how to react. So I kept quiet.

"I have a few suggestions to you, Mr. Sanders," the attorney continued. "Ms. Asaka's will entrusts you as the custodian of her daughter. This is legally valid. However, Mr. and Mrs. Asaka may contest the will in court, not by claiming that Ms. Asaka was mentally incapable of writing this will, but by claiming that they, Mr. and Mrs. Asaka, who have raised their daughter, are more qualified and eligible to raise their granddaughter than you, who is single and has no experience on that matter. After all, they are the real father and mother of Ms. Asaka, and the kinship does matter in a child custody dispute. They may win the case, depending on how their attorney presents it. This worries me. Of course I'll do my best to defend you. But please be prepared for the worst case."

I couldn't say anything. I just gazed at the table.

"One more thing." Mr. Cooper went on. "I understand that Mr. and Mrs. Asaka are now living in Ms. Asaka's apartment with their granddaughter. One possibility is that instead of contesting the will, they might take their granddaughter and simply fly back to Japan. I don't want that kind of complication, because once they leave this country, it will be hard for me to enforce the will, though it is not impossible. So my suggestion to you, Mr. Sanders, is that you take away the baby immediately from them, citing that you are now the official custodian of the child. The baby should live with you as soon as possible."

I still didn't know how to respond. After a while I only said, "I'll think about it."

I left the lawyer's office with a melancholy heart.

* * *

One thing I ruled out quickly was Mr. Cooper's second suggestion. I thought that Mr. and Mrs. Asaka would not flee with Annie to Japan against the legally executed will of their own daughter. This would be considered breaking the law and dishonorable. Japanese were honorable people, and the Asakas were an old family, who I thought must value honor more than anything else. So I decided to let Mr. and Mrs. Asaka live with Annie in Yukari's apartment until things were settled one way or the other.

As to the lawyer's first suggestion, I was not sure what to do. Mr. Cooper might be right. Mr. and Mrs. Asaka might contest the will as Mr. Cooper speculated, and they might win the case. Then what should I do? I didn't have an answer. For this, I had to wait and see.

My immediate concern was for myself. As the legally appointed executor of Yukari's will, I felt a heavy responsibility on my shoulders. But as I recalled Yukari's sacred request on her deathbed, I resolved to do the job. The most challenging task was to serve as Annie's legal custodian. This was easier said than done. Mr. Asaka's words echoed in my heart: "With due respect, Mr. Sanders, you are a single gentleman. Raising a baby is a woman's job. You can't take our granddaughter away from us." He was right in a sense. I questioned myself: *Can I raise Annie while I continue working?* Not only did I have to do it, but also I had to do it right so Annie could enjoy a healthy childhood.

* * *

One evening I came home earlier than usual. I was med-
itating on the situation in my apartment. A concierge called
and announced that Ms. Jane Clifford was in the lobby and
wished to see me. I was astonished because we had not seen
each other since the blessing of Anne at the Heavenly Rest.
Even on that day we did not speak. Jane had never visited my
apartment before either. I wondered what had brought her to
me this evening.

My room was a little messy. I didn't want her to become
too emotional or too intimate here. Besides, the walls of my living room were hung with my paintings and drawings, many of
which were nude figures. One stood out: my painting of "Blue
Roses and Three Friends," which was now covered by the black
drapery. I thought it was not proper to meet her in my room.
I replied to the concierge that I would come down to meet her
in the lobby.

It was a warm summer evening, but the air was dry. The
sky was still not completely dark yet. We decided to take a walk
north on Fifth Avenue toward Jane's apartment building. She
looked perturbed, but I did not detect any agitation or hostility. She walked closely beside me, without holding my arm.
Traffic was light, which kept the street tranquil, providing us
some privacy.

"I saw you at our church last month," Jane said in her
usual gentle voice. "Yukari was a beautiful lady. No wonder you
loved her."

I could not say a word for a while, but finally said, "I'm
sorry, Jane."

"No need to be sorry," she replied. "Recently our church made an announcement that Yukari had passed away, and that since her husband, Hans, had died three months before her, their child, Anne, who was blessed at the church, was now parentless. So the church is asking the congregation to pray for Anne and her deceased parents. You loved Yukari so much. You must be devastated. Please accept my sincere condolences."

Her tone showed a genuine sympathy for me. I was moved, particularly because she might instead have resented Yukari as her rival.

"Thank you," I said, though I couldn't continue further, for I didn't know what to say.

"You are welcome," she simply replied, and contemplated for several seconds. "I remember Yukari and Anne at the blessing for Anne's birth. It was a beautiful ceremony, full of love and hope. Now this. What a tragedy. I worry for the baby. What's going to happen to her? Does Yukari have her parents? Are they going to take Anne back to Japan? Or is she going to be adopted by someone? That's sad. Is there anything I can do for you and Anne?"

I told Jane about Yukari's will entrusting the custody of Annie to me. No sooner had I finished my story than she stopped walking.

"Are you going to raise Annie alone?" she asked. "Do you have a girlfriend to help you?"

"Jane, I cannot answer that question," I replied. "I'm thinking what to do myself."

"Is Annie living with you now?"

"No, she is still with Yukari's parents in her apartment."

Jane said eagerly, "When you take Annie, please let me hold her in my arms. I love a baby. And Annie is such an adorable child."

"Yes, I'll do that," I said to be polite.

"I'm good with babies. Do you want me to help you care for Annie?" she asked, her face bright.

"No, no," I said. "I appreciate your thought. But this has nothing to do with you. It's all about me. I have to find a way."

She clasped my arm tenderly. We walked for a while in silence.

"I'd be happy to take care of Annie as our child if you want," she said, squeezing my arm. "She is a beautiful child. I like her very much."

"Oh, no," I said hastily, "that would be too much. I could never ask you for that kind of thing. Annie is not your child."

"She is not your child either."

"It's true, but I can never ask you after insulting you so much."

"I've forgotten that," she said. Her voice was peaceful. "I just want to be part of your life. Why don't we get married and raise Annie together? Soon I'd like to bear a child for you. Then our child and Annie will be siblings. We can raise them together. Don't you want that? Besides, raising a baby is not an easy task for a single man like you. You need me. I love you, Mark. Take my offer. Let's get married and raise Annie together."

She stopped walking and kissed me. It was a warm kiss of love.

I was touched. I almost melted. I felt Jane like an angel. Her offer made perfect sense. But to take her offer was too selfish for me to consider. I had denied her love repeatedly before. So because both Hans and Yukari had died, I would accept Jane as my wife now? In order to make it easier for me to raise Annie, I would marry Jane? Besides, did I love Jane? Did I? ... No ... instead, I had loved Yukari. Now I could say that openly. I had loved Yukari, still loved her, and would love her forever.

Above all I wanted to cherish the memory of the sacred friendship among Hans, Yukari, and me. I wanted to live with that memory for the rest of my life. I had Annie with me, who was the fruit of our bond. I was willing to raise Annie by myself for the sake of Yukari and Hans, and our friendship.

"Thank you, Jane," I said. "I'm grateful for your thought. Please don't take this personally, but I'd like to do it by myself."

She sobbed quietly without a word.

My heart ached. I didn't want to torment her further. I hastily added, "But if the situation becomes too overwhelming to me, I'll ask for your help."

She inclined her head, still weeping.

With this, I resolved to do it alone, at least for now.

∗   ∗   ∗

A few days later in the evening I visited Shem Tov and Francine in midtown. This was my first visit to their home — a nice two-bedroom apartment. They used one bedroom for themselves and the other for Jacques's nursery, in which I saw a crib, toys, a rocking chair, a stroller, a baby bathtub, and other things for the toddler. Reflecting Jacques's gender, his toys included a model airplane, racing car, fire engine, and spaceship. He was already asleep.

I told them about Yukari's will and asked their advice on my raising Annie.

Francine spoke immediately. "I'm so glad you're willing to look after little Annie. We can help you. We went through this already. It's a challenge, but it's very rewarding."

"Yes, we'll assist you," Shem Tov said, nodding.

"My worry is whether or not I can successfully raise an infant while I work full time."

"We had the same issue," Francine said with eagerness. "After my three-month maternity leave, I had to go back to work. We were scared. But we brought Jacques, only three months old then, to the UN Childcare Center, which is right near the Secretariat building. They provide a professional day-care service for the children of UN staff members. We've been using it for over a year without any problem. We bring Jacques there at nine o'clock, and they take care of him very well. I visit the center during my lunch break and feed him. After five o'clock I pick him up and come home. It works well for us. So you can do it too."

"I also visit the center during my lunch breaks as often as my work allows," Shem Tov said. "It's rather enjoyable to see Jacques happily playing with the other babies. I must say the quality of the center's care is first class. You'll be surprised to see many UN staff members are doing the same thing, and they are all pleased with the arrangement. I see several single mothers there, as well as a few single fathers. So Mark, you won't be alone."

"Thanks for telling me this," I said. "It eases my anxiety."

"Your worry is understandable," Francine said. "I'll look after Annie too, when I visit the center during my lunch breaks. Don't worry."

"Actually, I'm glad," Shem Tov said, "because I've heard that having siblings is good for developing a healthy personality. Jacques and Annie will be siblings. So let's do it jointly. Let Jacques and Annie play together, and whenever you have questions or concerns, you can call us or visit us. We'll be always open to you and Annie." He reflected with a solemn face. "At least this is something Francine and I can do for Hans and Yukari. ... Poor Annie."

"Yes, Shem Tov is right," said Francine. "We'll help you. Let's do it together — for Yukari and Hans."

"Thank you," I said. "I'm grateful to you, Francine and Shem Tov, for your encouragement."

"Why don't you come to the childcare center during the lunch break tomorrow?" Francine proposed. "You should observe the facility by yourself. I'll be there."

"That's a great idea," Shem Tov said. "I'll come too."

* * *

The next day during my lunch break, I visited the UN Childcare Center, about a five- minute walk from my building. It was located on the ground floor of one of UN buildings. Outside was a small playground, equipped with slides and swings, where children were playing with joyful clamor. Inside was a toddlers' room, in which several toddlers were playing with their parents or the center staff. Next was a nursery room, where several women were breastfeeding or bottle-feeding their babies. I even saw a few men bottle-feeding their babies.

I met Francine, who was feeding Jacques with baby food. Shem Tov was beside her, watching Jacques with a fatherly grin.

"So what do you think?" Francine asked.

"This is a well-organized childcare center," I said. "I think Annie will like it here." I smiled with confidence and determination. "I can do it."

* * *

On Saturday I visited Yukari's apartment. I was right. Mr. and Mrs. Asaka had not left for Tokyo with Annie. They were all there. Mr. Asaka opened the door. I heard Annie crying. I saw Mrs. Asaka holding the baby and trying to bottle-feed her, but Annie seemed to be feeling blue.

With Mrs. Asaka's permission, I held Annie into my arms. She stopped crying. She was now three months old. She was much bigger, heavier, and prettier. Her skin was very smooth and pinky white, and her brown hair was longer and finer. She gazed at me for several seconds in silence with motionless brown eyes. Then something clicked in her. She broke into a big smile and made a loud cooing sound, opening her arms wide toward me and waving frantically.

I caressed her. She laughed. I talked to her in a friendlily voice. She responded by waving her hands and kicking her legs with delightful babbling. I amused her by playing the airplane in the familiar slow motion. She remembered it and cried for joy. I was happy, and her adorable clamor made my eyes wet. I hugged her close as she kept smiling and gurgling.

I asked Mrs. Asaka if I could feed the baby. Mrs. Asaka simply nodded.

I took the bottle and shook a few drops of the formula on the inside of my wrist. The temperature was comfortably warm. Sitting on the sofa, I cradled Annie in a semi-upright position and supported her head. I moved the nipple of the bottle to her mouth. She started drinking. I held the bottle angled up, making sure that the formula flowed well without air. Annie happily swallowed the milk.

Mrs. Asaka sighed and said with a Japanese accent, "It's amazing that she is enjoying the bottle-feeding from you, Mr. Sanders. I've never seen her swallow the milk from the bottle so quietly. With me she often cries. How happy she looks! Annie really loves you."

It made my heart warm.

In several minutes the bottle was empty. I held Annie straight up and gently rubbed her back, holding a small towel at her mouth. She burped, and I cleaned her mouth. I remembered all these motions from Yukari's nursing and was able to do them naturally. I felt happy for the baby. But then it struck me that Annie was now an orphan. I felt a pang in my heart.

An orphan ... it sounded awful. I could not leave her as an orphan. She had a full life before her. She might become a great violinist. She had to start getting violin lessons soon. She needed somebody to go through life with her. I remembered that I was entrusted as her guardian and custodian.

Some of Yukari's last words came back to me: "Please look after my child, my precious daughter. Please promise me."

I had promised her. She was so concerned that she even asked a second time: "Please look after our Annie." She'd said "*our* Annie." Obviously she meant that Annie was the child among Hans, Yukari, and me. And I had answered her, "Yes, upon my life." It was my pledge. I had meant it.

I held Annie straight up in a sitting position close to my face. Satisfied with milk, she was energetic and tried to reach my face with both her hands while smiling and cooing. I let her touch my face. Her fingers were tiny, but they were warm and so soft.

Poor child ... how much did she know? As I held her and caressed her, her innocent, angelic face made my heart heavy.

Mr. Asaka had not said anything, but had been simply observing me and Annie with thoughtful eyes. Now he said, "Mr. Sanders, please excuse us for a few minutes."

He gestured to his wife, and they went to the bedroom and closed the door. I did not find any hostility in his words or attitude. Rather, I felt he was warm to me. This was a stark contrast to the last Mr. Asaka who had stormed out of the attorney's office. He had changed, for which I was grateful.

I heard that they were discussing something in the bedroom, though I could not grasp the contents. I heard, too, Mrs. Asaka's sob.

Mr. Asaka came back, holding a paper bag. Mrs. Asaka followed, wiping her tears.

"Mr. Sanders," Mr. Asaka said with a solemn face, "I apologize that I didn't act courteously to you in the lawyer's office."

"There's no need," I replied. "I knew you were going through a difficult time."

"The Japanese consulate-general in Manhattan is a son of my old friend," Mr. Asaka continued. "I discussed my daughter's will with him. He consulted with his attorney. Their conclusion was that the will was formally drawn up in accordance with the law and is undisputable. My wife and I also witnessed that our daughter was mentally sound until her last moment, and she died with dignity. So we're resigned to accept her will as it stands. You have our blessing to exercise your authority as the executor of her will. My wife and I have decided to leave New York without anything of our daughter."

Mrs. Asaka shed tears.

"It pains us that we won't be able to look after our granddaughter," Mr. Asaka continued. "But observing you nursing Annie, and witnessing that Annie loves you, we feel you will offer her a good life. That's our comfort. We're old, and we feel probably this is better. We're thankful that God provided you for our granddaughter. We trust you to take good care of her."

"Yes, Mr. and Mrs. Asaka, I will," I said, "because I've promised Yukari. I'll protect Annie and watch her grow to be a professional violinist — or whatever else she wishes."

"My daughter told me about the family heritages among us," Mr. Asaka went on. "I am honored to be acquainted with you, for your great-great-grandmother met my grandfather in Washington DC more than a century ago." He presented the paper bag to me. "I know that my daughter's possessions are all at your disposal. But I found these. As you know well, one is a Japanese lacquer box, and the other is a Japanese fan. My family crest is painted on both. Please keep these with you, and when our granddaughter comes of age, tell her how she has inherited these. She should know that she carries the heritage of three families: yours, Hans's, and ours."

"Yes, I will, upon my honor," I said, receiving the paper bag.

I saw Mr. Asaka's eyes were teary. Mrs. Asaka wept. My eyes grew moist as well. I wanted to do something to alleviate their sorrow.

"Mr. and Mrs. Asaka," I said, "I've been thinking. I'd like to offer you a few things. First, according to Yukari's wish, her body will be cremated and the ashes will be scattered into the Atlantic Ocean near Manhattan. But we haven't done that yet, and her body is still at the hospital. So please let me propose that you take some ashes in an urn and bring them back to Japan with you, while the rest of the ashes go into the sea. I hope Yukari wouldn't mind."

The couple's faces brightened.

"Thank you, Mr. Sanders," Mr. Asaka said. "You are generous. I appreciate it."

"Yes, me, too, I am grateful," Mrs. Asaka said.

"Also, since Yukari gave me all her artworks, I'd like to present my pastel drawing, 'Yukari Nursing Anne,' to you. Please bring it back to Japan and keep it as a memento of your daughter and her child." I pointed to the framed drawing on the wall.

Mr. and Mrs. Asaka gazed at it with reverence, as if it were a Madonna and Child.

"Thank you," Mr. Asaka said. "It's beautiful."

Mrs. Asaka cried. Dabbing her eyes, she said, "Thank you. We'll treasure it."

"One more thing," I said. "If you want to take some of Yukari's possessions, like dresses and jewels, please take what you wish. This is also within my authority, so please feel free."

"Thank you, Mr. Sanders," Mr. Asaka said. "I understand our daughter and you were engaged and were going to get married. We would have welcomed you as our son-in-law. Please visit us with Annie as often as you can."

Wiping her tears, Mrs. Asaka said, "Yes, please come often. I'd like see Annie grow, my daughter's daughter." She broke into sobs again.

"Yes, I will," I said.

I caressed Annie in my arms and swayed her in a gentle motion. She murmured with joy.

This was the first time I felt I was her real father.

22

I moved Annie to my apartment with her belongings. One week later Mr. and Mrs. Asaka left New York, with only the urn and my pastel drawing, for which I thought they were very honorable. By this, Yukari's will could be executed in accordance with her wishes.

I had Yukari's music-related possessions sent to my apartment, including the three violins, piano, music sheets, CDs, books, music stand, and metronome, which Annie would use later. I kept all of Yukari's jewelry for Annie. I took my drawing of Yukari dancing, thinking that someday I would tell Annie its meaning. I gave Yukari's best dresses to her close friends in the Parnassus Symphony Orchestra. I also sent a few furnishings, particularly those related to Annie, to my apartment. The rest I gave to charities. Lastly I opened a bank account and a trust on Annie's behalf, and transferred all of Yukari's financial assets into them.

Now my new life as Annie's father had begun. I nursed her at home, brought her to the daycare center every weekday morning, visited her during my lunch breaks to feed her, picked her up after work, and took her home, while I continued working full time. It required some adjustments in my lifestyle, but soon this became a pleasant routine for me. Raising Annie while working full time weighed heavily on me. But I didn't mind, because the reward was immense. What joy to watch Annie grow!

Annie was a happy and quiet child. I often took her to visit Shem Tov and Francine, and in turn they often visited me with Jacques. Annie and Jacques became good playmates, though they were still babies. The support from Francine and Shem Tov was invaluable, as their practical suggestions on baby care augmented my inexperience.

Soon the news of my raising the infant daughter of Hans and Yukari as a single father spread throughout the United Nations, including peacekeeping missions and humanitarian missions around the globe. People seemed to remember me escorting the pregnant Yukari during the memorial service for the UNMIBH casualties, which had been simulcast on the TV through the UN satellite telecommunication link. The well-wishes from my colleagues and people whom I didn't even know poured in.

My director came to me to offer her admiration for my courage and compassion. Mr. Skoog, too, dropped by my office and thanked me. He brought a soft-colored stuffed rabbit for Annie, which she loved. Antonio, Jan, and Robert in UNMIBH jointly sent me by a diplomatic pouch a small rock taken from Mt. Igman in Sarajevo where the helicopter had crashed, with a warm note praising my decision. Justin and Ramez, too, stopped by in my room and thanked me, commending my determination.

The president of the Security Council walked into my room to show his appreciation. He informed me of the UN Memorial and Recognition Fund that granted scholarships to the children of UN staff members who had died in the course of discharging their official duties. He encouraged me to apply for it when Anne reached school age, as she was eligible for it.

Even the Secretary-General and his wife visited my office to express their gratitude. His Excellency and Madame presented me with a gold UN peace medal for Annie. I showed them a few framed photos of Annie on my desk, at which their faces lit with affection. I told them that Annie was enjoying the UN Childcare Center. The couple smiled and asked me to convey their love to her.

I felt honored and grateful for all these gestures.

One day, after picking up Annie from the daycare center, I went to the UN garden, holding her in the front-carrier. Summer roses were blooming. Among them, our blue roses stood out by their exquisite, striking color. This year they had more branches, from which dozens of flowers vigorously erupted in full bloom. Sumptuous was the sparkling light blue color on the silky smooth petals. The strong sweet fragrance wafted in the air.

At the top of the nearby flagpole, the UN flag waved majestically, complementing the blue color of our roses.

I showed Annie the blue roses, moving her face close to the blossoms. She liked them, trying to reach the blooms with her tiny hands, kicking her legs and squealing with delight. I explained to her in a friendly voice how these blue roses came to be, how much we — her mother, her father, and I, now her new father — adored them, how much even she, Annie, loved them while she was still living in her mother's womb, and my belief that the spirits of Hans and Yukari dwelled behind these blue roses. I didn't know how much Annie understood, but she gazed at the blue roses solemnly and made a lot of appreciative murmurs.

I heard Brahms's string sestet coming from our blue roses. I told Annie about her mother's double ensemble, and that when I had heard it the first time, her mother had announced the pregnancy with Annie, that her life had just begun. I hummed the familiar second movement. Following the melody, Annie nudged her left fingers and right hand as if she were playing the violin, tapping the strings and swaying the bow.

Accompanying the double ensemble and Annie, the blue roses oscillated in a gentle breeze. They were celebrating life with rejuvenating energy, determined to perpetuate their blooms twice every year as long as they lived. The sight was dazzling, and at the same time graceful and sublime. I hoped that Annie would grow like them, with their grace and perpetuity.

At that moment I felt Yukari and Hans were watching us in peace from behind the blue roses. To salute them, I raised Annie toward the sky and kissed her.

Annie smiled and clapped with joy, as if she were our blue roses.

The End

ABOUT THE AUTHOR

Yorker Keith lives in Manhattan, New York City. He holds an MFA in creative writing from The New School. His literary works have been four times recognized in the William Faulkner – William Wisdom Creative Writing Competition as a finalist or a semifinalist, including this novel, *Remembrance of Blue Roses*.